# Singer in the Snow

# Singer in the Snow

### BY
## LOUISE MARLEY

*Viking*

VIKING
Published by Penguin Group
Penguin Young Readers Group, 345 Hudson Street, New York, New York 10014, U.S.A.
Penguin Group (Canada),90 Eglinton Avenue East, Suite 700, Toronto, Ontario, Canada M4P 2Y3
(a division of Pearson Penguin Canada Inc.)
Penguin Books Ltd, 80 Strand, London WC2R 0RL, England
Penguin Ireland, 25 St Stephen's Green, Dublin 2, Ireland (a division of Penguin Books Ltd)
Penguin Group (Australia), 250 Camberwell Road, Camberwell, Victoria 3124, Australia
(a division of Pearson Australia Group Pty Ltd)
Penguin Books India Pvt Ltd, 11 Community Centre, Panchsheel Park, New Delhi – 110 017, India
Penguin Group (NZ), Cnr Airborne and Rosedale Roads, Albany, Auckland 1310,
New Zealand (a division of Pearson New Zealand Ltd)
Penguin Books (South Africa) (Pty) Ltd, 24 Sturdee Avenue, Rosebank, Johannesburg 2196, South Africa
Penguin Books Ltd, Registered Offices: 80 Strand, London WC2R 0RL, England

First published in 2005 by Viking, a division of Penguin Young Readers Group

1 3 5 7 9 10 8 6 4 2

Copyright © Louise Marley, 2005
All rights reserved

LIBRARY OF CONGRESS CATALOGING-IN-PUBLICATION DATA
Marley, Louise, date–
Singer in the snow / Louise Marley.
p.  cm.
Summary: In a land where the sun shines only once every five years, two gifted
young Singers are sent to a remote outpost where they struggle to refine their abilities
to create heat and light using their psi energy.
ISBN 0-670-05965-X (hardcover)
[1. Psychic ability—Fiction. 2. Self-realization—Fiction.
3. Coming of age—Fiction. 4. Science fiction.]  I. Title.
PZ7.M3444Sin 2005
[Fic]—dc22
2005005575

Printed in U.S.A.
Set in Centaur
Book design by Kelley McIntyre

*For the real Emily*

# A Note on Music

THE NEVYAN CLEF symbol is a C clef, indicating the one pitch all Singers must be able to remember and reproduce accurately. Both the *filla* and the *filhata* are tuned to C. The *filhata*'s central, deepest string is the bass C; from top to bottom, the *filhata* is tuned thusly: E-B-F-C-G-D-A. The *filla* is tuned with no stops on C.

The modes are natural scales of whole and half-steps; alterations, or accidentals, are considered variations and are used as embellishments, and can be half- or quarter-tones. Even those Singers without absolute pitch are required to memorize the pitch C early in their training.

The modes are employed customarily in the following ways:

First mode, *Iridu*: *quiru*, inducing sleep
Second mode, *Aiodu*: *quiru*, healing
Third mode, *Doryu*: warming water, treating infections
Fourth mode, *Lidya*: entertainment, relaxation
Fifth mode, *Mu-Lidya*: entertainment, relaxation

# *Glossary*

***caeru***: A fur-bearing animal; a source of meat and hides

**Cantoris:** The room in which a Singer does her or his work, and where the members of the House come to listen

**Cantrix (f)/Cantor (m):** A highly trained Singer who maintains the environment for one of the great Houses of Nevya

***carwhal***: A sea animal that lives mostly in the water

***ferrel***: A large predatory bird

***filhata***: A stringed instrument similar to a lute, used exclusively by Cantors and Cantrixes

***filla***: A small, flutelike instrument used by Singers

**House:** An ancient stone building that can be home to as

many as three hundred people, with apartments, large kitchens, nursery gardens, and manufactories

*bruss*: A large, shaggy animal used for riding and carrying, or pulling the *pukuru*

*keftet*: A traditional dish of meat and grain

*kikyu*: Small fishing boat(s)

**Maestro (m)/Maestra (f)**: Instructors at Conservatory; a term of respect

**Magister (m)/Magistrix (f)**: Hereditary or appointed House rulers

*obis* **knife**: A knife made of slender long metal pieces, used in conjunction with psi to carve stone and ironwood

**psi**: Mental power that can move tiny particles of air or sometimes larger objects

*pukuru*: A sled, which can be various sizes, with bone runners

*quiru*: An area of heat and light created by the psi of Gifted Singers

*quirunha*: The ceremony that creates a *quiru* large enough to heat and light an entire House

**Singer**: One who uses music to focus energy to create warmth and light

*tkir*: A large predatory cat with great fangs

*ubanyor* (m)/*ubanyix* (f): A sunken communal bath (for men/women)

*urbear*: A very large silvery-gray coastal animal

*wezel*: A thin, rodentlike animal, native to Nevya

# Singer in the Snow

## *Prologue*

EMLE'S MELODY FLOWED easily from her *filla*. Her slender tone rang against the ancient stones of Conservatory, the low notes warm and resonant, the high ones delicate and true. She felt the sure pressure of her breath against her lips, the precision of her fingertips on the little instrument's carved stops. She played in the second mode, *Aiodu*, perfect for creating *quiru*. The tune was going well, her tempo steady, her intonation perfect.

She closed her eyes, hoping. Always hoping. She stretched out her psi, the slender stream of her mind's energy, to stir the air to life.

She felt the strength of her psi as surely as if it were her own slender arm that reached out into the atmosphere of the practice room. She knew what needed to be done, and she knew how to do it.

But it was no different this time than it had been the last five times, ten times, the last hundred times she had tried. She came almost to the point of success, where she knew she could touch the tiniest parts of the air, excite them to light and warmth, create the *quiru* she longed for . . . and, at the crucial moment, the fibril of her psi collapsed.

As her cadence died away, a faint sigh escaped Maestra Magret. Reluctantly, Emle lifted her eyelids.

The practice room was bright, of course, and warm, because all of Conservatory was bright and warm. Though austere in its decoration, and spare in its furnishings, Conservatory never lacked for Singers' energy. Its daily *quirunha* was the most powerful on the Continent, performed by the best Cantors and Cantrixes of Nevya, the teachers of Conservatory. Their psi, borne on the wings of music, excited the invisible particles of air to create *quiru*, havens of warmth and light. Their Gift was all that stood between Nevyans and the deep cold.

But Emle's Gift failed to make *quiru*. The practice room was no brighter, no warmer than when she had begun.

Emle hung her head. *I am sorry, Maestra,* she sent. Her eyes stung, and she pressed the back of her hand to her eyelids. *I am trying, truly I am.*

Maestra Magret, a Singer and Cantrix whose silver hair spoke of her years of service, sent, *I know, Emle.*

*I have practiced so hard.* The back of Emle's hand shone with tears. She dried it on the hem of her tunic, and looked up into her teacher's faded eyes.

*Your music is lovely.* Magret stood slowly, leaning on her staff of ironwood. She had grown increasingly stiff over the last year. Someone should try to heal the swelling of her knees and ankles, the pain that made her rely more and more on the carved staff. Emle supposed that Magret did not wish to ask anyone to take time from their teaching to ease her pain, but someone should, just the same. Someone should help Maestra Magret, but it would not be Emle. Emle's healing, like her *quiru*, was ineffective.

More tears welled, and escaped to roll down her cheeks. Her nose began to run, and she groped in her pocket.

"Here, now." Magret spoke aloud, no doubt not wanting to intrude on Emle's misery. Or perhaps, Emle thought, not wanting to share in it. The Maestra handed her a clean white handkerchief. Pragmatically, as if Emle's whole life were not riding on this one great failure, she said, "It is time we speak to the Magistrix."

Emle's heart felt as heavy as the very stones of the House. She had lived in terror of this moment, had dreaded it for months, felt its imminence for weeks. Her anxiety had not helped her Gift, either. It seemed the harder she tried, the more it eluded her.

All of Conservatory's student Singers, except perhaps one, feared the Magistrix. They quailed before her fierce, dark gaze, dared not risk her infrequent reprimands. They yearned for her even more infrequent praise.

Emle's failure required the Magistrix's attention, and she knew it. She rose from her stool, dried her eyes, blew her nose. She spent all her courage saying, "Very well, Maestra." Her voice shook, but it didn't break. She tucked the handkerchief away to take to the linen ambry later. "I understand."

*Very good, Emle.* The touch of Magret's sending was gentle in Emle's mind. *Remember that the Magistrix has only your best interests at heart.*

Emle shielded her mind to hide her doubts. Magistrix

Sira possessed a fabled Gift. How could such a person under-stand—or forgive—Emle's faulty one?

The Magistrix of Conservatory carried the very survival of Nevya on her shoulders. It was to her the people looked to relieve the shortage of Gifted children. It was of her the Magistral Committee demanded answers and explanations. Sira held the very future of Nevya in her hands. She could not be expected to tolerate the blundering efforts of one young Singer.

Emle felt her heart's desire slipping through her fingers. Her father would be furious, her mother disappointed, her brothers scornful.

She replaced the stool in its corner with exaggerated care while she composed herself. She made a silent vow. If she was to be sent away, she would go with a brave face. She would behave with grace and courage.

She turned back to Maestra Magret with her spine straight and her head high. She was, after all, a Singer. Her Gift was flawed, her future uncertain, but she was a Singer. She would carry herself like one.

# *One*

AN ENORMOUS ICEBERG, calved from the Great Glacier, had floated for days off the southern coast of the Continent. When it crashed against the cliffs, its impact shook the very stones of the House of Tarus.

Luke lifted his head, distracted by the noise. He was on his knees in a loose box, soothing the labor pangs of one of the *hruss* in his charge. The old mare had borne one too many foals already, and for a whole day and night she had struggled to deliver this one. Luke's heart ached for her. He patted her rigid flank, and waited for her pain to recede for a moment before he stood. He slipped out of the stall and went to lean his long torso over the open half-door of the stables, drawing deep breaths of fresh cold air.

The stables were built at the back of Tarus. From the door Luke could see the whole bay, circled by icy cliffs that glittered in the morning sun. A low stone wall ran to the east and west along the broad cliff path, protecting people and *hruss* from falling to the rocks below. Luke squinted against the brightness to see the iceberg. The day before, it had been an enormous peaked mass, a dull, dirty gray above the frigid blue water. Now it had split, all at once, into three jagged floes, their raw edges clean and white. Fragments called brash ice choked the choppy water, shining like bits of broken limeglass. As he watched, another chunk fell from the original berg with a noisy splash. Behind him, the *hruss* shifted their great feet and whickered uneasily.

He called to them, keeping his voice low and even. "Whoa, there. Be easy, you big babies. Just ice falling into the sea." On his way back to the laboring mare, he patted a few broad, shaggy heads, tugged one or two floppy ears. Beyond the House lay the deep cold, but here, in the stables, the air was warm, ripe with the smell of *hruss* flesh and the peppery fragrance of freshly laid straw. Even now, as Luke knelt again beside the mare, the air brightened, and the heat intensified. In the Cantoris, the Singers were performing the *quirunha*, driving back the cold for another day, protecting the House through another long, frigid night.

Luke stroked the mare's tight flank, murmuring sympathy. He had tried, before the breeding season, to tell Axl that the mare was too frail to foal again, but his effort had won him only his stepfather's mockery.

Luke had worked in the stables for just three years, but he had been riding *hruss* since he was a tiny boy, first up behind his father, then on his own mount by the time he had two summers. They had lived at the House of Filus, far to the north, Luke and his parents and his little sister, until Luke's father's death in a hunting accident. When his mother had accepted Axl v'Tarus as her new mate, Axl brought them through the Southern Timberlands to the big House here on the shore of the Frozen Sea.

Luke's mother, Erlys, went to work in the linen ambry, with his little sister Gwin clinging to her trouser legs as she washed and dried and folded. Luke became Axl's apprentice, a job which filled the long Nevyan days with cleaning stables, spreading fresh straw, and repairing tack. The arrival of travelers from other Houses meant more beasts to feed, to curry, to stable.

He had grown too fast during the past cold seasons. He hardly knew where to put his big feet, where to fit his long legs. He kept to the stables whenever he could, in the company of dumb beasts, where heads didn't turn when he stumbled, as they did in the great room. For days on end, he spoke to no one but his mother and sister and Axl. His speech grew clumsy as well, as if from disuse. He fell into a habit of silence, walking through the House with his eyes down, his shoulders slumped. When he tried to speak to Housemembers, his tongue felt thick and his lips dry. Even to his own ears, Luke sounded like a half-wit, and so he spoke even less.

In Axl's presence, it was worse. His stepfather laughed at him. Even if Luke managed to speak his mind, Axl ignored him. In the matter of this old mare, for instance, he had dismissed Luke's concern as ignorance. And now, as the hours of labor dragged on, the master of *hruss* was nowhere to be seen. Luke had been alone in the stables since the previous afternoon.

"Luke?"

He scrambled up at the sound of his mother's voice,

and went to open the gate of the box. "Here."

She stepped into the stables from the corridor, her eyes searching the corners, the door to the tack room, the other stalls.

"I'm alone." Luke moved into the passageway so his mother could see him.

Erlys, a petite and delicate woman who looked much younger than her eight summers, smiled up at her tall son. "I brought your breakfast," she said, holding out a wooden bowl covered in a napkin. Her voice was girlish, too, almost as light and high as her daughter's. "You weren't in your bed last night."

"The mare's still laboring," Luke said.

"Axl should be back soon."

Luke took the bowl from Erlys's hands and went into the tack room. He sat on the bench that circled the walls, stretching out his legs. The *keftet* was rich with fresh fish, grain, and vegetables from the nursery garden. The bread, soft and hot, steamed with the fragrance of the softwood used in the big ovens. He devoured the bread in three bites, and took a huge spoonful of *keftet*. "Been gone awhile," he said.

"It's been eight days." Erlys sat beside him and put her hand on Luke's arm. He looked down at it, startled by how small it appeared. In the season just past, it seemed he had grown up all at once. He was now a head taller than Axl, though his shoulders were still narrow.

He took another bite and swallowed. "Where's Gwin?"

"In the Cantoris. She went to listen to the *quirunha*," Erlys said.

Luke had seen his sister in the Cantoris, her head tilted, her eyes closed as she listened to the music. She was dark like

Luke, but petite like her mother. She was impatient to claim two summers, like all Nevyan children, but in truth, she was only six years old, born in the second season of a long winter. He had been thirteen, not quite three summers himself.

Erlys stood up now, shaking the straw from her loose trousers. As he handed her his empty bowl, Luke noticed she wore new boots, beautifully made, with rich cuffs of *caeru* fur and thick hide soles. "Another pair of boots?" he asked, without thinking.

She glanced away, absently smoothing the binding of her hair. "Axl gave them to me," she said vaguely.

Luke bit his lip. Being *hrussmaster* at Tarus was respectable work, and important work, but it was not lucrative. They were plain Housemen, he and Axl. They wore the colored tunics of the lower levels, and lived in a small apartment not far from the stables. Luke could not imagine how Axl managed to bestow so many luxuries on Erlys, and her blithe acceptance of them irritated him. He thought sometimes, though with a pang at his disloyalty, that his mother behaved as if she were as much a child as Gwin, or even more so. She forgot Axl's slights as easily as she accepted his gifts.

He bent so his mother could kiss his cheek, and then he turned back to the laboring *hruss*.

WHEN THE AFTERNOON was almost gone, Luke went to close the top of the half-door. Temperatures dropped swiftly as daylight faded, and no Nevyan liked looking out into darkness. Every citizen understood from babyhood how deadly the deep cold could be. Luke had exercised the *hruss* and brought them back to the stables for their feeding. He had spent the entire afternoon cleaning the stable floor. The mare still labored. It seemed he would miss another meal.

He turned swiftly when he heard the door from the House open. He expected Axl at last, but it was the slight figure of his sister, Gwin, stepping carefully across the straw-strewn floor. Behind her came the junior Cantor of Tarus, timid Josu, the slender cylinder of his *filla* gleaming in his hand. His eyes darted anxiously here and there, and Luke knew he was searching for the *hrussmaster*. Axl's disdain of the Gifted was well-known.

"Gwinlet?" Luke said, eyebrows raised in question.

"Hello, Luke," she piped. She gave him a tentative smile. "I brought help."

Luke hurried to bow to the Cantor, feeling clumsy in the presence of this slender, fine-boned young man, whose somber clothes spoke eloquently of the upper levels. "Cantor Josu. I—I don't—"

"Your sister tells me that your beast has suffered since yesterday," Josu said. His voice was light and clear.

Luke couldn't think of anything to say. He had never spoken directly to one of the Gifted, and he marveled at Gwin's ease with them. He was painfully aware of the soiled straw that clung to his boots, that his hands needed washing and his nails were dark with grime. He ducked his head and stepped back to open the loose box.

The three of them crowded in, and Gwin looked up expectantly at the Cantor.

Luke stood awkwardly to one side as Cantor Josu stared

down at the *hruss's* swollen belly. The Singer's delicate nostrils flared at the scents of manure and sweating animal flesh, the tinge of blood in the air. Only Gwin seemed entirely comfortable.

Josu cleared his throat. "I have no experience with birthing, Houseman. My senior aids the Housewomen—at least, he did when he was well. But I can try."

The mare groaned, and Luke knelt beside her head. He stroked her shaggy neck. The heat of her body almost singed his fingers. "Poor old lady," he said under his breath. He looked up at the Cantor, wishing he could be articulate, at least at this moment. "Her gut's gone weak," he blurted, and then wished he could unspeak the words. It was the truth of the situation, but there must be a better way to express it, especially in the presence of one of Tarus's Cantors.

The ways of the Gifted were beyond Luke's understanding. They spoke to one another with their minds, an ability Luke could not comprehend. Cantors and Cantrixes had power over the very air, over the inner workings of the body.

Cantor Josu put his *filla* to his lips, his fingers on the stops. He closed his eyes as he began to play.

"*Aiodu,*" Gwin whispered to Luke. He had no idea what she meant.

The slender thread of music spun patterns as delicate and crystalline as snowflakes. Josu's fingers lifted and fell on the stops of the little instrument in a graceful dance as mysterious to Luke the stableman as the Gift itself. Gwin stood beside Luke, one small hand on his shoulder. Her eyes were closed, too, her face as intent as the Cantor's. A prickle of anxiety crept across Luke's shoulders as he looked at her, a vague unease that had nothing to do with the *hruss*.

The mare groaned again, and her sides heaved. Distracted, Luke pressed his hands against her, and felt the ripple of her flanks as the Cantor's psi helped her to push at her burden. He forgot his anxiety in wonder at it. He exclaimed, "Six Stars! It's working!" Gwin opened her eyes and looked with shy pride from the Cantor to her brother. Josu went on playing, and the air in the loose box grew brighter, warmed by his efforts.

A half hour passed before the foal, in a rush of blood and water, was delivered at last. The odors intensified in the over-heated stall. Cantor Josu, perspiring and a little pale, leaned against the wall with a handkerchief pressed to his nose while Luke scrubbed the new little beast clean with the rags Gwin brought. A few minutes later they helped the foal to stand on its wobbly legs. Gwin laughed to see it staggering around the loose box, nosing its dam, nosing Luke as if he could provide what it needed. Luke helped the old mare to her feet, and the foal began to suckle.

Luke straightened, pulling his sweat-soaked tunic away from his body. He stared at his boots as he mumbled, "Thanks." He wiped his face with his sleeve. "Might have lost her."

The Singer waved a slender hand, and backed out of the loose box. Gwin started to follow him, but Luke caught her back. "You're too dirty, Gwinlet," he whispered.

In the passageway, Cantor Josu stamped his feet to loosen the bits of straw that stuck to his thin-soled boots. He tucked his *filla* inside his tunic as he turned toward the House.

Before he could take a step, the door into the stables

banged open. Josu stopped where he was, and his pale face grew paler.

"Luke?" Axl's voice was deep, the baritone of a big man. Luke pushed Gwin gently behind him, and stepped to the door of the loose box.

Axl had handsome, even features and a shock of thick blond hair. His blue eyes, as he stood staring at the Singer, were icy. Courtesy demanded that he wait for the Cantor to speak first, but Luke could feel the edge of his stepfather's temper in the silence.

Josu, of course, should have nothing to fear from a mere master of *hruss*. But Axl's sharp tongue was famous throughout the House. He complained constantly to the Housekeeper that the *quiru* did not extend far enough, that the stables were too dark, that the water of the *ubanyor* was too cold.

Axl glanced to his right, where Luke stood. The brightness of the air in the stall gave clear evidence of a Singer's work. Axl couldn't address Josu, but he snapped at his stepson. "What's happening here?"

Luke felt his own temper growing, heating his chest, burning his cheeks, but he restrained it. He had been restraining it for three years, for Erlys's sake. Now he muttered through stiff lips, "The mare—long labor. Cantor Josu played, and—and the foal is born at last."

Axl's lips quirked. "Couldn't handle it alone, Luke? A simple foaling?"

It was a grossly unfair thing to say. Luke knew he was good with *hruss*. The beasts responded to him, trusted him. But he couldn't defend himself against Axl. He was not the one who would pay the price of such a conflict. He set his jaw, and kept silent.

Gwin crowded against the back of his legs, and her little hand stole into his, seeking comfort.

The young Cantor cleared his throat. "It was a simple thing, Houseman," he said uneasily. "A nudge only. Your son spent all of last night with the beast."

Axl bowed to the Singer, not quite as deeply as was proper, but elegantly. "I thank you for your help, Cantor," he said smoothly. "Especially in view of the shortage of the Gift, and your senior's illness. I'll certainly mention to the Magister your generosity in spending your afternoon in the stables." It was more a threat than a compliment.

Josu swallowed, the muscles of his throat working. He nodded to Axl, and then to Luke, and made his escape from the stables, sidling past the *hrussmaster*.

Gwin crept out from behind the shelter of Luke's legs, keeping her tight grip on his hand.

Axl's eyebrows lifted, and he gave the little girl a tight smile that turned Luke's heart to stone. "You here, too?" he said. "Does Erlys know?"

"Nothing wrong with Gwin being here," Luke muttered.

"Need a lot of help with your work, don't you, son?" Axl said lightly. "From the Gifted and from a slip of a girl." He strode to the loose box to look in. "Better get this mess cleaned up. Expecting a traveling party tonight."

Luke released his sister's hand, and bent to scrub the filth from her little boots with a handful of straw. "Off to Mama now, Gwinlet," he murmured. "I have work to do." Gwin scampered away without a backward look.

Luke walked back into the stall, a wary eye on his step-father. Axl behaved one way in Erlys's presence, and another in her absence. Luke, and even Gwin, moved warily around him. Gwin had learned to control her expression in his presence. She kept her voice small, and she played with her toys only when Axl was away. She struggled to keep her cubby-hole of a room neat enough that he would have nothing to complain of. When Luke thought of Gwin's attempts to smooth her bedfurs, to tidy her little assortment of brushes and ribbons, his chest grew tight with resentment.

He gritted his teeth and reached for the pitchfork. Axl, hands on hips, watched him begin his work before he turned away to the tack room.

Luke scraped the dirty straw out into the corridor and scattered fresh straw between the feet of the old mare and her suckling foal. He loaded the refuse into a wheeled barrow, and pushed it to the outer door. He pulled on his furs before he opened the door, worked the barrow over the stone step, and wheeled it around the back of the stables to empty it into the waste drop.

Full darkness had not yet settled over the Frozen Sea. In the bay, the fragments from the iceberg glowed crimson in the setting sun. The day had been long, and Luke thought the much-anticipated summer must surely be near. He let the bar-row rest and walked to the cliff edge to look down on the rocky, wave-lapped verge.

Tarus had no beach to speak of. The road approaching the House wound around the bay, skirting the cliffs. The fishermen pulled their *kikyu* directly up the cliff on a rope pulley, else they would be full of ice at daybreak. Only when the Visitor arrived, bringing the summer, could the *kikyu* stay in the water at night, bobbing peacefully on the waves, waiting for the fishing parties to go out in the morning.

Luke yearned for the summer—to be out of doors, to escape the endless labor of the stables and the disdainful eye of his stepfather. He loved working with *hruss*—their pungent smell, the feel of their shaggy fur, their trusting ways. But he longed to ride as his father had done, escorting hunters or traveling parties, learning the secret ways of the Continent. Luke knew how to build cookfires of softwood, how to locate the elusive *caeru* dens. His father had promised to teach him how to track the *urbear* that wandered off the glacier, to show him the landmarks to the passes and trails of the Continent. But his father died before he could fulfill his promise, and when Erlys accepted Axl, Luke's fortunes changed.

He sighed, and lifted the handles of the barrow once again. He was, he thought, little more than Axl's servant. He could not even protect the *hruss* from his stepfather's cruelty.

He glanced above the roofs of the House, beyond the halo of *quiru* light that enveloped it. Stars had begun to glitter in Nevya's sky. Time to get indoors, before the cold reached its icy fingers beneath his furs. The summer was not yet here. But soon, he told himself, one morning soon, he would look to the southeastern horizon and see the Visitor's pale face peeking above the mountains. Then, for a few short weeks, he would know the taste of freedom.

# *Two*

MREEN MOUNTED THE dais in Conservatory's Cantoris, her *filhata* tucked under her arm, her back tingling under the intense regard of her fellow students, her teachers, and the Housemen and Housewomen. It was her day, the day of her first *quirunha*, the ritual that would, if successful, proclaim Mreen a full Cantrix, Conservatory-trained and ready to take up the responsibilities of her own Cantoris. Every seat on the long ironwood benches was taken, the bright tunics of the lower levels mingling with the somber ones of the upper House. People without seats stood in the back of the room, before the tall limeglass windows, or leaned against the side walls. Mreen had prepared for the moment, but still, as she turned to look out at the curious faces turned up to the dais, nerves quivered beneath her breastbone. She smoothed her new black tunic over her trousers and took a slow breath.

She knew why so many people were in attendance. There had never been a Singer such as she. In fact, she could not truly be called a Singer. Though she walked in a perpetual haze of light, her own private, spontaneous *quiru* that hardly faded even when she slept, she could not sing. Neither could she speak. She was not capable of so much as a whisper. As an infant, her cries and laughter had been silent. As a student, her *quiru* were powerful and swift, but they were accomplished solely with the *filla* or, when she reached the third level, the stringed *filhata*. She had mastered the modes and their uses swiftly and easily. But she could not sing.

The Housemen and -women of Conservatory, who knew Mreen's wishes only if one of the Gifted voiced them for her, had gathered to learn how a *quirunha* might be with no singing.

Sunlight glittered blindingly on the snowfields from beyond the windows, and was reflected from the polished iron-wood benches and the smooth stone floor. The Magistrix of Conservatory stood near the doors, her arms folded, her tall figure limned in light. Her features did not move as she sent, *Are you ready, Mreen?*

Mreen bowed to the assembly as she responded. *I am, Magistrix.*

*Please begin, then.*

Mreen seated herself on the stool that awaited her and took her *filhata* across her knees. She stroked the strings, just once, checking her tuning. The bass C rippled out into the Cantoris, vibrating in perfect accord with the layered fifths of the other six strings.

At a normal *quirunha*, even a first *quirunha* as this one was, there would be two Singers on the dais. A senior Cantor or Cantrix would support the student in this all-important ceremony, which was as much a test as a proof that the junior Singer was ready. But they had decided—Magistrix Sira,

Maestra Magret, and Mreen herself—that she must perform her *quirunha* alone. She must prove her worthiness, demonstrate that despite being voiceless, she could serve her people, create the warmth and light that protected them from the deep cold and fulfill the duties of a full Cantrix.

Mreen bent her head above her instrument and closed her eyes. She plucked the C with deliberation, letting it fill the Cantoris, one solitary note to throb in the bones of its hearers. She placed her forefinger on the string to raise it a half step, and then another. The melody that swelled from her instrument was in the fifth mode, *Mu-Lidya*, rich and mournful and satisfying. She stated the tune first as monody, and then began to harmonize it with the other strings, letting the chords grow and change. She modulated to *Lidya* as she had planned, and then to *Doryu*. She closed her eyes, letting the music carry her, visualizing its form as she always did, seeing the pattern that grew and expanded and then curled in on itself as she changed modes, giving the music a new pattern, a fresh color, another meaning.

The image of her mother, the mother she had never known, took shape in her mind—laughing Isbel who had gone beyond the stars seventeen years before, Isbel who had died giving birth to Mreen, Isbel who should never have conceived a child. Mreen's heart filled with grief and shame, and she poured all of it into her music. She didn't hear the gasps from her hearers, didn't see the billow of light or feel the wave of warmth that swept out from the dais. She floated on the tide of melody, letting it carry her away from her secret sorrow, away from the Cantoris, and most especially away from the curious stares of the Housemembers. She had been born for the Gift. Almost effortlessly, she stretched herself past the walls of Conservatory, beyond the stands of irontrees, reaching, as if to the stars themselves, for her disgraced mother.

Mreen had no idea how long she played. She modulated to *Iridu*, a perfectly prepared, perfectly balanced modulation, and restated her melody, embellishing it with little quarter-tone flourishes, her fingertips tingling, her *filhata* as much a part of her as her own hands.

*Mreen.*

She heard the Magistrix's sending, but only faintly. Her mind was full of music.

*Mreen.*

Vaguely, she knew she must bring the piece to an end, but she had ideas yet to work out, a trill on the third degree of *Iridu*, resolving to a flurry of descending notes that would anticipate her cadence . . .

*Cantrix Mreen. You have made your point.*

Mreen drew a sharp breath, suddenly aware of what she was doing. Overdoing. She abandoned the trill and slowed her flying fingers on the strings. Smoothly, as if she had planned just such an abrupt ending, she modulated back to *Mu-Lidya*, and reached her cadence. She took a slower breath, and allowed the resonance of her final chord to decay in the hall before she opened her eyes.

No Nevyan ever complained of being too warm. Cold was every Nevyan's enemy, the ogre that stalked their nightmares, that waited beyond the circles of *quiru* light to seize them in its deadly grip. But at this moment, it was as if the two suns had shone directly into the Cantoris, warming the air to breathlessness, bringing perspiration to the brows and lips of everyone present. The air sparkled with a reddish glow, kindled by Mreen's powerful Gift. The dais itself shimmered with light, as it were afire.

Mreen stood, tucking her *filhata* under her arm, and bowed abruptly to the stunned assembly. As she stepped off the dais, one of her fellow third-level students in the front row came to his feet to begin the closing prayer. Mreen hurried up the aisle with the familiar chant flowing around her:

*Smile on us,*
*O Spirit of Stars,*
*Send us the summer to warm the world,*
*Until the suns will shine always together.*

It was not until she reached the doorway, where the Magistrix now stood, smiling her narrow smile, that Mreen realized Magistrix Sira had used her new title. Cantrix. She had passed her test.

Mreen bowed solemnly to Sira before she turned to receive the congratulations of her classmates, of the Housemen and -women. It was her moment. She saw that her fingertips were incandescent with residual energy. She looked up at Sira, supposing that her hair and her cheeks also shone with it, and she saw by the sparkle in Sira's eyes that it was true.

*You look very like your mother at this moment, Cantrix Mreen.*

Mreen bent her head. She knew she looked like her mother. When she held her mother's brushes in her fingers, she saw Isbel as clearly as she saw her own image in the reflective pool of the *ubanyix*. *Thank you, Magistrix. And thank you for stopping me just now.*

Sira gave a dry chuckle. *We would not want the Cantoris to catch fire*, she sent.

Mreen felt a blush add to the heat of her face, but the other third-level students came crowding around her, distracting her from her embarrassment. She was the first of her class to complete her studies, and she realized with a start that though they stood close to her, they took care not to touch her. She was now a full Cantrix, and the title set her apart.

Her cheeks suddenly cooled, and her fingers ceased their tingle. Even her halo of light, always brighter than the *quiru* around her, dimmed a little. She was an adult now, with an adult's responsibilities. Everything had changed.

EMLE STOOD WITH the other second-level students at the outer edge of the circle of well-wishers around the newly made Cantrix. As she listened to the jumble of silent congratulations and compliments, she watched the glow fade from Mreen's dimpled cheeks. Her private nimbus still brought out the red shades in her hair, but her green eyes darkened, and her eyelids drooped. She looked, for a moment, unhappy. But why, Emle wondered, should she be unhappy?

Emle bit her lip. It seemed there would be no *quirunha* for Emle, though she worked and studied harder than anyone. These other students would each have their turn, while she, Emle, would return home to Perl in disgrace. A failure.

Her mother would lose the large apartment she treasured. Her father would forfeit his rights to the first kills, the best cuts, the finest pelts. Her brothers would no longer be able to boast of their Gifted sister. They would never forgive her.

Emle stared at her feet, shielding her thoughts. Nothing should mar Mreen's triumph.

When she had mastered herself, she looked up to find Mreen's eyes on her, brows raised. Emle flushed. *Congratulations,* she sent hurriedly, forcing her trembling lips to smile. *Your* quirunha *was like none I have ever seen.*

No smile touched Mreen's lips. Her eyes slid away, even as she sent, *Thank you, Emle. The Magistrix stopped me just in time, I think.*

*No one can ever complain that a* quiru *is too* strong! Emle responded.

Mreen's mouth tightened, and she turned away. Emle wondered if she had offended her. She had not meant to, but it seemed she could do nothing right on this day. She took a step back, letting a flow of people come between her and Mreen. The dais still shone with abundant light. Even the sunlit windows faded in Mreen's *quiru.* Why, oh why, did Mreen have such a strong Gift that it must be reined in, while Emle possessed one so weak that no amount of effort seemed to strengthen it?

And what would she do with her life now? She could mate, she supposed. She had never given thought to that, having believed since she first entered Conservatory that she would be a Cantrix one day. She supposed she could become a seamstress, like her mother, or a cook, like her aunt. She could polish furniture or clean floors. Emle pictured herself on her knees, sponge in hand, scrubbing the *ubanyix*, listening as another Singer played a *filla* to warm the water. Emle would recognize the mode, would know she could play it better—how bitter a moment that would be.

She closed her eyes. When she opened them, Maestra Magret stood before her, leaning on her ironwood staff.

*Emle, the Magistrix would like to see you now.*

Emle put her forefinger against her trembling lips to steady them, glad she did not have to speak aloud. *I am ready, Maestra.*

*Good girl.* Her teacher's face was calm, her eyes level. *I will go with you.*

Emle followed Magret's bent back. They left the Cantoris, passing into the relative cool of the stairwell, and moved slowly up the wide, worn staircase. Their feet fit neatly into grooves worn into the ironwood by generations of students and teachers past remembering. Emle's fingers traced the *obis*-carvings of the banister as she climbed.

Magret knocked briefly on the door of the Magistrix's apartment, and it opened immediately. Ita, the Magistrix's Housewoman, held the door open for them to enter, and bowed as Magret passed her. "Maestra Magret," she said respectfully. "The Magistrix will be with you in a moment. I'll bring some tea."

Emle followed Magret through the door. Ita said cheerfully, "And you, Singer? Would you like something to eat?"

"Thank you, Housewoman," Emle said. "I am not at all hungry." Her voice sounded steady in her ears, and she took pride in this small accomplishment.

"Tea will be lovely, Ita," Magret said, lowering herself painfully into a chair. "Come sit beside me now, Emle."

"Yes, Maestra." It was customary, before the Housemen and -women, to speak so that those without the Gift could hear. It was also a matter of respect for a junior to follow a senior's lead, in this as in all other things.

Emle took a seat and accepted a cup from Ita. The finely carved ironwood transmitted the warmth of the fragrant tea to her fingers, and she let it strengthen her.

She felt Magret's eyes on her and looked up.

*Do not despair, my dear,* the old Maestra sent gently. *The ways of the Spirit are sometimes strange. Often what seems a tragedy becomes an opportunity.*

Emle doubted the old Singer could possibly understand her pain at this moment, but she pressed down the thought. It was hers to carry, hers alone. She sent, *Yes, Maestra. Thank you.* Magret's eyes flickered, and Emle knew Magret too had buried some thought.

There was no time to ponder what that thought might have been. Magistrix Sira was speaking with someone in the corridor, short, hard phrases in her deep voice. When she came through the door, her dark eyes were narrow and full of sparks. She dropped her long, lean frame into the chair beside the window and stared out through the limeglass for a moment, not speaking. Emle set her cup down and gripped her hands together beneath the table. Magistrix Sira was angry.

*Sira?*

Emle heard the sending. *Maestra Magret,* she suddenly

remembered, had been the Magistrix's senior, years before, at the House of Bariken. Emle supposed their relationship gave Magret special privileges. Surely no one else at Conservatory would dare send to the Magistrix without invitation. And certainly not without her title!

The Magistrix let her head fall back against the high carved back of her chair. *For every stride forward,* she sent, with a force that made Emle's head feel full, *Lamdon drives us two backward!*

*Tell me what has happened,* Magret sent mildly.

Emle relaxed her stiff posture. Whatever this was, it was not about her.

Sira sent, *It is the Magistral Committee.*

*Yes?*

Sira glared at the ceiling. *They passed the resolution.*

Magret, too, set down her cup. *Oh, Sira. And you fought so hard against it.*

*Cantor Abram resents me still. He opposes me in everything.* Sira rubbed her eyes with her fingers.

The Magistrix had almost eight summers, Emle knew. Her strong features were sun-browned and lined from years in the open. Her brown hair, which she kept cropped short in the manner of itinerant Singers, was streaked with silver, the color matching the slash that marred her right eyebrow. The students whispered stories to one another about how their Magistrix had acquired that scar, but no one knew the true one. Emle watched her from beneath carefully lowered eyelids. Sira was, Emle thought, both terrifying and magnificent.

*Who brought the news?* Magret asked.

Sira tilted her head back again and closed her eyes. *Cantor Kern sent word with an itinerant. He thought I would want to know before the emissary arrives from the Committee.*

*That was wise of him.*

*He is loyal to us, Magret, or I should say, to our cause. If the Spirit wills, all our own will be loyal to the cause, and to the Gift.* Sira opened her eyes and turned them to the snowfield beyond the window. *A child has arrived, too. Escorted by a hunter and an itinerant. No parents, no message. Just a Gifted child who is frightened and alone. And the hunter claimed he knew nothing about him.*

*How strange.*

*More than strange, Magret. It is disturbing.*

The Magistrix turned her head to Emle then, abruptly, with a fiercely intent gaze. *Emle.*

Emle tried not to look away or flinch. *Yes, Magistrix.*

*Maestra Magret tells me that your musical gifts are superb, but your quiru are inadequate.*

*It is true.* A rush of cold swept through Emle's body, and she wanted to tremble, but she would not. She made her lips firm, her eyes steady. She would not apologize for what she could not help. *I have practiced endlessly,* she sent. *I believe I practice more than any other student in the second level. It seems to do no good.*

The slanting afternoon light shone on the dark planes of Sira's face, as chiseled and clean as if they had been carved with an *obis* knife. *The Gift has its own ways,* Sira sent. *And we must find the way to use yours.*

Emle gripped her fingers tighter.

After a moment, the Magistrix sent, *There are the* obis-*carvers at Soren.*

Emle knew of the carvers, of course, as everyone did. *Obis*-carvers were oddly Gifted. They could neither send nor hear thoughts, nor create *quiru*, but they possessed enough psi to enable them to slice through the wood that came from the ironwood trees, the wood that was so hard it would not burn no matter how hot the fire. But Emle did not want to carve. She wanted to Sing. She would rather scrub floors than use her Gift in any other way. She swallowed, and did not answer the Magistrix.

*Emle, you are one of our own. You must not think I have forgotten what it is to be at odds with authority, or even with the Gift.* Sira leaned forward to put her elbows on the table. Her hands were long-fingered and thin, made for the *filhata*.

Emle looked down at her own entwined fingers. They, too, were long and slender and nimble. *If only it were something I could improve,* she sent. *My breathing, or my intonation . . .*

*Intonation can be very difficult to correct.*

Emle nodded. *I know. But a flawed Gift—I do not even know where to begin.*

*Sometimes,* Magistrix Sira sent, *the best way to solve a problem is to let it rest.*

Emle looked up.

*We have a new Cantrix, Emle. With a new assignment. But Cantrix Mreen needs someone to speak for her, until she settles in to her new position at Tarus.*

Emle's lips parted, and her mouth dried. *Speak for her?* she sent in confusion.

*Yes.* Sira raised her scarred eyebrow in Magret's direction, and the Maestra nodded.

*Of course*, Magret sent easily. *It will be much easier for Mreen to adjust that way. Until the people of Tarus learn the system of finger signs she uses—Emle, I believe you and the other students have learned them?*

*Yes, Maestra. We began when we first came, before we learned to send and listen.*

Sira inclined her head. *Mreen should no doubt have gone to Lamdon, where there are so many of the Gifted. But she is needed at Tarus. Cantor Mattu is tired and ill.* Sira linked her hands loosely on the table. *And this new resolution . . . I fear it will drive the Gift even further away.*

*Perhaps not, Sira.* Magret leaned forward. *We were making progress.*

The Magistrix nodded heavily. *We were. Not fast enough for the Committee, it seems.*

*They fear disaster.*

Sira snorted, a most undignified sound. *As do we all.*

*And so . . .* Magret sent delicately. *Mreen?*

Sira gave her old senior her thin smile. *Yes, Magret. You are right. We were speaking of Mreen.* She turned back to Emle. *The life of the Cantoris is an isolated one at best. With only a senior for company, I fear that for Mreen it will be too much to bear, since she cannot speak. It will take time for her Housewoman to learn to understand her. So few Housemen or -women learn to read, and in any case, writing everything she needs to say would be cumbersome and exhausting.*

*I am to go with Mreen to Tarus?*

*With Cantrix Mreen,* Magret reminded her.

Emle's cheeks burned. *Oh, yes, of course! I am sorry. I forgot.*

*An easy thing to do,* Magret sent.

Magistrix Sira stood up. Aloud, she said, "Are you willing, Emle?"

Emle stood, too, swiftly, energized by hope. She bowed from the waist, the perfect depth for her Magistrix. "I prepared myself to do whatever you asked of me. This request is easier than the one I expected."

Sira regarded her for a moment, and then turned to Magret. "You were right, Maestra," she said. "A remarkable girl." And to Emle once again, "You will remain at Tarus through the summer. Cantrix Mreen will be glad of your company, and of your strength of spirit. When you return, we will see how things stand."

Emle pressed all her thoughts low as she bowed once more. Mreen would be far better company than the *obis*-carvers. And there would be music.

Sira turned toward the door and then back, as if she had forgotten something. In a low tone, she said, "There is an odd coincidence. The riders who brought this little boy to us came from Tarus."

"I do not understand," Magret said. "Do they not know who his parents are? What House he is from?"

"They have a story." Sira's lips pressed into a hard line. "I do not believe a word of it."

# Three

THE SECOND-LEVEL STUDENTS whispered that Mreen's mother had been a Cantrix. If the story was true, it meant that Mreen's mother had committed the one unpardonable offense. All Conservatory students, from the beginning of their training, knew that Cantors and Cantrixes did not—could not—mate. When they reached the third level, they would receive formal instruction about the dangers of diluting the Gift, but long before that, the students told and retold the tales to one another, frightening themselves in the long dark nights, scaring the younger children in the dormitories. They learned of Houses growing cold and dark, of *quiru* collapsing, of people freezing to death. It was understood that itinerant Singers could mate—Singers who needed only to make the small *quiru* that would protect campsites at night as they escorted travelers or hunters through the frozen landscape of the Continent.

Emle didn't know if the story about Mreen's mother was a true one. If she had indeed been a Cantrix, she had endangered her Cantoris by conceiving a child.

But what a child! Perhaps the Gift fell so richly upon Mreen because her mother had sacrificed everything for her, including her own life. Sometimes, before Mreen had moved up to the third level, Emle gazed down the long row of cots in the dormitory and saw that she lay bathed in light even as she slept.

Everyone had assumed Mreen would be assigned to Lamdon, to be shown off there like one of their exotic flowers. How strange it was that she should be sent to Tarus, far to the south, a House on the cliffs beside the Frozen Sea. Rumors flew through the dormitory. One held that Mreen was being punished for her mother's transgression, but Emle refused to believe it.

And now, as Mreen's companion, she would travel outside the walls of Conservatory for the first time since her arrival as a small child.

She stood outside the new Cantrix's room with her traveling pack in her hands. She had tucked her *filla* into its inner tunic pocket. Her pack bulged with fresh linens, extra tunics and trousers, brushes and bindings for her hair, and one or two trinkets. She set the pack down beside the door, and lifted her hand to knock.

Before her knuckles reached the ironwood, Mreen sent, *Emle? Come in.*

Emle opened the door, and saw that Sira's own Housewoman was helping Mreen with her pack. Ita whirled, startled by the opening of the door. Of course, Emle realized, she had not known anyone was there.

Emle said awkwardly, "The Cantrix asked me to enter."

Ita dropped a small stack of snowy linens on the bed and faced Emle, her hands on her hips. "I can see she will need you, Singer," she said with asperity. Her black eyes snapped. "Until her own Housewoman understands her, those at Tarus will be at a loss."

Mreen, kneeling on the floor with an assortment of small objects spread around her, glanced at Emle. *Tell Ita I thank her for her help.* She gestured to her traveling pack, in which embroidered tunics, furred boots, and folded linens had been ingeniously arranged to maximize the space. *She repacked everything for me, and made a much better job of it.*

Emle cleared her throat. "Housewoman, the Cantrix thanks you, and assures me you have worked marvels with her pack."

Ita nodded, and bent to tie the strings. "The Cantrix is welcome," she said. She lifted the pack and moved it to the corridor. As she passed Emle, she cast her an oblique glance. "I wish you good fortune with your task, Singer." She marched down the corridor. Emle, not knowing what she should do next, pulled the door closed and stood uncertainly. Mreen, her halo of light shot through with faint shadows, was picking things up, turning them in her fingers, and setting them down again.

On the bed, its *caeru* leather wrappings spread open, lay Mreen's *filhata*, carved especially for her by the *obis*-carvers of Soren, and presented to her in preparation for her first *quirunha*. The intricate pattern of leaves and branches adorning the sounding board shone with fresh oil. The black tuning pegs glistened. It was a thing of great beauty, and Emle yearned to touch it.

Mreen set aside a bit of felted cloth like the ones babies sometimes sucked on, putting it next to a small panel of tooled leather on a wooden easel, a pouch lined with white *caeru* fur, and a *ferrel* feather. She lifted a stone—little more than a gray pebble—from the floor, and cradled it in the palm of her hand. Two bits of what also looked like stones, flat and shiny, lay where she had dropped them. Emle bent to see them better.

*What are these?*

Mreen flashed her a startled look, as if she had forgotten she was there. *Have you never seen metal?*

*No, never,* Emle sent. *Are they metal?*

*So they are.* Mreen scooped up the pieces. *These bits come from Observatory, where I lived as a little child.*

Emle cupped her palm, and Mreen dropped the bits into it. They were unevenly shaped, with edges as smooth as glass, and they felt weightless. Emle turned them over to examine the faint carvings in their gray surfaces. *What do the markings say, Cantrix?*

At the title, Mreen's eyes flashed at her once again, and then away. *No one can read them.* She put out her hand, and Emle gave the metal back, careful not to touch her. *But they speak to me,* Mreen added, in an offhanded fashion.

Emle shook her head, not understanding. *Speak to you?*

Suddenly, Mreen was laughing, her head lifting, her white teeth showing. The lack of sound made it oddly humorless, and her laugh looked . . . different, Emle thought. She supposed it was because Mreen so rarely moved her lips. *Oh, yes, Emle,* Mreen sent. *Mine is a strange Gift. The metal speaks to me.*

*What does it tell you?*

The silent laugh died, and Mreen looked hard at Emle, the green of her eyes very dark, like the thickest part of the ironwood forest. *Do you know the legend of the Ship?*

*I know it from the songs.*

Mreen nodded. *The songs, yes. But at Observatory*—she held up the metal bits in her hand, and they glinted in the light. *At Observatory the Ship is not a matter of legend, but of history. And these bits of metal give me impressions of stars, an endless sky . . . and of many hands touching them—so many, and from so long ago, I cannot distinguish one from the other.*

She bent forward to touch a small brush and comb. *These were my mother's. If I hold them, and concentrate, I see her face. And this stone*—she picked up the pebble again. *I carried it away with me when I came to Conservatory.* She turned her head toward the window, and Emle saw how her chin trembled. *It shows me my father, and his dear wife who cared for me as if I were her own babe. I have been away from Observatory for more than two summers, yet I miss them still.*

Emle sighed. The Gift demanded a high price. They came to Conservatory as little children, longing for their mothers, missing their fathers, their brothers or sisters, their familiar Houses.

Mreen dropped the pebble and the two bits of metal into the fur-lined pouch, and drew its string. *I will take this,* she sent. She picked up the tooled leather panel. *And this I will give to the Magistrix, to remember my mother by.*

*And the feather? The cloth?* Emle lifted them in her fingers. The bit of cloth was so old that bits of it crumbled away as she picked it up, and she set it down again with care.

*Childish things,* Mreen sent. Her thoughts in Emle's head

were harsh, even dismissive. *It is time to discard them.*

Emle stood up again and took a step back. She must not forget that Mreen was a full Cantrix now, an adult. She was only a second-level student, and she was half a summer younger than Mreen.

Mreen touched her temple with one finger and pointed the finger at the corridor. When Emle didn't respond, she repeated the gesture. Emle frowned, and then started at the knock on the closed door. "Oh," she said aloud, suddenly realizing that Mreen had used one of her finger signs. "I am sorry, Cantrix. I forgot." She jumped up to open the door.

A Houseman in a bright green tunic stood in the corridor. He bowed to Emle. "If the Cantrix is ready," he said. "And you, Singer."

"Yes," Emle said, trying to sound assured. She pointed to Mreen's pack. "You can take that down now."

*No, Emle. Wait.*

Emle amended, "Oh, wait, Houseman. The Cantrix is not ready after all."

Mreen scrambled to her feet and retrieved the tooled leather panel and its little easel from the bureau. She opened her pack and stuffed the panel inside, on top of her folded linens. With difficulty, she retied the thongs of the pack, and then stood back. *Now. He can take it now.*

When the Houseman had shouldered both their packs and retreated down the corridor, Emle helped Mreen to bundle up her remaining possessions. She looked around at the room, bare now of anything personal. *It is hard to believe you will not be back.*

*Do not say that,* Mreen sent sharply. *Every Singer's true home is Conservatory.*

Emle dropped her head. Another mistake. *Of course, Cantrix.*

Mreen moved to the window and stood looking out for several long moments. Emle waited in the doorway, wishing she could start all of this over again. When Mreen turned from the window at last, her face was set, her eyes remote. She sent nothing further as she led the way out of the room and down the wide staircase to the foyer, and the House-members gathered on the courtyard steps to bid her farewell.

THE HOUSE ASSEMBLED in ranks, some with their hoods drawn forward, many with their heads bared to the bright, cold sunshine. The tops of the ironwood trees swayed gently in a light breeze. The riders from Tarus were ready, the *hruss* stamping and snorting, eager to be off. Mreen glanced over her shoulder at the empty saddle awaiting her. It looked hard and uncomfortable, although Emle seemed delighted. The younger girl was mounted and ready, with one of the riders holding her reins. She had pulled her hood forward, and her eyes, sparkling with excitement, were very blue against the yellow-white of the *caeru* fur. The sunlight brought hints of gold from the strands of brown hair that escaped their binding to curl around her cheeks.

Mreen turned back to the gathering, and her face felt as rigid as the surface of the Great Glacier. She willed herself cold and still.

The students, following custom, sent their silent wishes to Mreen first.

*Congratulations, Cantrix Mreen!*

*I hope you like Tarus!*

*Go with the Spirit, Cantrix Mreen!*

The first-level students sent a jumble of half-intelligible good-byes. They were the only Gifted to be noisy, giggling, once in a while forgetting themselves in speaking aloud or whispering to one another. The second-level students hushed them, but in relaxed fashion. It was a day to celebrate. One or two of the young ones flashed Mreen finger-signs.

—*Good-bye!*—

—*Good luck!*—

After the students, the teachers, one by one, sent Mreen their good wishes.

The last part of the ceremony was Sira's, and she spoke aloud for the benefit of the Housemembers. Her deep voice rang across the cobbled courtyard. "Cantrix Mreen," she said. "The hope and pride of all of us, your friends and your colleagues, go with you. And remember—" Mreen lifted her head, anticipating the time-honored words that ended every farewell ceremony. "Remember that every Singer's true home is Conservatory. We await your eventual return, by the will of the Spirit."

*Thank you, Magistrix.* Mreen bowed deeply and turned to the rider waiting to help her onto her *hruss*. The rider, a weathered woman of nine or ten summers, put her hand under Mreen's bent left knee and boosted her into the high-cantled saddle. When Mreen settled herself, the rider tucked each of her booted feet into the stirrups and adjusted them for length. She tested the cinch and then mounted her own *hruss* with a nimble swinging of her right leg over the saddle. She kept Mreen's reins in her own hand and gave the Cantrix a quick bow before she turned to the leader of the traveling party.

"Ready here," she said briefly.

Mreen already felt the hardness of the saddle, and knew she would be sore by nightfall. She welcomed the physical discomfort as a distraction from her other emotions. And in any case, if she were a poor rider it would not matter. It was perfectly possible that, once having reached Tarus, she would never again ride out of its courtyard.

She took a last look at the assembled members of Conservatory. *Farewell, my friends,* she sent. She knew they would think her final message cold, even terse. But she dared not unshield herself to say anything personal. She relied on ritual. *May the Spirit of Stars keep you well and safe until we meet again.*

A silent chorus answered her, repeating the farewells and good wishes.

With her eyes on Sira's face, Mreen made one finger sign, the tips of her fingers touching her chest, turning outward. —*Farewell.*— She and Sira had never been apart since her birth. Sira's eyes were dark and unreadable as she repeated the sign.

At a call from the *hrussmaster,* the entire traveling party wheeled and clattered out of the courtyard. The *hruss'* broad hooves slid against the cobblestones, then trod firmly on the snowpack as they paced away from Conservatory on their way to the Southern Pass. They would follow the Pass into the Southern Timberlands. After three days, if all went well, they would turn west into a narrow path that followed the rocky cliffs that bordered the Frozen Sea. Two days' ride on the cliff path would bring them to Tarus.

Mreen twisted in her saddle for a last look at the slanted roofs of Conservatory, glowing with *quiru* light. The farewell ceremonies for new Cantors and Cantrixes always spoke of the return of the Singer to his or her true home, but she knew well that many never returned. Some worked in the Cantoris right to the moment of their passage beyond the stars. The need for their services was a matter of life and death to their people, and there were never enough of the Gifted. Many Singers held the memory of Conservatory only in their hearts.

Mreen felt Emle's eyes on her.

*Are you all right, Cantrix Mreen?*

*Of course,* Mreen sent. She could not bear, at this moment, to share her feelings.

Emle dropped her eyes, and Mreen felt a stab of compunction. Emle must have fears of her own. But just now, it was all Mreen could do to control her own emotions. She touched the pouch at her waist that carried the bits of metal, the stone from Observatory. She looked around her at the men and women who would, from this moment, depend upon her to keep them warm. Her heart thrummed in her ears. She had never felt so alone.

# *Four*

THE LINE OF *hruss* lumbered along the snowy trail, and the riders from Tarus, four men and one woman, rode in silence. The master of *hruss* led the way, with the most junior rider bringing up the rear behind Mreen and Emle. The riders kept watchful eyes on the forest around them and on the surface of the road beneath the *hruss'* hooves. They took special care to guide Mreen's mount, and Emle's, around the ironwood suckers that arched and twisted above the ground.

The wind sang in the highest branches of the ancient trees. Mreen tipped her head back to try to see their tops. She wondered how old they might be, how many winters had passed as they stretched out their huge roots, the great suckers that brought new treelings up from the frozen ground of the Continent. How many times had the Visitor shone on these trees? How many human lives had begun and ended while they grew?

The *hruss'* feet made plopping noises in the snow as they paced steadily south. Mist plumed from their wide nostrils, and their drooping ears turned back and forth, following the occasional commands from rider to *hruss*. Saddles creaked, and occasionally someone coughed, or grunted. All of it together made music of a sort, but she missed the stream of mental chatter that filled the students' wing of Conservatory.

Emle would answer, of course, if she sent to her, but Mreen had kept her mind strictly shielded from the moment her farewell ceremony ended. She feared revealing the panic that lurked beneath her silence, that intensified with every step her *hruss* took away from Conservatory. What if something went wrong? When had she ever called up *quiru* out-of-doors, under the naked stars, with the true threat of the deep cold all around?

It was all well and good to be a star student when the thick stone walls of Conservatory protected you, when there were senior Cantors and Cantrixes, even other student Singers, who could make the warmth and the light bloom, banish the darkness and the cold. But when the sun sank below the western mountains, and the air chilled, all these people would turn to her to keep them safe.

Mreen was born to be a Singer. She had known that since before she could walk. From her babyhood, she had walked in *quiru* light, slept in it, never knowing a moment's true darkness. At Conservatory, Mreen called up the swiftest, warmest *quiru* of any of the students, and she knew that Sira expected great things of her. But she imagined that under the pressure of all these eyes upon her—these weathered faces turned to her, knowing hands stilled at their work—she could falter. Her fingers could slip upon her *filla*, or her mind be distracted

by the evening wind, the imagined snarl of a *tkir* or the growl
of an *urbear*. She could fail. As her mother had failed.

She touched the bag of talismans at her waist, and she
prayed to the Spirit of Stars to sustain her.

When the road bent at a sharp angle, she let her gaze slide
sideways, just enough to see Emle riding behind her. The
younger girl rode as if she had been born to it, bracing her
slight weight easily against the cantle, her hands relaxed upon
the pommel. Her eyes, round with innocent pleasure in the
novelty of the day, were as blue as the clear sky above them.
When the nearest rider smiled at her, a charming blush rose in
her cheeks. Her soft, gold-glinting hair curled against her slender throat. She was lovely, Mreen thought. And so young. So
carefree. She made Mreen, though she had not yet completed
four summers, feel as old as the trees looming above her head.


EMLE WAITED THROUGHOUT the morning, and
then through the entire afternoon, for Cantrix Mreen to send
something to her, anything. Emle hoped she was concentrating on her new responsibilities, but she feared that Mreen
didn't want to share her thoughts with a lowly second-level
student, especially not one as troubled as Emle.

When the traveling party stopped for the midday meal,
the woman rider, called Karn, approached Emle to ask if the
Cantrix wished to relieve herself. Emle turned to Mreen.

Mreen had heard the rider's question. She gave a brief
nod, not even glancing at Emle.

Emle followed in silence as Karn led the way to a stand

of three intertwined trees where they could have privacy. She trudged behind Mreen as they walked back through the crusted snow. Even the brightness of the late-winter sun did not fade Mreen's steady halo of light.

One of the riders brought Emle a wooden bowl of *keftet*, dried *caeru* meat mixed with grain and some spicy seed. The fresh air had sharpened her appetite, and even through her unhappiness she relished this simple traveling food, the salty taste and refreshing texture. Her spirits rose a bit. Moments later they remounted and pressed on. The riders seemed to speak only when necessary, and she supposed it was part of their general watchfulness. Surely, escorting a full Cantrix was a heavy responsibility.

Emle let her fingers stray to the rough mane of her *hruss*. She liked the feel of it, the smell of the beast's flesh in her nostrils, the warmth of the saddle. She sighed, abandoning herself to the world of her senses. If Mreen disliked her, there was little she could do about it. It was simply one more mark against her, and not the most serious one. As the sun began to slip behind the trees to the west, Mreen's halo shimmered in the gathering dusk. Perhaps, Emle thought with a touch of bitterness, Mreen had received Emle's portion of the Gift in addition to her own.

She thrust the thought away with conscious effort.

*Emle.*

Emle lifted her head, startled. *Yes, Cantrix,* she answered hurriedly.

*It is getting dark. Should we not stop?*

*I—I do not know.*

Mreen cast her a glance full of some emotion. *Ask*, she sent, and looked away again.

Emle bit her lip, abashed. She turned to the nearest rider, and when she tried to speak, her voice was dry and creaky. "Excuse me," she said, and cleared her throat. "Excuse me, please—I am sorry. I did not hear your name."

He grinned at her. "Not that you'll need it, Singer, but I'm Pyotr. Pyotr v'Tarus, at your service." He gave a shallow bow. "How can I help you?"

She smiled, too, relieved at the easy exchange after the hours of tense silence. "It is the Cantrix," she said. "She wishes to know if it is not time to stop for the night."

Pyotr lifted the reins of his *hruss*, and touched its ribs with his heels. As he rode past, he said over his shoulder, "I'll ask Axl. But if the Cantrix wants to stop, she has only to say so. It's for her to command."

Emle saw Mreen's fingers come up and flash a sign. She nodded.

"Pyotr," she called hastily after the rider. "The Cantrix does wish to stop. If you could please tell the *hrussmaster*?"

The rider lifted one hand in acknowledgment as he made his way up the line. Moments later, the party slowed and stopped, and Pyotr hurried back to take the reins of Emle's beast. Karn took those of Mreen's, bowing, holding the stirrup so that Mreen could dismount. The two Singers stood by, their legs trembling with the unaccustomed exercise, as the riders untied their saddlepacks. One gestured with a sun-browned hand toward the fire that already crackled cheerfully amid a circle of bedfurs.

Mreen walked toward the fire, her back straight, her head high. Emle followed, marveling at the new Cantrix's composure. Was she not as sore as Emle? Emle's thighs and backside burned from the hours in the saddle, and her face and lips stung from the wind and sun.

Mreen glanced around the camp, and then moved to an ironwood sucker that arched high above the snow. She brushed it clean, and then settled herself as gracefully as if it were a carved chair. She reached inside her tunic for her *filla*. Emle stood to one side, ready to assist if Mreen wanted something, but feeling superfluous.

Mreen tested the *filla*, gently blowing a C, the central pitch for both *filla* and *filhata*, and then a sweet, clear A. Emle closed her eyes. The sound was slender under the open sky. Emle felt the rapt attention of the riders around her, waiting with confidence for the column of light and warmth to rise into the dusky evening, to close out the cold and the dark, to surround them in safety for the long hours of darkness.

Mreen drew a long, slow breath, and then began, at a leisurely tempo, a melody in the second mode, *Aiodu*. Emle thought it was exactly like Mreen to choose the simplest and least ostentatious of melodies for her camp *quiru*. Mreen had no need to prove herself. She knew her Gift. She would never suffer from the doubt that assailed Emle every time she played, because Mreen had never known failure.

Emle followed Mreen's psi as it reached into the air around them to excite the luminescence and the warmth from the matter that no one could see, but every Singer knew to exist. The melody unfolded, opened like the petals of a nursery flower, centered easily around the A that was *Aiodu's* primary. Mreen's psi was as strong as an ironwood branch, as flexible as a strand of *hruss* hair. She did not play long, and she forebore any cadenza. It seemed that almost no time had passed before her tune was over, her psi withdrawing, leaving a living, breathing silence around the campfire. Emle felt the warmth even before she opened her eyes.

The column of light was as wide as it was tall, reaching up to touch the tops of the irontrees where they nodded in the night wind, stretching across the road to include more trees and their twisting roots, well beyond where the band of *hruss* now tossed their heads and stamped, awaiting their evening feed. The riders grinned at one another, nodding, murmuring appreciation. They would boast, Emle thought, to their fellow Housemembers, that they had been the first to hear their fine new Cantrix play. They would brag that although their Cantrix did not sing, she created the swiftest, warmest *quiru* on the Continent. Even the *hrussmaster*, a big, handsome man with pale eyes, seemed impressed. He stood with his thick arms folded, his head tilted to one side, watching the Cantrix as she tucked away her *filla*.

*Thank the Spirit!* Mreen sent, with a sigh that made Emle turn in surprise.

*Pardon, Cantrix?*

Mreen sighed again, a small, lonely sound. *Their lives are in my hands, Emle. It was up to me alone, this* quiru, *and although I have never failed to accomplish it, such a failure now—for whatever cause—would be disaster. Tragedy.* She stared down at her hands, and Emle felt the shielding that came over her mind as strongly as if a rock wall had suddenly sprung up between them.

Emle sank onto her bedfurs. The season ahead of her seemed long and hard.

WHEN THE DARKNESS was complete, Karn led the two Singers out of the *quiru*. Emle stared up into the night sky, stunned by its blackness. Not since her journey to Conservatory from her home at Perl had she seen the night sky undimmed by a House *quiru*. The tiny white flames of the stars burned without heat. The snowfields cast a shallow glow that quickly faded into the immensity of the night. She felt the bite of the deep cold, even in this late season, and she heeded Karn's warning to hurry, that it was not safe to linger outside.

As they stepped back into the envelope of light, Emle said, "I have not looked on the stars for a very long time."

Karn smiled over her shoulder. "It's one of the best things about being a rider."

Emle smiled, too. "Remember the song, Cantrix Mreen— the one called 'Look Back'? Maestra Magret taught it to me herself. It was the first one I learned at the second level."

Mreen's eyes sparkled in the firelight. *I will take out my fil-hata,* she sent. *Sing it for us.*

*Oh, Cantrix, I did not mean . . .* Emle's cheeks warmed, and she was glad of the darkness. *I did not mean to suggest . . .*

Mreen's teeth showed in her silent laugh, and her cheeks, surprisingly, dimpled. *Please, Singer. Sing.*

It was lovely to see Mreen smiling. As she unwrapped

her *filhata*, laying aside the split-leather coverings, tuning the strings, Emle knelt beside her on her bedfurs. She glanced beneath her lowered eyelids at the riders sprawled comfortably around the remnants of the cookfire. Karn fed the fire with bits of softwood, and the riders murmured to one another, keeping a respectful distance from the two Singers.

Even itinerant Singers, of course, deserved respect. No one could travel without a Singer except in summer, and that was far too rare a season, coming only after five long years of winter.

Summer was coming soon, though. The years since the Visitor's last appearance had dimmed Emle's memory. What would it be like, to see the two suns at once? To see the softwood shoots blooming between the ironwood trees? She could hardly wait. A delicious sense of anticipation filled her as she drew breath. Her worries faded for the moment. She listened to Mreen's first, delicately plucked notes.

Mreen knew Emle's voice, it seemed. The song could be sung in several modes, the slightly mournful *Iridu*, the bright timbre of *Lidya*, or the rich, complex harmonies of *Mu-Lidya*. Mreen had chosen *Mu-Lidya*, the perfect mode to show off the sweetness of Emle's high notes. Emle cast the Cantrix a glance, flattered by the choice. Mreen's head was bent over her *filhata*, her fingers curled above its strings.

The riders watched Mreen, too, but when Emle began to sing, she felt their attention shift to her, and a quiver of nerves trembled briefly in her throat. She breathed it in, let it energize her voice, as she had been taught. She turned her eyes up to the gleam of the stars beyond the yellow *quiru* light. Caught up in the beauty of the night and the charm of the music, Emle could almost believe the words she sang, could persuade herself that there had been a Ship, that it had sailed down from the expanse of stars as easily as a *ferrel* feather drifts past the treetops to settle softly on the snow.

> *Look back, O Nevya,*
> *Look back to the Six Stars,*
> *And cry aloud,*
> *"Where? Where is the Ship?"*
> *From the Six Stars it came,*
> *From the reaches of the sky,*
> *Look back, O Nevya,*
> *And cry aloud,*
> *"Where? Where is the Ship?"*

Emle's voice felt as fragile as a breath. She sighed, wishing the sound had more strength in it, more depth. But when she lowered her eyes to meet Cantrix Mreen's, she saw a gleam in her eyes.

*Your voice fills the silence,* Mreen sent. *Be glad of it.*

*Yes, Cantrix,* Emle sent in response. She dropped her gaze to her empty hands, but not before she saw the nods of appreciation from the riders. It must have gone better than she thought. Perhaps the thinness of the sound was due only to the open air, the night breeze. She hoped so. And she wondered if Mreen, despite her great Gift, might envy her, because she could sing. It was a strange thought, and she pressed it low, so Mreen would not hear.

# *five*

THE DAYS OF riding were misery for Mreen. Every inch of her body ached. Her face itched from the wind. Her eyes burned from the glare of sun on snow.

But it was the *hrussmaster*'s strange eyes that made her the most uncomfortable. They were ice-pale, and the *quiru* light glittered in them when he looked across the fire at her. Of course he did not address her or touch her, but there was no protocol to dictate he should not look at her.

Mreen wished there were such a rule. She turned to avoid his gaze, and sent to Emle, *I do not like that man.*

Emle was brushing her hair, rebinding it, and she glanced up in surprise. *Who?* Her eyes looked past Mreen, searching for the offender.

*Oh, please, Emle, do not look at him.* Mreen folded her arms around herself, feeling a chill despite the warmth of her *quiru*. It was their last campsite before reaching Tarus the next day, and Mreen was more than ready for a real bed, an hour in the *ubanyix*, and a comfortable meal. They had ridden along cliffs all day, and Mreen had been fearful of the height, exhausted by the constant salt wind from the Frozen Sea.

Emle, though, seemed perfectly at ease with the days of riding, sleeping in the rough. She bloomed with health and energy. Her eyes found Mreen's. *Do you mean the* hruss-master?

*Yes.* Mreen held her gaze. *I touched something of his.*

*You did? What was it?*

*He carries a wallet—you know, one of those little folded leather carriers, with pockets for bits of metal and so forth. They make them at Amric, tooled with flowers, and leaves. It fell from his belt, and I picked it up so the snow would not spoil it. . . .*

Emle watched her, her lips a little apart. *And you saw something?*

Mreen gave a small shake of her head. *No. I only held it for a moment, and then laid it on a stone. But I heard something. I heard—* She shook her head again, disliking the memory, unsure of what it meant. *It was a child crying, as if in the distance, but distinctly.*

*A child?*

*A small child, like one of the first-level students. Sobbing as if its heart would break.*

Emle's eyes slipped past her to where the master of *hruss* sat beside the fire, and then slid quickly back. She put her fingers to her lips. *Cantrix—did you—*

*It is impolite to listen to the thoughts of others, Emle.* Mreen let her lips curl, and she saw Emle smile in answer, then press her fingers to her mouth to suppress a giggle. It was a relief to feel young and foolish for a moment. *His mind is a jumble—I would learn nothing.*

At Conservatory, the students learned slowly, over the years of their study, to refrain from trespassing on others' thoughts. By the time they reached the third level, most of them felt they must set an example for the younger ones, and they disciplined themselves carefully. But, sometimes— sometimes it was just too tempting. Or necessary. Still, when Mreen had tested the *hrussmaster's* mind—Axl, his name was, Axl v'Tarus—she found only shadow and cloud, nothing she could grasp, no clear thought. And the moment she had laid down the wallet, the crying faded from her hearing.

A shadow fell over the two of them where they knelt on their bedfurs. Mreen looked up to find the master of *hruss* standing over her. Her back stiffened.

Emle scrambled to her feet. "Hrussmaster," she said hastily. "Did you want something?"

His eyes flicked over her, and then back down at Mreen. "I came to be certain the Cantrix has everything she needs. And that her saddle is comfortable."

Emle took a step forward, inserting her slight body between Mreen and the master of *hruss*. Mreen marveled at the younger girl's strength of spirit.

"The Cantrix says that her saddle hurts her at every step," Emle said brightly. "But it will pass, and she begs you not to concern yourself."

Mreen relaxed, and sat back on her heels.

"If there is anything I can do . . ." Axl said smoothly.

"No, thank you, Hrussmaster. I will see to the Cantrix's comfort myself."

Axl grunted, and turned away without speaking again. Mreen stared at his broad back, stunned by the wave of loathing that surged from him. Emle sank back onto the bed-furs, and Mreen saw that she felt it, too.

She thought of it again later. The riders had taken their bowls away to be cleaned. The stars sparkled wanly through Mreen's tall, strong *quiru*. She held her *filhata* in her lap, and had strummed the first chord of the oldest song of all. The riders squatted or knelt, smiling with anticipation, ready to enjoy the music. Karn had confided to Mreen and to Emle, when she had escorted them outside the *quiru*, that she and the other riders were sorry to see the trip come to an end. The weather had been good, Conservatory had provided extra food for their meals, and there had been entertainment every evening of a quality no itinerant Singer could provide.

The strings of the *filhata* made a sweet, clear sound, despite the lack of reverberation in the open air. When Emle began to sing, Mreen noticed the *hrussmaster* standing just beyond the circle of riders.

*Sing the light,*
*Sing the warmth,*
*Receive and become the Gift, O Singers,*
*The light and the warmth are in you.*

Emle's pretty voice made the ancient tune sound as fresh as if she had just composed it.

Axl frowned, and Mreen, though her fingers played on, felt the chill again, creeping across her chest and belly, prickling at her arms. Why, she wondered, did the master of *hruss* hate the Gifted? She couldn't guess. But she was certain it was true.

LUKE SAT WITH Gwin and Erlys in the great room at Tarus, enjoying a moment of leisure after the morning meal. The late winter sun glowed on the polished surfaces of the long tables, the rows of chairs, the *obis*-carved lintels of the doorways. Axl had been away for the past twelve days, off to Conservatory to escort the new Cantrix to Tarus, and the respite had been a great relief to Luke and his sister. Erlys had been cheerful, smiling as she bent over her soap pots, chattering freely when they met in the great room for meals. Now the three of them sat nibbling at the last of the nut bread, talking of the coming summer.

"I want to sleep outside!" Gwin proclaimed.

Luke laughed, and tweaked her braids. "Not all that warm, Gwinlet," he said. "A *ferrel* might try to nest in your hair!"

"But the itinerants sleep outside," she protested. "I know, because the last ones who were here had a little boy, and he told me!"

"They sleep outside because they have to," Erlys said mildly. "In the snow and the wind. You wouldn't like it, Gwin."

"I might! Will you let me try it?"

Erlys smiled at her daughter. "We'll see. We'll have to ask your father."

Gwin's face clouded, and she stared down at her plate.

"Gwin . . ." Luke warned, but it did no good.

"He's not my father," Gwin said in a small voice. "Don't call him that."

Erlys's smile faded. She spread her small hands in a gesture of helplessness. "But he is your father now," she said plaintively. "Your stepfather, anyway. I don't know where we would be without him."

"Happier," Gwin said.

Luke put his hand out to cover his sister's, just as Erlys touched his other hand. "Couldn't you give him a chance?" she asked. Her eyes reddened with quick tears, as they so often did now. "Just try to get along?"

"We do," Gwin said, tossing her head at her mother. "But he doesn't."

"We would have nothing on our own," Erlys said, in a voice almost as thin and high as Gwin's. "My first mate died when you were just a baby. And left us poor as *wezels*!"

Luke set his jaw. "The House wouldn't let us starve," he said.

"Axl loves us," Erlys said, though weakly.

"He doesn't." This, of course, was from Gwin, and loudly. Erlys cringed. Luke knew that Gwin's outspokenness was often the cause of Axl's outbursts.

He gripped his mother's hand. "I'm almost grown. I can take care of you. Both of you."

"You couldn't, Luke," she said, her voice growing even smaller. The bright morning seemed to dim around them, the cheery warmth to subside. Suddenly Luke could see only dirty plates, snow-grimed windows, the new shadows beneath Erlys's eyes.

"Luke," Erlys began. "Gwin . . . I'm doing the best I can."

"Let me go to the Magister," Luke managed to say through stiff lips. His voice caught and broke. "Tell him."

Erlys paled, and pulled her hand free. "No, no, you mustn't, Luke. It's my own fault; I don't do things the way he likes, and—things will be better, you'll see. He loves me."

Luke had no answer for that. He had heard Axl shouting at Erlys, heard the heavy slap of his palm against her back, the thud of her body when he shoved her against a wall. He had seen the bruises on her cheeks and arms that she tried to explain away. He knew he was right. These were matters to be reported to the Magister, who had power over every Houseman and -woman. But Erlys had begged him to leave it alone, and he couldn't go against his mother's wishes. He turned to Gwin, searching for something to say.

Gwin's head was tilted to one side, her eyes closed as if she were listening for something.

"What is it, Gwinlet?" Luke whispered. Erlys turned to Gwin, too, her face pale as snow.

"They're here," Gwin said.

"Who?"

"The new Cantrix. The riders." Her eyes opened, and they were very dark. "Him."


EMLE COULD JUST see the massive stone walls of Tarus rising in the distance, and she kept peering ahead, catching glimpses through the ironwood trees. A low stone wall lined the cliff path. As they approached the House, she saw that the wall continued on all along the great bay, where the water was calmer, a darker green than the distant sea. Tarus itself rose majestically above the curve of the cliff, its tiled roofs glowing with *quiru* light. Emle thought it must be twice the size of Conservatory.

The travelers turned out of the cliff path and into a stableyard with an enormous fenced paddock. They passed through a stone arch that opened into a wide, clean-swept courtyard. The steps leading up to the double doors were broad and shallow.

Emle freed her feet from the stirrups, and slid easily down from the *hruss*. Her soreness had subsided halfway through their journey. Pyotr grinned at her as she shook out her tunic and smoothed her trousers.

"You could be a rider, Singer," he said. "You've taken to *hruss* like an *urbear* to ice!"

Emle laughed as she pushed back her *caeru* hood. "I am almost sorry our journey is over, Pyotr," she said. "The House will seem confining after this."

He nodded. "So it will."

Karn helped Mreen down from her mount as a little group of people emerged from the House's great front doors, and stood on the steps leading to the courtyard. They all wore the brown and black and dark-blue tunics of the upper levels.

Mreen stood before them, her head bowed. "Excuse me," Emle said softly to Pyotr. "The Cantrix needs me now."

Emle sidled between the riders and *hruss*, and came to stand at Mreen's shoulder. *I am here, Cantrix,* she sent.

*Thank you.* Mreen slowly, deliberately, put back her hood and lifted her eyes to the group assembled to welcome her.

Emle had grown used to the halo of light surrounding Mreen, and she supposed the riders had also become accustomed to it. But she heard the general intake of breath as Mreen shed her *caeru* furs and started toward the steps, and she felt the little wave of shock that ran through the House-members. She turned her eyes to Mreen, and tried to see the new Cantrix as these strangers saw her.

Mreen had taken extra care to bind her hair into smooth auburn coils. Her green eyes glittered in the sunshine, and her cheeks were pink from the days of riding.

And the light!

Emle supposed Mreen was excited about meeting the people she would soon serve, her new Magister, his mate, her new senior Cantor. No doubt it was anticipation that made her halo so bright, shot through with sparks. It shimmered around her, as if she walked in limpid, cool flame. Tarus's new Cantrix looked like the Gift itself, personified.

*Introduce me, please,* she sent to Emle.

Emle bowed to her, and then to the welcoming group, and spoke aloud. "This is Cantrix Mreen v'Conservatory. She gives you greetings."

Several people bowed, and a thickset man with graying hair began a little speech of welcome, and a list of introductions.

Emle took a step back. The welcoming party swept Mreen into their midst, and in moments they had carried her with them back into the House. No one had waited for Emle.

She stood, with her heavy saddlepack at her feet, unsure of what to do. She didn't know if she should follow Mreen and intrude upon the welcoming ceremony, or wait for someone to come back for her. The riders began to lead the *hruss* away over the cleanswept cobblestones as she hesitated.

The great ironwood doors swung closed with a clicking of a heavy latch. She looked behind her and saw that the courtyard had emptied, the last *hruss* and rider just rounding the corner of the House. She bit her lip, and then hefted her saddlepack with both arms.

She followed the riders through a stone arch to the stableyard. The stables lay to her left, the paddock to her right. Gates and doors stood open, *hruss* milled about, and riders called to one another, unloading saddlepacks and bedfurs. Beyond everything, the waters of the bay glistened in the last rays of the sun.

Emle hung back, not wanting to plunge through the crowd. She watched as the confusion resolved itself, the *hruss* unsaddled and stabled, the riders disappearing into the House. No one noticed her. And, she thought forlornly, no one had missed her, either.

She stamped her foot, remembering her vow to herself. She was a Singer. And sooner or later, Mreen would need her. She struggled across the stableyard, lugging her saddlepack, and approached the stables.

The upper part of the half-door had been left open. She heard a voice inside, a bass rumble, a halting answer in a higher tone.

Emle's nose and cheeks were beginning to sting with cold.

She tried to open the bottom half of the door, but it was latched from inside, and her hands were full. "Excuse me," she called. "Could someone open the door?"

The voices fell silent. She tried again. "Is someone there?" A pause. She added, with a little laugh, "I must come inside, I think, or I will freeze solid."

At last she heard the thud of boots on the straw-covered floor of the stable, and she looked up to find the *hrussmaster's* tall figure looming over her.

"You're at the wrong door, Singer," he snapped.

Emle caught her breath at the impatience in his tone. She was unaccustomed to being treated with anything less than respect by the Housemen and -women at Conservatory. More often, they addressed her with affection. She lifted her chin. "I am sorry, Hrussmaster," she said, glad to hear the edge in her voice. "I am new to traveling. I did not know which door to use."

"You should have followed the Cantrix," he said.

"No doubt." Emle's teeth were beginning to chatter. "But Cantrix Mreen was surrounded by her welcome party, and meeting the Magister and her new senior, and I did not wish to intrude." She stepped back a little so that he could open the door, and gave him an expectant and, she hoped, commanding look.

His eyes flickered slightly. Slowly, as if reluctantly, he opened the bottom door, and stood aside for her to pass through into the warmth of the stables. She moved around him carefully, loath even to let her furs brush him as she passed. Her pack had grown heavy, and she hugged it close to her body with arms, which had begun to ache. He made no offer of assistance.

He shouted at someone in the back of the stables. "Luke!" She jumped, her ears pained by the volume. "Luke, come make yourself useful. This Singer can't find her way."

Emle turned forward to meet her guide, letting her pack slide to the floor.

A youth, taller and thinner than the *hrussmaster*, stood in the passageway between the stable boxes. He was as dark as Axl was pale, his hair a glossy black, his brown eyes dull. His shoulders slumped as if he carried a heavy weight upon them. "Yes," he mumbled. "What . . ." His voice trailed away as he stared at Emle.

"Don't stand like there like you're witless," the *hrussmaster* barked. "Take her to the Housekeeper. She'll know what to do with her."

The stableman bent to pick up Emle's pack, lifting it as if it were packed with feathers. He ducked his head to her, and turned to lead the way. There was an inner door, she discovered, at the end of the passageway. When they reached it, he gestured for her to precede him. "Housekeeper," he mumbled, not meeting her eyes. "Top of the stairs."

She put her foot on the single step leading up into the corridor, and then paused. She could not help but see the misery that pulled his mouth down, the flush of shame in his thin cheeks. "I do apologize, Houseman," she said softly. "It seems I have offended your master in some way, and caused you trouble as well."

"No," he muttered. "Axl's always angry."

She smiled. "You do not need to come up the stairs with me. I will find the Housekeeper myself." She reached for her pack. "Thank you for your help, Houseman."

"No—please—" His eyes touched her face, then shifted to his boots. They were none too clean, and Emle felt his agonizing embarrassment as an ache in her own throat. He tried again. "L-luke," he stammered. "I'm Luke."

"Luke," she said. "And I am Emle. Singer Emle. I am your new Cantrix's companion."

He put the pack into her hands, careful not to touch her fingers. "Uh—if you need something . . ." He didn't seem to be able to finish the sentence, and an uncomfortable silence stretched between them.

Emle gave up, and finished his thought for him. "I will ask, Luke. Thank you." She tried to adjust the weight of the pack. The House *quiru* was warm, and she began to long to take off her furs. At that moment she heard Cantrix Mreen.

*Emle? Where are you?*

The sending came sharply, as if Mreen were angry, but Emle felt only relief at being remembered at last. *I am here, Cantrix. I have just come in from the stables.*

*The stables? Why?*

*I will explain in a moment.* Hastily, Emle bowed her head to the stableman. "I hope I will see you again soon, Luke. I will mention your kindness to the Housekeeper."

He bowed, his tall, thin body bending awkwardly. He opened his mouth to say something, but then closed it, and turned abruptly away, to go back into the stables. Emle hurried down the corridor to find the stairway to the upper level.

# Six

MREEN KNEW WITHIN moments of meeting Cantor Josu that it would be she who would lead their Cantoris. She remembered him from Conservatory, when he had been a third-level student and she still at the first level. His was a fragile nature, as delicate as his slender frame.

He bowed. *Hello, Cantrix Mreen. Welcome to your new— welcome to Tarus.* Even his sending felt timid. *Congratulations on your investiture.*

*Thank you, Cantor Josu.* She bowed to him carefully, to show the correct depth of respect. She hoped that such formality would soon pass. They would, after all, be working together for a very long time. And the day would soon come when he would be the only person, in this entire House, to whom she could fully express her thoughts.

He colored as if he knew what she was thinking, and turned to lead the way up the steps. The warm air of the House made her instantly uncomfortable in her heavy furs. Around them the welcoming party walked in silence, waiting for the Gifted ones to open the conversation. In the foyer, Mreen paused, looking expectantly at Josu.

He hesitated, and his senior hobbled forward, supporting himself with a staff.

*You must speak for Cantrix Mreen,* he sent.

Mreen caught her breath at the weakness of the old Cantor's sending, the wave of fatigue that swept out from him as he stood beside her shoulder. She bowed to him, too, careful to hide her pity. *You must be Cantor Mattu,* she sent. *I am so pleased to meet you at last. Magistrix Sira sends her warmest greetings.*

His smile was tremulous, and she knew that she had not deceived him. His eyes were full of some deep and complicated emotion. Cantor Mattu's day had passed, Mreen thought. His work was done. She had to press down her feelings again, as her breast filled with gratitude that she was at the beginning, full of health and energy, with all of life before her. She wondered if Mattu had felt the same when he came to Tarus as a young Cantor.

And Josu seemed to have remembered his duties at last. Aloud, he said, "Cantrix Mreen. Welcome to the House of Tarus." He gestured to his right. "Perhaps you would like to look at our Cantoris."

Obligingly, Mreen moved to the open doorway of the Cantoris. Tarus, though so large, was laid out like the other Houses, with a great staircase curving up from the foyer to the upper-level apartments. Corridors ran beneath the stairs to the lower-level apartments, the stables, the nursery gardens, and the waste drop.

The whole group, except Mattu, followed her into the Cantoris. Mattu leaned against the doorjamb, watching from a distance. Mreen admired the *obis*-carved lintels, the slender ironwood beams that stretched across the ceiling, the intricate stonework of the floor, and Josu spoke her thoughts for her. They all crossed the foyer again to the great room, where the tall limeglass windows glowed with late afternoon light. Housewomen were laying the long tables for the evening meal, and they bowed and retreated hastily before the Magister's party.

A plump, middle-aged woman stepped forward as they left the great room. Josu said, "Cantrix Mreen, this is our Housekeeper, Gerta."

The Housekeeper beamed. "Welcome, Cantrix," she said. "This young woman—" she indicated a tall, slender girl in a bright green tunic, who kept her eyes cast down. "This is Lispeth, your new Housewoman. Lispeth grew up here at Tarus and will be useful to you. She reads, also, which will be a help, will it not?"

Mreen nodded to the girl, whose fair hair gleamed in the sunshine, but Lispeth only stared at her feet. Mreen could not think how to greet her if she would not look up. With a little shrug, she turned back to Gerta.

The Housekeeper seemed to notice nothing amiss. "And now, Cantrix, you must feel in need of the *ubanyix*. It's all ready for you. Lispeth will show you the way. Come now, bathe before another moment passes, and everyone will rejoin you later." Gerta stood with her hands folded before her waist, as if waiting for Mreen to agree with her suggestions.

Mreen raised her brows at Josu. *Do the Housemembers understand?* she asked him. *About me?*

*Oh, yes,* Josu responded hastily.

And Mattu added, *Conservatory told us you are unable to speak. But your—*He paused, and gave her a gentle smile. *Your light speaks for you.*

Magister Kenth and his mate took their leave. Mattu, also, disappeared, and Mreen felt certain he had risen from his sickbed only to greet her. He would travel soon to Conservatory, she imagined, but she doubted he would be strong enough to teach. It was sad, but Cantor Mattu, at least, would die at home.

She sighed, and then noticed that Josu still stood uncertainly beside her, as if he did not know what to do next.

*Cantor Josu,* she sent politely. *Perhaps we could talk later, if that would be convenient to you? A bath just now would be most welcome.*

*Of course,* he sent, a little too swiftly, as if relieved to have this first meeting come to an end. *Lispeth will show you to the ubanyix, and then to your apartment. I will meet you again at the evening meal.* He pointed out the head table. *I suppose we must discuss how to go on. It has been difficult, with Cantor Mattu so ill.*

*I am sure it has. Yes, let us talk then.*

She followed Lispeth down the corridor. The girl never spoke, nor even met her eyes. Mreen glanced at her curiously, sure that her new Housewoman was even younger than she. Could she truly read? she wondered. Would she be able to learn her finger signs before Emle returned to Conservatory?

Mreen sighed, aware all at once of how fatigued she truly was, weary of the dirt beneath her fingernails and the reek of *hruss* upon her clothes. The *ubanyix* was as large as everything else at Tarus. The rim of the great tub was elegantly scrolled, the soap dishes carved into elaborate flowers.

Mreen gave up worrying, and hurried to strip off her soiled riding clothes. She stepped down into the water. Though it was steaming slightly, it still felt too cool to her hot skin. Lispeth had already bowed and was on her way out the door, when Mreen lifted her hand, her fingers curved in the sign that meant she needed her *filla*. Of course, Lispeth would not have understood even if she had been watching.

Mreen recalled, with a guilty start, her companion.

*Emle!* she sent, concern making her sending too forceful. *Where are you?* She feared she must sound petulant, even angry.

To her relief, Emle responded immediately. *I am here, Cantrix.*


GWIN CAME TO FETCH Luke from the stables. He was busy putting away the traveling party's tack, and as he hung bridles and lifted saddles onto their rack, she chattered busily, telling him everything she knew about the new Cantrix. He smiled, listening to her. It was good, he thought, to hear her prattle on like any other child. He knew when they reached their apartment, she would fall silent, speak only when spoken to, slip away to her own little room as quickly as she could.

"She has a light around her all the time!" Gwin was exclaiming. "Her own *quiru* light that never fades, and she can't speak at all, Luke—not a single word. She is completely silent, and only Cantor Josu and Cantor Mattu can understand her!"

"Are you sure, Gwinlet? Maybe she's just quiet. Her first day." He picked up a length of rope that lay in the straw, coiled it, and hung it neatly on a peg. He dusted his hands, and looked around the tack room to be certain he hadn't missed anything.

"Of course I'm sure, you silly!" his sister said. "Everyone is saying she has no voice at all—doesn't sing or talk or even whisper." Her voice dropped, and she said with wide eyes, "She uses her fingers—like this." She twisted her little hands into a shape, and then dropped them.

"You saw her do that?"

"Well, no, not yet. But I heard about it from the House-keeper."

Luke laughed. "You were talking with the Housekeeper, you little rascal? Did you have a lot to say to her?"

"No, Luke, not me! I heard Gerta tell Mama, when she came to bring some towels to mend. And Luke, you're to come now, so we can go to the evening meal together."

"Together?"

Gwin's smile faded, and the sparkle in her eyes dimmed. "With Mama and Axl. I wish it was just us, though. You and I and Mama."

Luke squatted beside Gwin, and touched her hair with his fingers. "It's hard, Gwinlet," he said softly. "But it's done now. We have to try, for Mama."

In a small voice, she said, "I know." And then, with a rebell-ious pout, "But I don't see why she needed a new mate."

He leaned forward to kiss her forehead. "When you're older, you'll understand," he said.

"You're older," she said, with perfect logic. "Do you understand?"

He groaned. "No, Gwinlet. Not really."

She gave a sharp, satisfied nod. "Me neither."


MREEN'S CONFUSION MADE her abrupt. *The water is cold,* she sent, before Emle had even closed the door to the *ubanyix.*

*Shall I bring your* filla *to you?* Emle asked. She still had her furs on, and her saddlepack in her hands. She dropped all of it on the floor near the door. *Is it in your tunic?*

*Yes. And I am sorry, Emle.* Mreen lifted a hand, and let it splash down into the water. *Actually, I . . . I am embarrassed to have . . . have lost you!*

Emle lifted Mreen's soiled tunic and felt for its inner pocket. *I found my way.* She pulled out the *filla,* and crossed to the tub. She handed it to Mreen, and went back to the bench to pull off her boots.

Mreen dried her hands on a folded towel before she picked up the *filla.* Sitting on the little shelf that circled the tub beneath the water, she played a short figure in the third mode, *Doryu.* She added nothing—no flourish, no cadenza, no embellishment at all—yet she felt a wave of pure envy from Emle. She laid the instrument down, watching as Emle stepped down into the now-steaming water.

*Emle,* Mreen began, and then paused. She could not think how to go forward.

*Yes, Cantrix?*

It seemed best, Mreen decided, to be direct. *You are angry with me. I do not blame you.*

At that, Emle did raise her eyes. *Cantrix! Why should I be angry?*

*Because I left you.*

Emle shook her head. *You were meeting your new senior, your new Housemembers! I understood perfectly.*

*I was very nervous,* Mreen admitted. *I still am.*

Emle didn't answer that. She reached for the binding of her hair, loosening it so that it fell in thick brown waves into the water of the *ubanyix.*

*Perhaps,* Mreen tried, *you will remember all this when you take your own Cantoris. . . .*

Emle lifted her face again, and the misery in her eyes startled Mreen.

*Emle?*

*Surely you know I will never have my own Cantoris,* Emle sent. Her eyes blurred with tears, and she looked down at the strands of her hair floating in the warm water. *I could not even warm your bath for you.* She wrapped her arms around herself as if she were chilled. *I may just as well forget Conservatory, forget the* filhata *and the* filla *and the modes I worked so hard to learn, the scales I played a thousand times. I might just as well mate and have a dozen babies!*

Mreen sucked in her breath in shock. *Emle!*

Emle scrubbed at her eyes with her wet hands, and Mreen saw how long and well-shaped her fingers were, perfect for the strings of the *filhata.* She thought of Emle's voice, as clear and pure as icicles, with high notes that were the envy of every Singer at Conservatory. Emle was a marvelous musician, in every way. By the Six Stars, whatever could be the matter with her Gift?

Emle dropped her hands. Her eyes were bleak, but dry. *I am sorry, Cantrix,* she sent. Her chin trembled, and then firmed again, and she sat up straighter, pushing her wet hair away from her face. *I did not mean to complain.*

Mreen reached behind her neck to undo her own hair. It didn't fall in heavy strands like Emle's, but massed in a tangled cloud. She ran her fingers through it, trying to smooth it, to pull out the knots. She nodded at Emle. *No need to apologize to me,* she assured her. *If I were you, I would be just as unhappy, and just as desperate.* She put out her hand to touch Emle's wet shoulder. Emle's skin was smooth, her arm finely muscled. Yes, Mreen thought, perfect for the *filhata*. She sent, very firmly, *But, Emle—no more talk of mating and babies. Not now. Not yet.*

Emle managed a small smile in return. *No, I promise, Cantrix.*

*By the will of the Spirit, your Gift may yet flower. You must tell yourself that.*

*Yes, Cantrix,* Emle sent obediently.

Mreen reached for the soap, and slid lower in the water. How small her own problems seemed compared to Emle's! She wondered if there was not something she could do to help the girl, but if Maestra Magret and Cantrix Sira had not thought of something . . .

*Cantrix?* Emle's sending was determinedly cheerful. *May I help you with your hair?*

*Thank you, Emle. It is so hard to work with!*

Emle scooted closer on the shelf, and began to work with

a wooden comb on Mreen's tangled curls. Mreen tipped her head back, and gave herself over to the comforting touch.

Of course, she thought, Sira had sent Emle here, and Sira was always wise. Perhaps coming to Tarus would be just the something Emle needed. Mreen sent a swift plea to the Spirit of Stars that it might be so.

THE DRIED FISH of Tarus was famous all over the Continent, but until that first night in the House by the Frozen Sea, Emle had never tasted fresh fish. It had been caught just that morning in the bay below the cliffs, pulled out, she supposed, between the chunks of ice she had seen shining in the waters. The cooks had simmered it in its own broth with vegetables and grain until it made a fragrant chowder redolent of the sea air she had been breathing for the past two days. Her appetite was sharp from the days of travel, and the chowder was rich and sweet in her mouth.

She glanced across at Mreen. They both sat at the high table with the Magister and his mate, with Cantor Josu on one side of Mreen and Cantor Mattu on the other. Emle, who had no official position other than Mreen's companion, sat at the end, where her voice could speak for Mreen if necessary. Mreen's eyes were on her bowl, but her hands rested in her lap. Emle put her own spoon down, and wondered why Mreen was not eating.

Feeling emboldened by their frank discussion of the afternoon, Emle skirted strict protocol to send tentatively, *Cantrix Mreen? Are you feeling well?*

Mreen lifted her eyes, and found Emle's. *He hates me,* she sent. *And I do not know why.*

*Who? Who hates you?*

Mreen moved her eyes slightly, to one of the long tables below, where the Housemen and -women sat chattering and laughing over their evening meal. Emle followed her gaze.

Just as she looked at him, he dropped his eyes, but she knew he had been staring at Mreen. *The* hrussmaster.

*Yes,* Mreen responded. Emle watched her pick up her spoon, and taste the chowder. *I think he hates all the Gifted, but me especially.* Her eyes lifted to Emle's. *By the Spirit, this is the most delicious fish I have ever tasted.*

*I know.* Emle took another spoonful, and then frowned across the table. *Cantrix—why should Axl hate you in particular?*

*Because,* Mreen sent without emotion. *Every time he looks at me—or anyone does—they can hardly forget who and what I am.*

Emle could hardly argue with that. Even now, in the brightness of the great room, Mreen sat bathed in light, her freshly washed hair glinting redly, her dimpled cheeks aglow. *It is true,* Emle sent to Mreen. *You are the very embodiment of the Gift. But without the Gift—where would all these people be? Including the* hrussmaster, *and his family?*

Mreen looked down at her spoon, turning it in her fingers. *Emle,* she sent. *Find something of his, something he has worn or carried. But do not speak of this to anyone.*

Emle laid her own spoon down, and watched Mreen, but the Cantrix sent nothing else. It was an order, Emle thought. It was not a request. And she did not feel at liberty to refuse.

# Seven

LUKE SPENT MOST of the meal staring in wonder at the new Cantrix, until his stepfather kicked him under the table and snapped, "Luke, close your mouth. You look like a great fish."

Luke ducked his head to hide the heat in his cheeks. Gwin's little hand found his beneath the table, and squeezed his fingers.

"But, Axl," Erlys said hastily. "It is a wonder, to see one of the Gifted like that. She glows!"

"She ought to save that energy for when it's needed," Axl growled. "She flaunts it."

"But," Gwin offered, so softly her voice was almost inaudible. "They say in the kitchens that the Cantrix can't help it. That she shines like that all the time, even when she's sleeping."

Erlys turned to Axl. "Is that true, Axl? Even at night, she is alight like that?"

He didn't answer her, but frowned at Gwin, his handsome face creasing. "Gossip," he said. "I've told you before." He took a spoonful of chowder, and glowered at the little girl over his bowl. "The business of the Gifted is no business of yours, Gwin, nor yours, either, Luke. Gwin, you quit wasting your time in the Cantoris. I'd better not hear of you hanging around bothering the Cantors again."

Gwin's cheeks flamed now, too. Luke tightened his hand around hers, and they waited, as they had learned to do, for Erlys to distract Axl's attention.

Erlys reached for the bread platter, urging another slice on her mate. Luke glanced up at the far end of the head table, where the young Singer sat. Emle's eyes roamed the room, and she seemed to be enjoying her meal. She was so pretty, he thought, prettier than any of the girls at Tarus, or at Filus either. Her gaze reached his table, and he dropped his own, hoping she hadn't caught him staring. Axl was right about one thing—he had no business with the Gifted. And if his stepfather caught him mooning over a Singer, he would find a thousand ways to embarrass him.

Luke picked up his spoon to finish his meal. Evening chores awaited him in the stables.

Already, in this late season, the days were growing longer, though the Visitor had not yet shown its face above the south-eastern horizon. Luke took advantage of the mild weather to walk around the outside of the House, past the kitchen doors, which were left open to release steam and heat. Slender columns of smoke rose from the three chimneys above the big ovens. The cooks and servers bustled about in the kitchen, carrying pots to the stone sinks, stacking bowls and cups on the wooden sideboards. Luke walked on past the waste drop, and the glass-roofed nursery gardens. He paused at the opening in the stone wall, where the narrow, slippery stone staircase led down to the bay. The wooden hoists jutted from the cliff, but no *kikyu* were strapped into them now that the danger of being frozen into the ice was past. He strolled on into the stableyard, looking over his shoulder at the green waters of the bay.

The iceberg was greatly diminished, its peaks slumped into rounded shapes, dim as old snow. The brash ice had melted. The sky was shading to violet. Luke's heart lifted. The Visitor could rise tomorrow, or the next day, surely within the week. The snow was melting from the cliff path, and before long, slender softwood shoots would nod in the light of the two suns. There would be feasting, and celebration, and excursions into the timberlands. He stretched his arms out and turned his face up into the evening light, filled with joy. For a few weeks, at long last, there would be freedom.

He turned, grinning like a little boy, and then stopped abruptly, stumbling over his own feet. He felt his grin fade, and his throat went dry. Emle—Singer Emle—stood just inside the half-door of the stables, watching him.

"S-singer!" he stammered. He stood rooted to the ground in an agony of embarrassment. He must have looked a fool, a hulking overgrown idiot, just as Axl always said.

Emle smiled up at him from beneath her eyelashes. They were long and curling, gilded by the evening light. "Hello, Luke," she said. "What has happened to the iceberg?"

He forced his feet to move. His legs felt impossibly long, his hands huge and awkward as he reached for the latch. "Melted," he muttered. He opened the door, and stood before her with his hands behind him, wishing he could think of the right thing—anything—to say. He glanced warily past her shoulder. He would hate to have this lovely girl see his stepfather berating him.

Her smile faded. "I hope you do not mind me coming here."

"No," he managed. He didn't know what to do next. He could hardly offer her a chair. He looked down at her feet, so dainty and small in their soft slippers. His own were enormous in comparison, his boots thick-soled and heavy. He brought his gaze back to her face, and found that she was looking around with lively interest.

"I love the way the stables smell," she said. "And is that a new foal, in the box there? It is so sweet! What long ears it has!" She moved across the passageway to lean over the gate to the stall. The mare lifted her head to regard her, and then dropped it again, unalarmed. The foal stepped to the gate, and put its muzzle into Emle's hand. She laughed as it nibbled at her fingers.

Luke felt some confidence where *hruss* were concerned, and he was relieved to have Emle's attention diverted. "Soon be as big as that one," he said, pointing to the next box, where another beast hung its broad head over the gate, watching the humans with wistful eyes.

"That one looks friendly, too."

"Too much, sometimes." Luke rubbed the big *hruss*'s forehead, and it pushed its nose against his chest. "In *quiru*—outside—they'll step all over you if you're not careful. It's not just the warmth, either. They want to be with humans."

Emle smoothed the foal's drooping ears. "Have you traveled a great deal, Luke?"

"No—not since—I mean—my father died."

"You lost your father. I am sorry." She gave him a glance warm with sympathy. Her eyes were the clear blue of a morning sky, and Luke's cheeks grew warm for the second time that evening.

He longed to be gracious, easy with his words, but he couldn't think how. After a long, embarrassing moment, he mumbled, "You need something?"

She stepped back from the foal's reach, and wiped her palms on her trousers. "So I do, Luke," she said. "Or, I should say, Cantrix Mreen does."

MREEN AND EMLE had carefully prepared their request so as not to give away their purpose. Emle doubted, though, that anyone would suspect Mreen's special talent. Their challenge was only to think of something to ask for that would make sense to the stableman or the *hrussmaster*. Emle had been greatly relieved to find Luke alone in the stables. Though she was not so sensitive as Mreen, the master of *hruss* made her distinctly uncomfortable. Luke's awkwardness simply made her feel sympathetic. She wondered if he ever left the stables, except for meals.

She followed him down the passageway and into the tack room, where the air was rich with the smells of *caeru* leather and saddle soap. Her feet crunched on fresh, crisp straw. Luke stretched his long arm up to a row of pegs above a long worktable, and brought down a length of leather thong. He held it out in his hand, letting it dangle so Emle could take it without touching his fingers.

"I am not a Cantrix, you know," she said, trying to speak lightly. She let her fingers brush his palm as she accepted the thong. "There is no taboo against touching me."

He looked startled. "But—you're a Singer."

"A student only."

"Isn't it the same thing?"

She coiled the thong around her fingers. "I am here only to serve as Cantrix Mreen's voice. Until her new Housewoman learns to understand her finger signs."

"You'll be a Cantrix, in your turn?"

"By the will of the Spirit," she said, and sighed. He looked confused, and she confessed, "I have some trouble with my Gift."

"I'm sorry." He sounded as if he meant it, though he looked so sullen. She wished he would smile. His face was lean, but it had good lines. He had a nice mouth, and a strong chin. He wore his black hair long, tied back in a queue, and his neck and shoulders were muscled. He straightened one of the saddles on its peg and said, "Guess we all have troubles."

"So we do."

He hesitated, and then said in a rush, "The riders say your voice is beautiful."

Emle smiled, remembering the nights in the open, singing beside Mreen under the undimmed stars. "They are kind to say so."

He gestured to the length of thong. "Wouldn't the Cantrix

prefer a ribbon? My mother works in the linen ambry. She could come upstairs. . . . Or the Cantrix's Housewoman could come down."

"No, no, thank you," Emle said. "This is right. The panel is made of leather, you see, tooled leather, something that belonged to Cantrix Mreen's mother. She saw the thongs the *hrussmaster* used on her saddlepack, and—" Emle paused. She sensed someone coming, someone whose thoughts preceded her in a jumble of images and feelings and colors.

"Let me split it for you, then," Luke said. "It will look nicer." He reached across the work bench for a leather knife.

The knife was slender and curving, its *obis*-carved blade shining in the light, and its point wickedly sharp. Emle gasped and stepped backward, the thong clutched to her breast. Her stomach clenched.

"Singer? What's wrong?" He looked chagrined, as if he had made some mistake.

For a moment, she could not answer him. She swallowed, shaking her head, and finally managed, "I—I am sorry. I—I do not like knives."

"Oh." He laid it down again. She forced her eyes away from it, and turned, without thinking, to face the door.

It was the little girl, the one who had been sitting beside Luke at the evening meal. His sister, surely. She was dark, as he was, with long, straight hair hanging in untidy strands about her narrow face. When she saw Emle, she stopped where she was.

"Gwinlet," Luke said. "Have you met Singer Emle?"

The child stared up at Emle in silence. She had a quality

of stillness about her, of holding herself back.

Emle said, "Hello." A familiar sensation prickled at her temples, the tingle of psi.

"Hello," the child said. Her voice was pitched very high.

Emle smiled at her. "I believe I saw you at the *quirunha* earlier, did I not?"

Gwin said gravely, "Our new Cantrix doesn't sing."

"No, she does not. Nor speak."

"Why?"

"Gwin . . ." Luke warned, but Emle put up her hand.

"It is a good question, Luke. I am happy to explain." She smiled at the little girl. "It seems, Gwin, the Spirit gave Cantrix Mreen no voice."

The little girl put her head to one side, considering this. "Are you her voice, then?"

"So I am." Emle knew she sounded mournful, and she saw Luke turn a quick, sympathetic glance her way. He caressed his little sister's head with his hand. Emle was touched by his gentleness with Gwin. Her own brothers—burly, rough-handed boys—had possessed no tenderness for their sister.

"Enough, Gwinlet," Luke said now. "Don't trouble the Singer anymore."

*Emle? Where are you?*

With a start, Emle remembered her errand. *I am still in the stables. I am coming.*

She turned to go, and saw that Gwin had already preceded her to the door, as if she too had heard Mreen's call. Emle looked down at the tiny girl, and her temples tingled again, but she only said, "I must go now, Luke. Thank you for your help."

He smiled at her, and she found that her instincts had been right. His smile softened his face, brightened his brooding eyes. He said, "Anytime."

MREEN TOOK THE THONG Emle handed her, and pulled it slowly through her fingers. It was pliable, warm from Emle's hand. When Mreen held it to her nose, she thought she detected the tang of *hruss*, even the scent of outdoors, of the thick pitchy needles of the irontrees. That, she supposed, was imagination. But the sound she heard in her mind, when she closed her eyes and focused upon it, was not fancy. She heard it through her psi, but it was as real as breath.

It was faint, hardly stronger than the fragment she had heard when she held the *hrussmaster*'s wallet in her fingers. A single cry—thin, startled, choked off. And then, like a treble ostinato, the weeping that went on and on and on.

Mreen had discovered her odd ability as a tiny child, still living at Observatory with her father and her stepmother. Once she had touched the great piece of ancient metal that was Observatory's pride, and had received a glimpse of the stars, the darkness of the heavens, and a rush of clouds and winds flying past, as if she had been lifted on *ferrel* wings high above the mountaintops. At Conservatory she had grown used to the images of students who had trod the stone floors of the practice rooms before her. And of course, the few possessions left to her by her mother brought her visions of Isbel's face.

Mreen held the thong a moment longer, hoping for something more.

She opened her eyes to find Emle watching her. *Did you hear?* she asked.

Emle shook her head. *No. What is it?*

Mreen closed her eyes again, clenching the bit of thong. She saw, dimly, a campsite ringed by great ironwood suckers, a fire burning in its center, shadowy figures around the fire. There were no details, nothing to clarify what she saw, only the high-pitched weeping. *I see a traveling party,* she sent slowly. *But I cannot see who is in it. There is the child crying. And that is all.*

*What does it mean?*

Mreen opened her eyes, and put the leather strip on her bedside table. *I do not know, Emle. But it must mean something. And it alarms me.*

# *Eight*

EMLE FELT A BIT sorry for Josu. Despite his sweet tenor voice and sure touch on the strings of the *filhata*, it was clear that Mreen's Gift intimidated him. He deferred to her so often—bowing, apologizing, waiting for her to choose a mode, state a melody, set a tempo—that Emle could hardly blame Mreen for growing impatient with him.

One morning, several days after their arrival, Josu approached Emle in the great room after the meal. "May I ask you something, Emle?" he said.

She bowed to him, smiling encouragement, winning a shy smile in return. "Of course."

"I thought you might know—" His cheeks flushed a faint pink, and he avoided her eyes, looking past her to the tall limeglass windows.

She followed his gaze, taking pleasure in the unmarred blue of the sky. No new snow had fallen in some time, and Emle, like every Housemember during these gradually lengthening days, paused whenever she passed a south-facing window, hoping to be the first to see the Visitor's face over the horizon.

Josu cleared his throat. "It seems," he said softly, "that I have done something to offend Cantrix Mreen. I thought you might tell me what it was."

Now Emle understood why he spoke aloud. He didn't want Mreen to hear his thought. Had he not been a full Cantor, she might have laid a comforting hand on his arm, but of course, such a gesture would be improper. She turned to face him. "Cantor Josu, I thought the same when I first became her companion, but now I know better. It is simply her manner."

"Her manner?" Josu frowned. "But she is so—so—"

"She seems angry?"

Josu's features drooped. "I am afraid she does not like me," he said. "And yet—it is possible we shall work together in this House for years. How will we manage?"

In the hallway, Housemembers began to gather to go into the Cantoris. Mreen sent, *Emle? Are you there?*

*Yes, Cantrix.* Emle smiled again at Josu. "I am sure Cantrix Mreen likes you," she said. "But she is afraid, and it makes her abrupt."

"Afraid? Of what?"

Emle answered, "She is afraid of failing."

Past Josu's shoulder, she saw Mreen come into the foyer, her *filhata* under her arm. Even in the clear sunlight, she glowed. The Housemembers parted to let her pass. Several bowed, but none spoke to her. And they were careful not to touch her.

Josu said, in a low tone, "But, Emle—Cantrix Mreen's Gift is immense."

"Yes. But something troubles her. I do not know what it is."

Mreen was already on the dais when Emle followed Josu up the aisle between the long benches. Mreen, tuning her *fil-hata* strings, glanced up briefly at Emle, and then back down at her instrument. *At last,* she sent. *I thought perhaps you had something better to do.*

Emle responded as mildly as she could, *You could not have thought such a thing, Cantrix.*

Mreen's lips curved, and her cheeks dimpled briefly as she adjusted the peg of her C string. *Perhaps not, Emle. But my Housewoman insists on tidying my bureau, and I could not find my extra strings.*

Josu stepped up on the dais beside Mreen, and Emle took a seat in the very center of the foremost bench.

*I taught her the sign,* Emle sent.

Mreen's ghost of a smile faded. *Lispeth flees at the very sight of me. She was out of my room before I could get her attention.*

*I am sorry,* Emle answered. *I will speak to her again.*

Mreen gave the slightest shrug. She looked to Josu, and played a short figure in *Iridu.* He nodded agreement, and the *quirunha* began.


DURING CANTORIS HOURS, Emle sat on the dais to interpret Mreen's instructions to those who came for healing.

Emle regretted the weakness of her Gift more then than at any other time. At Conservatory, second-level students almost always cared for the first-level students, easing their earaches, their sore throats, their upset stomachs. In this, as in making *quiru*, Emle's psi was ineffective. She could see the problem in her mind without difficulty, and she knew exactly what needed to be done. But try as she might, the fibrils of psi she extended groped uselessly about. If one came close to the point of actually touching something, it broke and scattered, doing no harm, but doing no good, either.

Mreen, of course, suffered no such impairment. Mreen healed burned fingers, soothed bruised muscles, lowered fevers with a speed that made Josu raise his brows in admiration. Emle sat close by, included in the circle of Mreen's halo of light, and gave voice to Mreen's advice.

The very last case of the day was a young, tired-looking woman complaining of headache. Mreen sent her psi directly to the pain, bringing the Housewoman quick relief. *Tell her to rest now*, Mreen sent to Emle.

Emle nodded, and spoke automatically. "Salli, the Cantrix wants you to rest."

The Housewoman bowed, but as she straightened and turned to leave, Emle saw that her eyes had filled with tears. "Why—wait, Salli. Just a moment," Emle said.

Salli turned back to face the dais, her head hanging. Two tears coursed down her cheeks, and she gave them a surreptitious dash with the back of her hand.

"Do you not feel better?" Emle asked. "I would have thought that the Cantrix . . . that your pain was gone."

"It is," the Housewoman said, so softly Emle had to lean forward to hear her voice.

"Then why do you weep?" Emle asked. "Is there something else?"

"It is only that I know the pain will return."

"You have headache often?"

Salli sniffled. "Almost every day." She lifted her head, and Emle saw how tired she looked, how even her hair seemed to droop with fatigue.

"Is it always the same?"

Salli shrugged. "About the same."

"When does the pain begin?" Emle asked.

"Usually in the night."

"What are you doing then?"

"Trying to get my baby to sleep."

"Is there a problem with the baby?"

Salli grimaced. "Only that he likes to sleep in the day and be awake at night. And then my other one, my little girl, wakes up early in the morning and wants her breakfast. It seems I barely fall asleep before one or the other of them is crying."

"And your mate cannot help?"

"He's a hunter. He's not home often."

*Emle. What are you doing?*

Belatedly, Emle realized that she had spoken without consulting Mreen at all. She bit her lip. *Oh! I—I did not mean to—*

Mreen frowned, and Salli stared at the two of them, alarm in her face. Mreen did indeed look very stern at that moment.

Emle held up a hand to ask Salli to wait as she struggled for a way to explain herself. *Cantrix, we have seen Salli in the Cantoris twice before.*

*So we have.*

*I thought perhaps—if we could understand the cause—*
Mreen's frown eased. *Very well, Emle. Continue, please.*


MREEN WATCHED AS Emle spoke with the House-woman. Emle's eyes shone with sympathy, and she seemed to forget herself entirely as she listened to Salli's troubles. It was no wonder the Housemembers liked her, and Mreen knew they did.

She sat back, holding her *filla* loosely in her fingers. A bubble of sorrow rose in her throat. She might as well have been making *quiru* high in the mountains, entirely on her own, for all the comfort she gained from the company around her. Had Isbel felt this same way, this isolation from everyone? Mreen swallowed, and forced away her self-pity. Sira had said that her mother's senior had been a cold, cruel man. She, Mreen, had Josu, who was timid, but pleasant. And, for the moment at least, she had Emle.

Emle murmured a few last words to Salli, and the House-woman bowed and withdrew.

*What did you tell her, Emle?*

*At Perl, when hunting parties were away, the women took turns with each other's children. I suggested she arrange something like that, and try to spend an hour or two alone, in the* ubanyix, *in the gardens . . . something that would refresh her. I said I would speak to the Magister about this. . . . I hope that meets with your approval, Cantrix.*

*I would never have thought of such a thing, Emle.*

Emle lifted her hands, and her eyes begged for approval.
*It was just that I remembered.*

*You did well. You will be a wonderful healer someday.*

Emle's shielding sprang up, and Mreen felt a stab of sympathy. *Come,* she sent. *The Housewoman is not the only one who needs some time to herself! I would love to bathe, would you not?*

*So I would,* Emle responded. *Thank you, Cantrix.*

Mreen tucked her *filla* inside her tunic, and gave a long, weary sigh. *Could you call me Mreen, do you think, Emle? I am weary of formality.* She touched the younger girl's shoulder. It was good to touch another person, to feel connected, though briefly.

Emle bowed, and her pretty smile made her cheeks glow. *Thank you, Mreen.*

It had not occurred to Mreen that Emle might also feel lonely. She could speak, could make friends, meet people— but perhaps that was not so easy as it seemed. It was something Mreen would never know.

She dreaded the day that Emle would return to Conservatory, and leave her behind.


LUKE, SITTING CROSS-LEGGED on a *caeru* rug beside his bed, was braiding a nosepiece for a hackamore, carefully twisting the leather strips into the pattern, smoothing out any rough spots. Gwin sat on her bed in her little cubby, drawing with a stick of charcoal on a sheet of thick paper. She hummed a little melody to herself as she worked.

"What is that tune, Gwinlet?" Luke asked.

She glanced up. "I don't know its name," she said. "But I know it's in *Doryu. Doryu* is for warming water."

Luke grinned at her. "And how do you know that, little one?"

"I listened outside the door when Cantor Josu warmed the water in the *ubanyor*. And I know it's *Doryu* because there are other tunes in the same mode. Like this." She began a new melody, her narrow face brightening with her pleasure in the music.

Luke shrugged. "I can't tell one mode from another," he admitted. "But I like hearing you sing."

She grinned up at him. "This one is in *Doryu*, too, only it has words. Listen:

*Little one, lost one,*
*Sleepy one, small one,*
*Pillow your head,*
*Dream of the stars,*
*And the Ship that carries you home.*
*Little one, sweet—*

"Enough of that racket!" Axl's deep voice cut through the heavy wooden door of the bedroom like the blade of an axe.

Gwin's voice broke as if cut in two. Her eyes dropped to her paper, and she clutched the stick of charcoal as if she had been turned to ice.

Luke clenched his jaw. Pure anger welled in him until his hands began to tremble. Deliberately, he laid the nosepiece aside, and came to his feet.

Gwin stared at her drawing. "What are you doing, Luke?" she whispered.

"I've had enough," he said. "I'm going to tell him."

"No!" She dropped the charcoal, and jumped off her bed to come to him, to seize his arm with her little hand. "It doesn't matter," she said, sounding all too much like Erlys. "I don't need to sing."

Luke knelt beside his little sister, and gently lifted her hand from his sleeve. "Gwinlet," he said. "Why shouldn't you sing in your own room?"

She shrank back, hugging herself. Her pinched face made her look as if she had ten summers instead of not quite two. Fury propelled him into the common room of the apartment.

Axl upturned a wallet on the table beneath the window, and the bits of metal glinting on the wood startled Luke so that for a moment he forgot his purpose. "Why—how did you come by so much metal?"

With a practiced hand, Axl scooped up the bits and poured them back into the purse. "What business is that of yours?" he growled. He stood, weighing the leather bag in his palm.

Erlys appeared in the doorway to the bedroom she shared with Axl, and stood with one slender hand on the doorjamb, her face, like Gwin's, drawn with fear.

Luke felt no fear. He felt only anger, clean and strong and hot. "The metal's not my business," he said in a level tone. "But my sister is."

Axl's handsome face darkened. "So?"

"Don't shout at her anymore."

"Oh, Luke," Erlys breathed. She took a hesitant step into the common room, and then stopped when Axl put up one heavy hand.

"Go back in the bedroom, Erlys," he commanded, and then to Luke, "I don't take orders from a half-grown boy."

Luke stood as tall as he could. "Not half grown," he said. "Full grown." He stepped closer to Axl. He was now a full head taller than his stepfather, though Axl's shoulders were broader, his neck thicker than Luke's. "Why shouldn't a little girl sing if she wants to?"

"Luke," Erlys moaned.

Axl whirled on her. "I told you," he snarled. "Get back inside! I'll take care of this."

Erlys quailed before him.

Luke's heart began to pound. The air in the apartment was thick with rage, his and Axl's. He took the one long step that put him between his mother and Axl, and he shouted, "Don't bully her! Take it up with me!"

Axl laughed, and tried to push past him.

Luke stood his ground. It was the closest physical contact he had ever had with his stepfather. Axl had never actually struck him, beyond a casual shove or a slap on the shoulder. It was Erlys he hurt, who bore the full brunt of his temper. Hurting Erlys was how Axl controlled them all. "Get out of my way, half-wit," he snapped.

"No! Don't touch my mother."

Axl's hands balled into fists. He had to look up slightly to meet Luke's eyes. He leaned close, to hiss directly into his face, "Don't touch her?" He laughed again, a nasty, rumbling sound. "She's my mate, and I'll touch her if I want to."

"Our father never struck her."

"Your father got himself killed," Axl sneered. "Let a stupid *hruss* fall on him. He was a half-wit like yourself, no doubt."

"He was trying to save the beast," Luke said through clenched teeth. "She got her leg trapped in an ironwood sucker, and she . . ."

"He didn't have the brains to get out of the way, though, did he?" Axl spoke the foul words casually, as if they meant nothing. "Nor do you, apparently," he added, and shoved again at Luke.

Luke shoved back, grunting, furious.

"Luke! Let it be!" Erlys cried. Gwin dashed from her cubby and ran to her mother.

Axl roared, "Erlys, come here. Come here right now, or you'll be sorry!"

Erlys, with a whimper, freed herself from Gwin's entangling arms, and tried to sidle past Luke. When he put out his arm to stop her, she began to sob.

Axl grated, "I'll show you who's master, you great fool!" He reached past Luke to seize Erlys's arm.

Luke batted his hand away.

He saw Axl's blow coming, but there was no time to evade it. It exploded against his cheek. He staggered backward, gasping with pain. The second blow caught him directly on the eyebrow, with a thud of knuckles meeting bone. Erlys wailed.

Gwin made no sound at all. She placed herself directly in front of Erlys.

When Axl came at him again, Luke seized Axl's wrist. He grunted with effort, as Axl twisted in his grasp, but he held on.

The years of labor in the stables, of hauling straw and feed, of lifting saddles and shoveling wet straw, had made him strong. Axl's face reddened as the realization swept over him, and he ripped his arm free to strike again. Luke, without thinking, drove his own fist directly into Axl's midriff. He had reach, and the element of surprise, and Axl's belly was soft with fat. The blow drove the breath from Axl's lungs. Axl lurched backward to crash against a wall. He gasped, and bent to put his hands on his knees, struggling for air.

For a long, frozen moment no one moved. Luke and Gwin stared at Axl in horror as Erlys wept aloud, her mouth open like a child's. Luke's blackened eye began to burn, and his fist throbbed from its contact with Axl's ribs. He trembled with shock and disgust. Slowly, he backed to a chair and sat down.

Axl caught his breath at last. He straightened slowly, and lifted one thick finger to point at Erlys. "Listen to me, Erlys. You'll learn to control your brats, or else."

"Leave her alone," Luke said. His throat had gone dry, and his voice rasped.

Axl's lip curled. "You don't know what's good for you," he said. "I'm still *hrussmaster* of Tarus, and you're my apprentice. You'd better not try anything like this again."

He snatched his wallet from the table and stamped out of the apartment, slamming the heavy door behind him. Erlys ran to Luke. Gwin stood where she was, her face as still as stone.

Erlys, sobbing, tried to press a damp cloth to his bruised face, but Luke pushed her hand away. There was more trouble ahead, he knew. Axl would find some way to hurt him. And Luke had no idea how to stop him.

MREEN, RECLINING IN a cloud of fragrant steam in the *ubanyix*, sat up suddenly. *Do you hear that, Emle?*

Emle, in the midst of washing her hair, straightened, too. The wet hair dripped warm water over her cheeks. *What is it?*

Mreen put a hand to her throat. *I am not certain.*

Emle closed her eyes and listened to the wild, unformed burst of psi. It was a silent, involuntary cry of misery and fear. She opened her eyes. *Not Cantor Josu. Who else in this House is Gifted?*

The mental cry rose again, and Mreen winced. *By the Spirit, Emle, she is terrified.*

*Who?*

*The little one. The* hrussmaster's *stepdaughter. Gwin.*

Emle stared at Mreen, feeling foolish. Of course. She should have seen it herself. *She is Gifted.*

Mreen covered her eyes with her wet hand. *Yes. Something is happening, and she—*

There was one more cry, a despairing outburst that told them nothing. Emle could not even place it. A moment later it subsided, but it left Emle shivering in the warm water.

Mreen dropped her hand, and met Emle's gaze. *The poor little thing.*

*She is Gifted, but she hides it. Why?*

Mreen slid under the water again. *This is Magistrix Sira's fear,* she sent. *That if Lamdon forces the Gifted to be taken to Conservatory, whether they will or no, families will hide their Gifted children from us. Perhaps Gwin's family knows of the resolution.*

*But Mreen,* Emle began, and then hesitated. How could she be sure? Perhaps Luke already knew of his sister's Gift, and simply kept it to himself. She could not imagine Luke forcing his little sister to do anything she did not want to do. And their mother—Emle had seen Erlys, a small, frail-looking woman, in the great room. Erlys was not one to stand up to the Magistral Committee.

Or to her mate. Emle shivered again.

*It is the* hrussmaster *she hides it from,* she sent to Mreen.

*Ah. Of course you are right.* Mreen had picked up a bar of soap, but now she slipped it back into its niche, and gazed unseeing at the curls of steam rising from the water. *But, Emle—the cry I heard when I touched the thong, or when I held his wallet—it was not Gwin.*

*You are certain?*

Mreen nodded. *Yes. If it were the same child, I would recognize it.* She took her hair in her hands and twisted the water from it, then tossed it over her shoulder and reached for the towel waiting beside the tub. *We will keep her secret, too, Emle. Magistrix Sira will come, in the summer, and we will ask her what to do. Until then, we will not tell Josu, nor Magister Kenth. No one.*

Emle nodded, and reached for her own towel. Poor little Gwin! She wondered what had happened to frighten her so.

# *Nine*

EMLE ROSE EARLY the next morning to practice a few minutes before the morning meal. She played a few scales to warm her fingers and her lips. When she felt ready, she tried a long passage in *Mu-Lidya*, one that required a long, steady breath. She had just drawn another to repeat the exercise when a commotion in the corridor distracted her. She laid her *filla* aside to investigate. Before she reached the door, Mreen called to her.

*Emle! Did you hear? It has come at last!*

Emle opened her door. Several people hastened past her toward the broad staircase, pulling on their furs they went. They smiled at her, and at one another. Laughter rose from the foyer below, and those on the stairs hurried faster, joined by others just leaving their apartments. Mreen emerged from her own room, her furs over her arm.

Emle laughed, and bounced with excitement. *This is a great day, is it not?*

Mreen's dimples were lovely to see. *Oh, so it is, Emle, so it is! Come with me, let us see it for ourselves!*

Emle dashed back into her room for her furs, and they tripped down the corridor to the staircase, eager as children. They joined the stream of people moving through the big doors, down the stone steps, flowing around to the back of the house, where the stableyard overlooked the bay.

Emle lifted her face into the cool morning, letting her hood drop back on her shoulders. She saw that even in their haste, the Housemembers were careful not to jostle the Cantrix, and left a little space around the two of them. Several greeted Emle, bowed to Mreen, and then pressed on. The great room was empty, the morning meal delayed. Every Housemember, cook and seamstress and Magister and hunter alike—more than three hundred people—hurried to witness the great event. The very air felt giddy with the sense of holiday, of celebration.

And there it was! So long in coming, so much anticipated—the sign of renewal and rebirth—summer at last.

The Visitor's face was pale, Emle thought, pallid before the more vivid yellow of the sun. It had seemed bigger to her five years before, but then she had been no more than a child. She supposed it had swelled in her memory, grown larger as she dreamed of how the Continent would change when it arrived. The Visitor melted the icicles, banished the snow from the meadows and paths, made the roof tiles drip water onto the cobblestones below. And she imagined now, seeing the tiny disc so clearly above the southeastern horizon, that already this day was warmer than the one before, the air brighter. She could almost feel the stirrings of the softwood saplings in their long-frozen beds, the stretching of their slender trunks toward the light of the second sun.

Emle stood with Mreen, a little apart from the rest of the House, watching the Visitor rise higher. They had a fine vantage point at the edge of the cliff, resting their hands on the stone wall. Around and behind them, Housemembers exclaimed over the sight. Parents lifted small children to their shoulders, held babies up so they could see. Emle gazed for long moments at the Visitor, and then smiled over her shoulder at the crowd of happy faces. A sharp salt breeze sprang up from the bay, ruffling her hair in its binding, chilling her exposed ears.

Emle reached up with her hands to pull her hood forward. The movement made her turn her body a little to the left, and she caught sight, just within the half-door to the stables, of the only person who had not rushed outside to be part of the celebration.

She recognized his tall, lean form in the shadows, though he kept his face hidden, out of the light everyone else sought so eagerly. Josu had arrived, and stood now beside Mreen. Emle worked her way through the crowd toward the stables.

At her approach, Luke drew back, but she squeezed past a little knot of people to get closer, sure Luke could not want to remain indoors on this wonderful morning! And later there would be dancing in the courtyard, and special songs, and perhaps a speech by the Magister. Soon the cooks would begin preparations for a special meal, a celebration.

Emle peered into the stables, a little blinded by the brightness of the daylight. "Luke?" she called softly. "It is Emle. Will you not come out? It is glorious to see!"

For a moment it seemed he would not answer. And then

she heard his deep voice, speaking softly, but clearly. "I was the first to see it, Singer."

"Come out, then," Emle cried gaily. "Come out and join us!"

"No," he said abruptly. "Not now."

"But now is the moment!" she persisted. The merriment grew behind her, and she glanced back to see that the cooks and the servers had carried the morning meal out on great trays, each one requiring two to balance it. All of Tarus, it seemed, was now sitting on stones or ironwood roots, on riding blocks, some even perching on the rock wall above the cliff, holding bowls of *keftet* that steamed in the chill morning air.

Emle leaned over the half-door to peer into the gloom of the stables, but she caught only a glimpse of Luke's long legs as he moved out of the passageway and into one of the loose boxes, away from view. "Look, Luke, everyone is having their *keftet* here, in the stableyard, to watch the Visitor pass! Surely your chores can wait. Come out!" She reached for the latch, intending to open the door, to coax him into the sunshine.

"No!" he said. "I can't! Leave me alone!"

Emle, shocked, lifted her hands from the door. "I—I am sorry." Heat burned in her cheeks, and she took a step backward, not knowing whether to be hurt or humiliated. Or both. "Forgive me." Her voice trembled.

Before she could turn away, he stepped into the straw-strewn passageway, not into the light, but far enough that he could call to her. "No, Singer . . . wait. I didn't mean . . ."

Emle stopped. A sudden, powerful rush of emotion

flooded her mind, drowning her perceptions, a wave of confused and unhappy feeling spilling from some other, unshielded, undisciplined mind. Emle put her hand to her throat.

Luke's sister, little Gwin, also lurked in the shadows of the stables, her slight figure almost hidden by a stack of leather feed buckets. Emle took a step forward again, thinking to call to her. At the same moment, Luke moved just enough to show his face in the light and then withdrew into one of the boxes.

The glimpse was enough. Emle gasped at the dark bruise, the swelling of his eye and cheek. He was hurt, surely. He should have come to Cantoris hours, let Mreen or Josu reduce the swelling, examine his eye for damage. Emle opened her mouth to tell him so, but then thought better of it. Both Luke and Gwin were keeping secrets. Luke, no doubt, had good reason for hiding his injury, from her and from everyone else as well. He would not welcome attention being drawn to it. And Gwin . . .

Emle turned her back on the stables, and looked out into the festive gathering. She spotted the *hrussmaster*'s blond head and his mate's dark one close by his shoulder. Did Erlys not wonder where her daughter was? Her son?

Mystified, she made a slow progress back to where Mreen and Josu stood admiring the rising of the second sun. For Emle, though on this day she had reached three summers at last, the brightness of the day was dimmed. She saw Mreen's puzzled glance.

*What is it, Emle?*

Emle only shrugged and shook her head. She did not know what she should do.

Fury burned in Luke's heart when he saw that the young Singer had seen his bruised face, had been about to speak to him, and then had turned away out of sheer pity. Of course, he told himself, he had not wanted to expose his shame, the shame of his family. His mother had begged him to keep the incident quiet, and Gwin, too, had wept on his shoulder, fearful that more disaster would befall them if word of Axl's behavior reached the ear of the Magister. But Luke thought he could bear it no more.

But now the Visitor had risen at last. He would be free, at least for a time. He began to pack for a trip into the mountains, to let the *hruss* stretch their legs, perhaps to attract a wild one or two to Tarus's herd. He would have a few days of liberty.

Gwin tagged after him as he assembled his things for the journey, pestering him with questions. "What's that for, Luke?"

"That's a saddlepack, silly. To carry some food, some softwood for a fire, a pot and a bowl." He took a roll of bedfurs from the high shelf where they were stored, and tied it to the wide skirts behind the cantle of the saddle.

"Why do you need so many furs?" she asked. "The Visitor's here!"

"Yes, but it's still cold in the mountains. I won't have a Singer."

"You should hire an itinerant."

"I have no metal, Gwinlet." He grinned at her. "Do you?"

She sighed. "No. I don't have any metal."

"I know, little one. No one does." Luke tried not to think about Axl's metal. He lifted the saddle to its peg, and tugged on the ties to make sure they were secure.

Gwin tilted her head. "Cantrix Mreen has metal."

He straightened. "The Cantrix has metal? How do you know that?"

Gwin glanced at the open tack room door, and then moved closer to him to whisper, "I heard her, when she was showing it to Emle. She carried two bits from Observatory."

Luke stared down at his sister for a long moment. "Gwin. How could you hear . . . the Cantrix has no . . ." And then, in a burst of understanding, he knew. His knees weakened, and he sank onto the bench beneath the saddle pegs. "Oh, Gwinlet. By the Spirit. You can't be."

Her eyes seemed dark and ancient to him, full of sadness. "You mustn't tell anyone, Luke. You mustn't."

"But—" He stared at her, trying to comprehend the miracle. "But you could go—" He broke off, stunned by the marvel. His little sister, little quiet Gwin! A Singer, a Cantrix even! "Oh, by the Six Stars, whatever will Mama say?"

"You mustn't tell her!" Gwin whispered fiercely. "No one must know! They would send me away!"

"But don't you want to go, Gwin?" Luke whispered, too, seizing her hand. It was cold in his fingers. "Don't you want to go to Conservatory? To learn to play the *filla*, the *filhata* . . . to know all the modes, and their uses?"

She stood very still. "So I do," she said. "But I cannot."

He stared at her, stunned by the change in her speech pattern. Already she seemed distant to him. "Why?" he finally blurted. "Why can't you?"

"Because of Mama," she said. "Because he would hurt her."

"Oh, Gwinlet," he said, helplessly. "You must think about this."

"I have thought about it, Luke." Her childish voice was as solemn as any adult's. "I have thought of nothing else for months."

"But, Gwin . . . She's your mother. You aren't hers."

She only looked at him. He gazed back, knowing that in some obscure way he was wrong. That Erlys, in refusing to free herself from Axl or to protect herself, had placed both her children in this position. And yet, despite her weakness, he loved her. They both did.

Luke held out his arms, and Gwin stepped into them. She pressed her face into his shoulder, and he hugged her, hoping to comfort her. But who would comfort him? Perhaps being an adult meant he was on his own, that he could no longer expect others to care for him, to protect him.

On this day, he had four summers at last, but that no longer seemed the marker of his adulthood. The events of last night made him a man. He had taken his future into his own hands, for better or worse. He had stood his ground, and he must accept the consequences.

He swallowed a lump in his throat, and held his little sister tighter.

# Ten

THE SUN-DRENCHED HOURS of summer seemed to Emle as ephemeral as soap bubbles, shining and fragile. Each day something special happened. Sometimes the entire House took their midday meal in the courtyard, and afterward Emle played her *filla*—tunes in *Lidya* and *Mu-Lidya*. The children and the younger adults danced beneath the two suns, whirling and leaping, laughing until they could hardly stand. Once, the youngest Housemembers, giddy with freedom, led everyone on a merry chase through the timberlands, where only patches of stubborn snow still clung to the shadiest spots, and where Emle found wildflowers growing among the softwood shoots—bright, tiny blooms of scarlet and white and vivid blue, flowers she had not known existed. And by the fifth day of summer, the guests began to arrive, from Perl and Amric and Soren and even far Isenhope, riding in merry groups of five or six or more, to visit their relatives, greet old friends, share news and gifts, and simply be together.

Although the work of the House went on—the washing

and cooking and cleaning, and the daily *quirunha* and Cantoris hours—everyone, including the Gifted, carried their burdens lightly and hurried to finish essential chores in order to be out of doors as much as possible. Emle and Mreen strolled along the cliff one warm evening, carrying their furs over their arms, admiring the dim disc of the Visitor on the horizon, rolling its way to the northwest.

They settled themselves on a round boulder, which had already sprouted a thin cushion of green moss.

Mreen stroked the moss with the flat of her hand, and mused, *Last summer we were both at Conservatory. With all of our teachers and our classmates . . . I wonder if we will ever see them again.*

Emle leaned back on her hands, gazing out over the calm sea. *I suppose I will,* she sent. *The Magistrix promised me I could return.*

*Ah, yes. Of course you will. But I would imagine some of my class have gone on to their own Cantorises. Those you will not see.*

*That is true. A sad thing.*

Mreen nodded. *My own sister Trisa—well, in truth, my stepsister, but we are as close as sisters—she is Cantrix at Observatory. I do not know when I will see her again.*

*When did you leave her?*

Mreen's eyes clouded as she gazed to the north, where the distant peaks still glistened with late-season snow. *I was not yet five years old,* she sent. *And she was fourteen. Perhaps she would not even know me now. Perhaps even my father and my stepmother would not recognize me.*

Emle shook her head, smiling. *Mreen—everyone knows who you are! There is no one like you on the Continent. I would imagine your family recognized your Gift before you did!*

*You are right, Emle! Trisa knew it first.* Mreen's dimples flashed, and she pulled her knees up to wrap her arms around them. *And now, Emle, tell me about your first summer.*

*My first summer.* Emle sighed. *I have difficulty remembering my first summer.*

*You were very young.*

*Yes. Only four years old. And*—Emle paused. *And it was when my Gift was discovered.*

Mreen raised her eyebrows. *Tell me about it.*

*I*—*I am not sure I can. I know how odd it is, but*—*I cannot quite remember. Something happened*—She paused again. Something blocked her memory, as if a curtain had been drawn across it, or as if she had shielded her mind, and could not open it.

Mreen sent gently, *Just tell me about your family, then.*

*I have three brothers, older than I. We are not close as you and Trisa. Indeed, they were not sorry to see me go to Conservatory.*

*Because of your Gift?*

Emle shivered a little, and pulled her furs over her shoulders. *Yes, I suppose. I think so.*

Mreen pulled on her own furs, and hugged herself inside their warmth. The salt breeze freshened as the dusk approached, tingling in their nostrils, teasing loose strands of hair about their cheeks. *Do you want to remember, Emle?*

Emle gazed unseeing into the darkening sky. *I am not certain of that, either. I do not know if it is better to forget, or to bring it out and*—*examine it, I suppose.*

Mreen simply sat for a long time after that, offering nothing but the warmth of her shoulder, the companionship of her silence. When the Visitor set, it seemed to drop all at once beneath the horizon. Almost immediately, the chill of evening spread up from the water and over the cliff edge.

*Come, Emle.* Mreen stood, brushing bits of moss from her tunic. *We should go inside.*

*Yes.* Emle stood, too, feeling as if she had missed an opportunity somehow. *Mreen, do you think I should try harder to remember? It seems as if I have forgotten because—because it hurts me to remember.*

*I cannot answer you, Emle. I do not have any experience in such matters.* Side by side, they walked across the stableyard to the stone arch leading to the front steps. Mreen put her hand on Emle's shoulder. *I do know, though, that some hurts take a long time to heal.*

Emle glanced at her and saw that the gleam of her halo dimmed, and vague shadows shifted through it. She supposed she was not the only one who carried distressing memories.

LUKE WATCHED THE Visitor sink below the horizon from his campsite in the lee of an ironwood grove. Above his head the stars came alive, one or two at first, then a dozen, then a thousand—far more than he knew how to count. His tiny softwood fire did nothing to dim their sparkle, and there was no *quiru* to fade them. He lay with his head pillowed on his bedfurs and lost himself in the spill of stars across the wide black sky, his ears soothed by the humming of the wind through the tree branches and the rhythmic munching of *hruss* cropping grass.

He had ridden up to this mountain meadow with three *hruss*, on the pretext of giving them some exercise and a few days of the tender new grass. It was a relief to be away. Once his face healed, he and Axl had kept an uneasy distance. Luke knew his mother was trying desperately to smooth things over, fluttering around Axl, fawning over him. It turned Luke's stomach. He loved her, but he couldn't understand her.

He had to accept her choice. Erlys had given up their family's home, their peace, their closeness, in order to have Axl. Luke was weary of trying to puzzle it out. At least, for two or three days, he would be his own man.

Erlys had fussed endlessly, even over this, with Axl glowering in the background. "Will you be safe?" she cried softly. "Axl, someone should go with Luke. There are—I don't know—*tkir*, or *urbear*, or he could fall and be hurt."

"No *urbear* in the summer," Luke said.

Axl rumbled, "He thinks he's grown, Erlys. Let him find out what it's like."

Only Gwin seemed to understand. On the morning of his departure, she had slipped out into the stableyard to press a leather bag into his hands. When he opened the drawstring, he saw that it was full of dried fish, raisins, and half a loaf of fresh bread. He kissed her, and rode away before Axl could find some last chore for him to do. She stood braced on the paddock fence and waved until he turned onto the cliff path, out of her sight.

The Continent in summer was like another world. The air was rich with the scent of swift-growing softwood, of grass, of flowers so tiny they were almost invisible. As he rode, Luke saw *wezels* darting beneath arching ironwood roots, a fat *caeru* peering at him from the mound that marked its den. "I'll remember you," Luke murmured, looking around for landmarks. "But we don't need you now."

He turned from the road where a path branched up toward the foothills, through heavy stands of ironwood and half-grown softwood, climbing to the broad mountain meadow where the *hruss* could crop their fill.

He had almost reached the meadow when he spotted the wild band. He was passing the mouth of a canyon tucked between two wooded slopes, when he glanced up, and saw a tiny band of wild *hruss*, led by one stallion. Two of the mares had foals—leggy, half-grown creatures with manes and tails still stiff and short. Luke reined in his mount, and the two following stopped obediently. The wild ones threw up their heads to watch. Luke's little band whickered at the strangers, then dropped their heads and began to graze. A tiny stream bubbled nearby, run-off from the quickly shrinking snowcap above their heads.

Luke looked around, satisfied with the spot. "Might as well camp right here," he said to himself. "Maybe tempt one or two new ones into Tarus's stables."

He put the *hruss* on loose hobbles and cleared a space for his cookfire. There were no ironwood roots to sit on, but a few scattered boulders made an enclosure. It would be, he thought, home enough for a few nights. He arranged his saddle and bedfurs, and laid the fire.

He made a small pot of *keftet* with a handful of grain cooked in water from the stream, adding dried fish to flavor it. He sat cross-legged, enjoying his simple meal, watching the flames crackle in the darkness. It occurred to him that he should feel lonely, a half-day's ride from the nearest human. But he felt free.

He stared into the fire for a long time, listening to the comfortable sounds of the *hruss* breathing nearby, shifting their big feet, occasionally jostling one another. He thought of his father, gone now beyond the stars, and wished he could share this moment with him. He tipped his head back and amused himself by searching for the Six Stars among the uncountable number flung across the sky. He tried to sort out six in a group, but he kept losing track of the clusters he had already scanned, and finally, chuckling, he gave it up. He doubted anyone could pick out the six from which the Ship of legend was supposed to have come. Pondering the old story, he rolled into his bedfurs and fell into a deep and easy sleep, lulled by the wind and the fresh air.

By morning, the band of wild *hruss* had moved closer to his campsite. Luke laughed to see them, their floppy ears twitching, their nostrils flaring. He laid out little mounds of grain for them to taste, keeping his movements gentle and slow. He knew, if the wild ones attached themselves to him, they would follow him home.

"Sorry, fellow," he murmured at the stallion, who still kept his distance at the far end of the canyon floor. "They like company. Spirit made them that way, I guess." The stallion looked young, with sleek lean flanks and a well-made head. Luke poured a bit of grain on a flat rock, as close to the stallion as he dared get. "Listen, my brother. You're welcome to join us, too," he offered. The beast only tossed his head, making his ears flop and his fine black mane stream in the breeze.

"No," Luke said quietly, "I didn't think so. But I'll leave this here, just in case."

FOR TWO DAYS, he tramped the meadow and explored the little stream up to its source, a quickly shrinking snowfield on the flank of the mountain. At night he cooked his meal and savored the solitude, and slept soundly until the suns shone on his face and the *ferrels* flew down from the mountaintop, their shrill calls startling even the drowsing *hruss*. At the edges of the meadow, the new crop of softwood was already as tall as his shoulder. He stepped carefully among them, knowing, as all Nevyans did, how precious each one would be when the generous warmth of summer gave way to the first cold season. They would be left to grow as long as possible, and at the first threat of deep cold, day parties would come out to harvest them, sledding them back down the steep slopes to be trimmed and stacked behind the wall of the nursery garden, to cure in the warmth of the *quiru* where it stretched past the House walls. For the long years of winter, the stock of softwood would provide cookfires and campfires.

On his third morning in the mountains, Luke woke slowly, reluctant to leave his bedfurs, but knowing it was time to break camp and turn for home. He had promised his mother.

He smiled at his swollen band of *hruss*. The wild mares and foals now grazed side by side with the hobbled *hruss*, all of them glossy with the good food and easy living of summer. Luke stood at the edge of his camp after he had cooked and eaten a light breakfast, and gazed up the meadow, where the black-maned stallion stared back at him, head high, ears flicked forward.

"Last chance, my brother," Luke called. "I don't like to leave you here alone."

The stallion stamped a foot, and swished his glistening black tail.

Luke sighed. "You're a beauty, that's for sure. Wish you'd change your mind."

He saddled his beast, and loaded the two pack animals. With a last check around his campsite, kicking dirt into the fire to make certain it was out, he mounted, and took the reins of his pack animals in his hand. He glanced over his shoulder at the stallion as he started down the path. The mares and foals followed closely. The stallion whinnied, one long, lonely call.

"Can't talk them out of it now," Luke said, half to himself. "Even if I wanted to."

He felt bad for the black-maned *hruss*, but he led his increased band down the mountain with a deep sense of satisfaction. He had set out with three beasts. He would return with seven.

He indulged himself by picturing a triumphant return to the House. Erlys and Gwin would be proud. Axl would be silent, for once, and perhaps even the Magister would offer a word of praise. Erlys would see that it was true, that he could take care of the family himself.

And perhaps that young Singer would notice.

Emle. Luke imagined her golden brown hair curling from beneath her white fur hood, her blue eyes shining with admiration at the four new *hruss* in the paddock. She would be in the company of the other Gifted, he supposed, but she could be simply strolling with Gwin, enjoying the light of the two suns. . . .

At the thought of Gwin, his stomach tightened, and his daydream evaporated. If Gwin was walking with Singer Emle, would they be talking with their minds, in the way of the Gifted? Had the Gifted ones of Tarus discovered Gwin's secret? If they had, surely they would send her—be forced to send her—to Conservatory. Everyone knew about the Magistral Committee's new provision. It had been announced in the great room by the Magister, read aloud in its long, boring detail. All Gifted children were to be sent to Conservatory, regardless of their families' desires. Even itinerants, now, must send their children to be trained. No mention was made of how this new rule was to be enforced, but the Committee had power over all the Houses.

One of the hunters had muttered imprecations as the Magister finished his reading, and the woman across from him, also one of Tarus's hunters, raised her eyebrows and wondered aloud how they were to hunt in the cold seasons without itinerant Singers. It seemed the Magistral Committee did not concern itself with the problems of hunters.

"Let 'em get a bit hungry, and they'll think about it," the man had grumbled.

And Axl leaned forward to say, "Let the Cantors and Cantrixes escort hunting parties. They have plenty of time on their hands."

It had been said with a smile and a light tone, but both the hunters looked away, and Luke knew they didn't want to be associated with such a remark. And Gwin would be part of all of it, if her secret were discovered.

The long, commanding call of a *hruss* interrupted his thoughts. Luke twisted in his saddle and saw that the black-maned stallion had followed him after all. He was keeping his distance, but he was there.

"Well, my brother," he said cheerfully, as he turned to watch the steep path in front of him. "You won't regret it. I promise you."

THE DAY WAS bright, warm enough that Luke tied his furs behind the cantle of his saddle and rode in his tunic, relishing the sunlight on his bare head as he led his band of *hruss* down off the mountain. As he topped the last rise, he paused for a moment, enjoying the sight of Tarus spread out beneath him, the waters of the bay sparkling behind it. The walls of the House were massive, spreading from east to west, the nursery gardens tucked behind, the Cantoris and great room nestled in front, and the clean gray cobblestones of its circular courtyard, made gay now by the brightly colored tunics of Housemembers enjoying the morning.

As Luke turned into the cliff path, the *hruss* lined out nicely behind him. The foals danced alongside their dams. Even the stallion followed more closely as the day wound down. From time to time Luke turned to encourage him, and the *hruss*'s ears pricked at the sound of his voice. It was almost evening when they reached the stableyard.

Axl was working on a section of the paddock fence. He

had a hewn timber in his hands, and was just lifting it into place as Luke and his *hruss* rounded the last bend and rode out of the trees. Axl stopped when he saw Luke. He stared at him for a long moment, then turned back to his task, hammering in four ironwood pegs with quick, powerful strokes. When it was done, he laid his hammer down with exaggerated care and pivoted, his back to the fence, to watch Luke.

Luke dismounted in the center of the stableyard, glad to see the paddock was empty. He moved to the gate and opened it, leading his mount in, still saddled. The other beasts followed, the wild mares sniffing at the fence, but trusting the leaders. The stallion came last, prancing, his head high and his eyes rolling. For one agonizing moment, Luke thought he might not pass through the gate. Under his breath, he whispered, "Come on, Brother. Don't fail me now." As if he had understood, the black-maned *hruss* lifted his head high, staring at Axl, and then trotted through the gate and into the paddock to begin a circuit of the fence, smelling everything, his silky tail high and streaming.

Axl stood with his fists on his hips, saying nothing. Luke closed the gate and set about removing packs, unsaddling his mount. He finished, and faced the *hrussmaster* with his hands full of gear.

Axl gestured at the new *hruss* in the paddock. "What's all this?"

Luke felt the old surge of resentment, but he reminded himself of his nights in the open, the freedom of the wind on the back of his neck, the sense of competence that seeing the stallion join his band had given him. He met Axl's eyes, remembering the sensation of that thick fist against his cheek, and the strength of his own hand blocking the next blow. And he saw, by the flicker of Axl's eyelids, that he had not forgotten, either.

"I rode out with three *hruss*," Luke said. "And I came back with eight."

"Why in the name of all the Houses did you have to bring a stallion?"

Luke felt a sudden heat rising in his neck. Had he made a mistake? But a stallion would be beneficial, expand the domestic herd, widen the breeding possibilities. He drew a breath. "Why—why not a stallion?"

Axl crossed his arms, and leaned against the stable wall, a triumphant smile beginning to spread across his face. "You great fool," he said lightly, as if it were a pleasantry. "We can't put two stallions together in the paddock. They'll fight each other. Everyone knows that. We'll have to keep them separate, one in a box, one outside. We'll be moving them back and forth every damned day."

Luke dropped his eyes. "Take care of it myself," he mumbled.

"Of course," Axl said, his voice dropping a note. "If I remind you, day in and day out."

Luke's cheeks burned now. He had worked hard in these stables, and had become a good *hrussman*. If he had made a mistake, it was an honest one. But he knew who would pay if he resisted Axl now. And since his mother would not stand up for herself, he must protect her. "No need to remind me," he muttered.

Axl snorted and turned back to his chore. "By the Ship," he said, very clearly, "I could have found a dozen able apprentices, and I'm stuck with you."

And how many mates could he have found, Luke wondered, who would put up with him? But he only bent to pick up his saddle, and carried it into the tack room. He looked back at the paddock where the new *hruss* were now dozing in the late afternoon sunshine. Axl stood just outside the paddock, a piece of wood in one hand, a hammer in the other. He was looking at the *hruss*, too, and smiling to himself.

# *Eleven*

EMLE, IN HER tiny apartment next to Mreen's, woke early the morning after their talk. She dressed in a fresh dark tunic, and brushed and bound her hair.

It was still early, though the morning was bright beyond her small window. Only the kitchen girls would be about, or people beginning to gather in the great room for the morning meal. Emle tucked her *filla* inside her tunic and hurried down the staircase to the *ubanyix*.

The corridor was empty, and when she pushed open the heavy door, she found the bath also empty. Fresh towels had been laid out by the linen mistress the night before, and the niches were stocked with cakes of soap. The Housekeeper had filled the tub with fresh water. Emle imagined the Housemembers waited for Mreen to come down and warm the water before having her morning meal. Emle stepped inside, and closed the door behind her. She drew out her *filla* and put it to her lips.

With eyes closed, she played a straightforward *Doryu* piece, one she had learned in the first level. She knew it perfectly, its twisting half-steps, its minimal quarter-tone embellishments, the little runs built into the melody. She played it again, and then once again, without modulation, without variations. *Doryu*, the simplest and most straightforward of the five modes, was always best for water. Water was harder to excite than air. The tiniest parts of water were slow to awake, to move in response to the music. Emle tried to send out her psi easily, to unreel it as easily as Luke might uncoil a length of rope in the stables, to flex it as effortlessly as she flexed the muscles of her arm. She finished the piece, knowing she had played it well, even perfectly. But that barrier was still there. Just as her psi reached the water, it sundered, as if cut by a . . .

A knife?

Something about the thought shocked her.

She stopped playing, and opened her eyes. Nothing had changed. The water was still tepid, the *ubanyix* no brighter than it had been when she came in.

Emle's eyes stung as she left the bath. She put her *filla* back into the inner pocket of her tunic and turned toward the great room, her steps dragging. Why, O Spirit, she thought bitterly, Why give me a Gift I cannot use?


MREEN DRESSED SLOWLY, thinking of the long day ahead. It was time for the morning meal, but first she must warm the water in the *ubanyix*. There would be Cantoris hours, and the *quirunha*. The Housemembers, she supposed, would avoid her in the great room, as they always did. Lispeth would duck her head, so she could not read the finger signs Emle was trying so hard to teach her. Cantor Josu would be silent, as he so often was, which pained her.

Mreen held out her hand. She concentrated for a moment, and watched the light around her hand and arm intensify, glow with warmth and power. She was so accustomed to the nimbus that surrounded her, and Conservatory had become so used to it, that she had not realized how much it would separate her from everyone else. Only Emle treated her as if she were a normal person—a friend.

She let her halo subside to its usual glow, and picked up one of her mother's brushes to try to tame her mass of hair. Isbel's image rose before her as her fingers curled around the carved wood. Mreen saw the curling auburn hair, her own round chin, her dimples. Could Isbel possibly have felt as isolated as she herself did?

Mreen sighed. The Gift felt heavy this morning.

Cantoris hours, however, were brief. Somehow, in the summer, ailments seemed less troublesome, pains less serious. Mreen supposed it to be the warmth, the fresh air, the general sense of well-being and holiday that the whole House seemed to share.

Their last task was an infant, wailing with earache. It was a simple thing for Mreen to relieve the pressure and soothe the pain. It took only moments, and a brief melody in *Aiodu*. Everyone in the Cantoris smiled when the baby's cries ceased, and the tired mother slumped with exhausted relief. She stood up, and managed a bow while cradling her child on her shoulder. She spoke to Emle. "Please tell Cantrix Mreen I thank her."

Emle leaned forward. "Housewoman. The Cantrix can hear you perfectly. But you can also thank her like this." She lifted her hand to make the sign, and then stopped, abashed, glancing uneasily over her shoulder.

Mreen shrugged. *Go on.*

Emle turned back to the Housewoman. "This way," she said. "Touch your forefinger to your heart, and then lift it toward the Cantrix. This is her finger sign to say thanks."

The Housewoman's eyes slid uncertainly to Mreen, to Josu, and back to Emle. Emle nodded encouragement. "Try it."

The Housewoman resettled her baby on her left shoulder and lifted her right hand. She straightened her forefinger, touched her chest, and lifted it.

Mreen responded with a quick flutter of her fingers. The Housewoman stared blankly at her. Emle sent, *Mreen, if you will make the sign a little slower, she can see it.*

Mreen pressed her lips together. She should be able to think these things through herself. Emle was watching her, her brow furrowed with concern. Mreen supposed she thought she had given offense. Mreen blew out her breath, and carefully repeated her sign, moving her fingers slowly in succession, one, two, three.

"Housewoman," Emle said. "The Cantrix made the sign that means 'You are welcome.' Did you see it?"

The woman grinned, and all at once Emle saw that she was little more than a girl herself. She patted her child's back as she said, "So I do, Singer Emle! Wait till I tell them in the ambry! I'm the first Housemember to speak the Cantrix's language." She bowed again, and left the Cantoris. Her baby had fallen fast asleep, its long eyelashes curling against rosy cheeks.

Emle turned on her stool. Mreen turned to her, smiling. *Emle. Thank you. Do you think they will all learn my signs? Will you teach them?*

Emle nodded. *So I will, with your permission. I think your Housemembers will be very glad to be able to speak with you.* She chuckled. *Even Lispeth!*

Mreen shook her head. *Lispeth? May the Spirit will it!*

At that, even Josu laughed.


THE TRAVELING PARTY arrived just as they all walked out of the Cantoris.

Emle waited for Mreen, and followed her out into the foyer. They found the double doors open to the courtyard, and a little group of riders just dismounting at the foot of the steps. Mreen stopped so abruptly that Emle almost bumped into her. There had been many visitors since the summer began, traveling parties arriving every few days. Emle tried to peer past Mreen's shoulder to see why this one commanded her attention.

*Emle.*

*Yes?*

Mreen turned to face her, holding out her *filhata*. Her eyes were sparkling, the brightest green Emle had ever seen. *Will you take my* filhata, *please.*

Mreen thrust the instrument into her hands, whirled, and ran down the broad steps. Her halo shone like a sunburst, frothing and sparking around her head.

Emle stood dumbfounded, holding the *filhata*, watching the reserved Mreen hurl herself into the arms of a tall, dark-haired man. A woman stood by, beaming.

Emle didn't realize Josu stood beside her until he sent, *Who are those people?*

*I do not know, Cantor.* Emle held the *filhata* to her awkwardly, both arms around the curved case. *I do not know any of them.*

There was another man, a little shorter, broad-shouldered, with thick, graying hair. Mreen untangled herself from the first two and bowed, deeply, to this new man. He laughed aloud, bowed in return, and then he, too, embraced her.

*Cantor Theo v'Observatory,* Josu sent.

Emle glanced at him. *Do you know him?*

Josu's thin cheeks turned pink. *No, Emle. I . . . I listened.*

*Josu!*

*I am sorry. Please do not tell Mreen!*

Emle covered her laugh to protect Josu's dignity, and turned her face away so he would not see her merriment. After all, she thought, Josu had only five summers himself.

*He was trained by Magistrix Sira, a long time ago,* Josu told her. *When they were both held captive at Observatory.*

*Captive?*

*So the story goes. I do not know how much of it is true. They say he was an itinerant Singer, but now he has been Observatory's Cantor these three summers.*

*And the others?*

Josu gave a slight shake of his head. *I do not know them.*

The stableman, Luke, came around from the back of the house. He hung his head, and seemed to shuffle, his heavy

126

boots scuffing at the cobblestones. The travelers gave their *hruss* to him, and he led the beasts away after making an awkward bow. Something tugged at Emle's heart as she watched him go, but she had no time to think about it. Mreen, with her guests at her side, fairly danced up the steps and into the foyer.

*Cantor Josu,* she sent. *Emle. This is my father, Kai—*Mreen wound her arm through that of the taller man—*and this is my dear stepmother, Brnwen.* Mreen smiled at the woman with a warmth that twisted Emle's heart with envy. Emle bowed, shielding her thoughts.

"Hello," she said quickly. "Welcome to Tarus. I am Emle."

Mreen's fingers flashed, too quickly for Emle to catch the signs, but Brnwen nodded and smiled. "Mreen tells me you are Singer Emle," she said. "And you must be her senior," she said, turning to Josu. "Cantor?"

He bowed, too, and said politely, "Josu. It is good to meet you."

Both Brnwen and Kai bowed, and then the broad-shouldered, older man stepped forward. "And I am Theo," he said. "Cantor Josu. Singer Emle." He bowed, and then grinned. *Greetings from the Cantoris of Observatory. Cantrix Trisa will want to hear every detail of Mreen's new home.*

*Trisa is my stepsister,* Mreen sent happily. *And Cantor Theo's junior.* She flashed her parents another sign with her fingers, and the three of them turned into the great room, moving to one of the window seats, where they sat together, hands touching, cheeks touching from time to time. Emle could hardly tear her eyes from them.

*Emle?*

She turned, dismayed, fearing she had been rude. Josu was staring at her, one eyebrow lifted. *Yes, Cantor. I am sorry.*

*I will show Cantor Theo to the* ubanyor. *Could you find Gerta, and arrange rooms for Mreen's guests?*

*Yes, yes.* Emle bowed quickly. *I am on my way now.* She bowed again, blushing before Cantor Theo's easy smile, and hurried away in search of the Housekeeper.


THE EVENING MEAL was a festive one. Mreen shared a table with her parents and Cantor Theo. Emle sat near them, but she might as well have been alone. Mreen was absorbed in her guests, in Theo's conversation, and her fingers flew faster than Emle could follow. She propped her chin on her hand, and gazed distractedly around the room until her eyes fell upon Luke.

He, too, sat with his family, but his eyes were cast down, his shoulders slumped. Next to him little Gwin, too, was silent. She stared at Cantrix Mreen and her visitors, her face very still, her eyes flickering as she followed Mreen's finger signs. Across from Luke sat Erlys, smiling too brightly, pressing part of her own portion of chowder on Axl, giving him an extra piece of dried fruit. As Emle watched, Erlys cast an anxious glance at her son, who looked, if it was possible, more sullen than ever. Like herself, Emle thought, he was in company, but alone.

When the meal was over, Emle rose quickly, smoothing her dark tunic. She watched Axl and Erlys leave the room, with Luke shambling behind them. He was a head taller than his stepfather, but his slumping shoulders made him look somehow smaller. Emle hurried around the row of tables.

"Luke," she said softly, just at the doorway. He stopped, and his spine straightened a bit when he saw her, the droop of his mouth easing.

"Singer," he mumbled. "Do—what—"

"Gwin tells me you were in the mountains for three nights, all alone."

His head lifted. "So I was," he said softly. He glanced after his mother and stepfather, who had gone beneath the staircase toward their own apartment.

"Tell me," she said, trying to put a gay smile on her lips. "Sit with me, and tell me what it was like. Were you not afraid?"

He stared down at her, his face blank with surprise. "Sit—sit with you?"

If she had not, at that moment, felt herself to be as much an outsider as Luke, she might have given up on him. But something about the stiffness of his face, the weariness in his dark eyes, made her persist. "Yes," she said firmly. "With me." She turned to lead the way to one of the tall windows. The cushioned benches beneath them were favorite spots for people to congregate and chat. "Yes, Luke. I want to hear all about it." She curled herself in one corner of the window seat, and waved him into the opposite one. "I would have been terrified!"

# Twelve

LUKE LED EMLE through the back corridor of the House toward the stables. He felt a bit as if he were moving in a dream. The other Housemembers glanced at him curiously, and he supposed they were wondering why she bothered with him. One or two stared in openmouthed surprise. His feet felt lighter than usual, more nimble, as they had in the mountain meadow when there was no one watching him. He had managed to tell her all about his trip, about the new *hruss*, about the beauty and peace of being alone under the stars. He was sure he had not described it well, but at least the words had come to him, and she had smiled as if she understood perfectly.

She was, he thought, the easiest young woman to talk to that he had ever met. Her eyes shone in the yellow *quiru* light. Her hair made him think of the soft mane of a newborn foal, but he would never say so. He feared it sounded wrong, though to him it was the nicest comparison he could make.

And now, she had asked to see the new *hruss*, particularly

the foals. Luke prayed that Axl would not be in the stables.

They reached the outer door, and Luke held it open. Emle smiled up at him as she ducked beneath his arm, and his heart missed a beat. Or perhaps it missed several beats. He found himself smiling, too, as he guided her through the passageway and out to the paddock.

The twilight was just shading toward darkness. The new *hruss*, crowding forward to meet them, looked clean and strong. Luke felt a proprietary pride in their shining coats, their clear eyes, and their trim fetlocks, which he had spent hours over this very morning. Emle exclaimed, "Oh! They are so beautiful, are they not, Luke? And the foals . . . such long legs!" The foals ambled over to sniff at their fingers, pushing one another to get closest to Emle and Luke.

"You see how easy they are with us," Luke said. "And they were running wild only a few days ago."

"I think you must be wonderful with them," Emle said. Luke's neck warmed under her praise.

"Which one is the stallion?"

"He's there, at the far end." Luke pointed. "He's shy," he added. "Maybe a bit stubborn. But just stand here, very still, and in a moment he'll get curious."

The mares came to the fence, and Luke patted each of them, and gave them a bit of grain he had scooped up in his palm. The stallion lifted his head, and flicked his ears forward. "Ho there," Luke said softly. He dug a little more grain from his pocket, and held it up, above the mares' heads. "When you're ready, Brother. I'll wait."

"Brother?" Emle whispered.

"I guess that's his name. It just sort of happened."

Beside him, Emle stood very still. Luke didn't look down at her, but he sensed her concentration. When the stallion took a step toward them, and then another, Luke heard Emle's quick breath. "He is the most beautiful beast," she whispered.

"So he is." Soon the *hruss* stood across from them, nibbling grain from Luke's cupped palm, his great eyes turning from Luke to his mares, and then to Emle. Luke murmured, "One new person for you to know." The stallion lowered his head and allowed Luke to rub his forehead and then smooth his drooping ears. "He was very good about being groomed this morning," he told Emle. "And tomorrow I will try him with a saddle."

The inner door to the stables opened and closed with a loud bang, and voices sounded in the passageway.

Emle started, and glanced up at Luke from beneath her eyelashes. His heart sank. "Oh, no," he groaned. One of the voices, he knew, was Axl's, and the other, he feared, was the Magister's.

Emle touched his arm. "Come, Luke," she whispered. "I think the *hrussmaster* does not care for either of us. Let us hide ourselves!"

And with a bubble of a laugh, she dashed away into the darkness. Luke called under his breath, "Be careful, Emle! Be careful of the drop!" He hurried after her, fearing she might trip in the darkness, and almost stumbled into her. She had taken shelter behind an ironwood branch that overhung the rock wall. They stood together, panting, just beyond the reach of the light.

Axl emerged from the stable door with the Magister, matching his steps to Kenth's slow ones. They leaned against the paddock fence, just where Luke and Emle had stood a few moments before.

Kenth said something that was hard to catch, but Axl's response, in his rumbling baritone, carried easily through the twilight.

"A beauty, isn't he?" he said, with an inflection delicately judged between pride and modesty. "By next season we can double our herd, Magister. Tarus will have foals to spare, and we can sell a few."

Kenth said something else.

"Yes," Axl answered him. "And Clare, and Filus. I'll try to teach Luke enough before he goes, but he may need help. He's a bit slow."

Luke stiffened. Emle, beside him, drew a sharp breath.

"I have to keep him busy," Axl added. "He's moody."

Kenth said something, and Luke thought he heard "father."

"Of course," Axl responded. "Very hard on him. But he has to come out of it sooner or later. That's why I sent him up to the mountains after the wild band. Easier to do it myself, but I thought it would be good for him. I don't know why it took him three days. Dawdling, I suppose, like boys do."

Luke wanted to burst from his hiding place and confront his stepfather. He should have guessed, he supposed, that Axl would take credit for it, for all of it. Axl made him sound like a difficult boy, when he had just achieved something any man could be proud of. And Emle . . . Emle would think him a liar. That he had made up the entire tale.

After a time the two men strolled back into the stables. The wind came up off the bay, bringing the scent of salt and fish, and the warning that the nights could still be cold. "Singer Emle," Luke managed to say, though his voice was rough. "Cold. Have to get indoors."

"All right, Luke," she whispered. "Lead the way, and I will follow."

He held back the drooping branch, and then he walked ahead of her. His feet felt clumsy and enormous again, his body all awkward angles, his arms too long, his legs too thin. He thought, if he had Axl before him at this moment, he would not be able to restrain himself. He longed to defend himself, to explain to the Magister the truth of the matter. But how could he? He could not admit to either of them that he had been listening. Nor could he put Emle in such a position.

He opened the stable door, and after Emle had gone through, he took time with the heavy latch. When he turned, he found her standing in the passageway between the stalls, watching him. Her eyes, so luminous earlier, had darkened.

He searched for something to say, but his mind was a blur of misery and humiliation.

It seemed she, too, had nothing to say. After an agonizing interval of silence, she murmured, "I suppose I had better see if the Cantrix needs anything. Or her guests."

He could only nod. His tongue felt frozen.

She turned toward the House, and he followed at a little distance. At the door she glanced back. "Thank you for showing me the *hruss*," she said softly.

He nodded again, feeling as clumsy and stupid as Axl

claimed him to be. But what was there to say?

Emle went through the door into the corridor, and the door swung slowly shut. Luke stood in the straw-strewn passageway, hating himself, hating Axl, and longing to know what to do, how to redeem himself. Suddenly, he could bear it no more. He rushed to the door, and pulled it open again.

"Singer Emle!"

She was just at the turning of the hall, and she spun back to face him, her mouth opened in surprise.

He reached her in two long strides, and stood looking down at her, sure his face was flaming, his hair a tangle, his eyes wild. "Emle," he repeated, a little louder than he intended.

"Yes?" She stared up at him. At least she didn't look away, embarrassed for him. He didn't think he could have borne that.

"I—I told you the—the way it was. The way it really was. I didn't—I wouldn't—I don't want you to think—"

His voice faltered, and he spread his hands, feeling a complete fool. But Emle smiled, and then she laughed, a gay, musical sound. "But I know that, Luke," she exclaimed. "Of course I know!"

"You know—what do you know?" he stammered.

"I know that Axl, your stepfather, told the Magister a terrible lie."

"But—how—" Luke wanted to pinch himself. He couldn't seem to finish a sentence.

Emle put a finger to her lips. "You must not tell anyone," she said, twinkling up at him. "My Gift is flawed, it is true, but I hear thoughts very well indeed."

"You hear thoughts?"

"So I do, Luke. But I am not supposed to eavesdrop. My seniors would be very unhappy with me if they knew."

"But how can you hear the thoughts of the unGifted?"

She shrugged. "Perhaps they are not thoughts exactly. They are more like moods, or impressions. It is like looking out at the waters of the bay, the colors changing in different light, different weather. And the thoughts of your stepfather . . .'' She stepped a little closer, and whispered, "They are very dark, Luke. Murky and thick, like the sea on a cloudy night. I think Axl tells more lies than truths."

WHEN LUKE SLIPPED quietly into the family's apartment, he found Gwin huddled on her cot, a wooden doll in her arms. From the large bedroom, its door closed, Luke could hear Axl's voice, heavy and harsh. Erlys's answering tone was as light as a child's, and it sounded as if she had been weeping.

"What's happening, Gwinlet?" Luke whispered.

Gwin looked up at him, and he saw that she, too, had been crying. Her face was red, and tears still clung to her eyelashes. "Oh, Luke," she said, and burst into soundless sobs.

"What is it?" He crouched down beside her cot, letting her throw herself against his shoulder. She said something, but it was muffled against his tunic, and he couldn't understand her. Gently, he held her back a little. "What was that? Tell me again."

"Luke," she cried. "He wants to send you away! He's telling Mama you have four summers now, and you shouldn't live with your parents anymore. And he's sending you to Arren!" She buried her face against him once again, and he just held her, patting her back, murmuring wordless comfort. Above her head, he stared at the wall.

It was tempting to take the opportunity of leaving Tarus, to let Erlys deal with Axl however she might. He could start again, in a House where his stepfather had not spread stories about him. He knew hardly anyone at Tarus, after all. He would only be leaving Gwin.

But he couldn't do it. Gwin had no one else to protect her.

He soothed her as best he could, and dried her tears with a corner of her bedfurs. "Never mind, Gwinlet," he said softly. "I'm not leaving. Not for a long time, anyway."

"He'll make you go. He said so."

Luke stayed where he was for a moment, kneeling beside her cot. The voices in the bedroom were quieter, but he thought he heard his mother's soft weeping. Luke shook his head, and stood up. "No," he said firmly. "He can't make me go. Wait here, Gwinlet."

She watched, wide-eyed, as he crossed the common room and knocked on the door of Axl's and Erlys's bedroom. The sounds within stopped abruptly. A moment later the door opened, and Axl came out. Erlys came to the doorway, where she stood with her eyes on her feet.

"What is it, son?" Axl said. He folded his arms and smiled up at Luke. "It looked to me as if you still had chores to finish in the tack room."

Luke's pulse quickened. He took a deep breath, and moistened his lips with his tongue. "Chores are done. Gwin tells me you have plans for me, and I've come to say I'm not going. I'm not leaving my family," he said stiffly.

Axl turned his head just enough to give Gwin an icy look, and then he turned slowly back to Luke. "This is my family now," he said. "And I will make the decisions."

"Not for me, you won't," Luke said. His voice broke a little, but it was from anger, not fear. The sensation, growing familiar now, flared in his chest. He breathed again, trying to control it.

"Luke . . ." Erlys moaned from the doorway. Luke glanced at her. She looked just as Gwin did, her eyelashes wet, her face red with weeping.

Axl didn't even look at her. "Erlys, go back in the bedroom," he ordered. She backed out of the doorway. "Close the door," he growled. She did, slowly, softly. The click of the latch was loud in the silence.

Axl's eyes were fixed on Luke. "Son, you're a grown man now. Time for you to make your own way."

"I do good work for you."

At that, Axl snorted. "If I direct your every move," he snapped. "Great clumsy fool. Let someone else take you on as apprentice, and you'll see life is not so easy."

A rush of fury almost took Luke's breath away. He put one hand on the wall to steady himself. "It's not true," he hissed. "I've been a good apprentice. I've carried more than my share of the work in the stables."

Axl cocked an eyebrow. "Really? Do you think people will believe that?"

Luke straightened, feeling his hands form into fists without his volition. "Have you been telling them otherwise, Axl?" His voice rose, and he clenched his fists to keep from lashing out. "What have you been saying about me?"

For answer, Axl only laughed.

Luke took a step back, not trusting himself. He didn't like the way Axl made him feel. It was not true, he told himself, that he was clumsy, or a fool. It was unfair, and there was nothing he could do about it. Except refuse to give in. "I won't go," he said again. "I'm not leaving my mother and sister."

"I told you," Axl repeated. "They're my family now. And it's high time Erlys and I had a little time alone."

"What about Gwin? She's just a little child. You can't send her away."

Axl's eyes flickered away from him and then back, and he hesitated, ever so slightly, before he said, "We're talking about you, Luke. And I'll be speaking to your mother about your selfishness." His lips pursed. "I'll hold her responsible for your actions."

Luke knew what that meant. He took another step backward and said, in as level a voice as he could manage, "If you touch her again, I'll kill you, Axl. That's a promise."

Axl stared at him for a long moment, his eyes narrowed to slits. "And now you threaten me?" he snarled. "I'll have to mention this to the Magister, Luke."

"If you do," Luke responded, before he could stop himself, "I will tell him what goes on in this apartment, though my mother has begged me not to!"

Axl's face darkened, and Luke saw that he, too, made fists of his hands. Luke braced himself, ready, even eager, to do battle. But Axl saw, and remembered the last time. He straightened, and his hands opened.

"You're a fool, Luke," he said softly. "And you have no idea what I can do." His lips curved in a humorless smile. "We'll see about all this." He turned and opened the bedroom door. His voice was so low Luke could barely make out his words, but something about them filled him with dread. "We'll just see."

# Thirteen

EMLE WATCHED FROM a distance as Mreen, as had become her habit over the past days, joined Cantor Theo in the great room to sit together over a cup of tea. Brnwen and Kai sat on either side of Mreen, saying little, but beaming with affection. What a lovely family they were, Emle thought. Mreen had lost her own mother, but the Spirit of Stars had sent her this sweet woman who cared for her, loved her as if she had given birth to her.

Emle walked out into the sunny courtyard. She was growing accustomed to being alone a good deal. She knew Mreen and her family did not intentionally shut her out, but they had little enough time together, and she was loath to intrude. The peak of summer had passed, though the Visitor still lent its warmth to the Continent. The softwood shoots had thickened and begun to turn into the trees that would be harvested when the cold season began again. Emle wandered out among them, touching their slender trunks.

She turned to her left, making her way through the trees

down to the cliff path, and wandered along it for a little distance, feeling every stone of the path through her soft-soled boots. It was cool in the shade of the ironwood trees, and she wrapped her arms around herself, shivering a little in her thin tunic. When she came to a clearing, she stopped, and stood looking out over the Frozen Sea. Not frozen now, of course. Perhaps the sea needed a different name during the summer, when the fishermen's little *kikyu* moved freely through the waves, no longer having to dodge chunks of ice, or to fear being caught on the sea when darkness fell.

Emle tried different names aloud, to see how they sounded. "Salty Sea," she said, thinking of the taste of the fish that came from it. "Great Sea." And then, with delight, "Summer Sea!" She cried it aloud, letting the wind carry her voice out over the water. "Summer Sea! I will make a song about it!"

She heard the sudden crunch of a boot on the rocks behind her, and she whirled. When she saw that it was Luke, she laughed with relief. "By the Spirit, Luke! You startled me."

He thrust his hands into his pockets. "Sorry."

Emle smoothed her hair back into its binding with both hands. "You must find me very silly. You have caught me shouting names at the very ocean."

"Summer Sea," he said somberly. "I hope to hear that song one day."

Her laugh died. "Luke . . . but what is the matter? Has something happened?"

He hesitated, turning to gaze out over the water as she had. She watched his profile, thinking that he had changed a great deal in the brief time she had been at Tarus.

"My stepfather," he said at last, "is trying to send me away."

"Oh." She felt cold again, suddenly. "Oh. And you do not wish to leave your family."

He turned his face to her. She hardly recognized him, indeed. Something old looked out of his face, something grave and oddly weary. "I don't want to leave Gwin," he said in a tight voice. "I think Erlys has made her choice."

"I suppose—I suppose your mother loves her mate?"

He looked away again, and his jaw tightened. "I don't know," he said. "If that's love, I wouldn't want it for myself."

Emle bit her lip. She was not at all sure she knew the right thing to say. But, she thought, she could listen. "Would you like to tell me, Luke?"

He was silent so long, she began to fear she had offended him. But then he leaned against the stone wall, gazing out over the water, and began to speak.

"I hate him," he said. "I can't help it. When my mother accepted him, I tried to get along with him. At first it was all right, but then he began to . . . to say things. Insults. Things he knew would hurt. And he would say them where people could hear." He took a long breath, as if saying so much at one time wore him out.

Emle stood very still, waiting.

"He controls us by hurting my mother," Luke said bitterly. "It got worse when I stood up to him. But I had to do it." She saw the flexing of muscle in his arms, the way his fingers curled into fists.

"The bruises . . ." Emle murmured.

"Yes. I hit him, too, Emle. Brawling, like . . . like I don't know what. Who behaves that way? And since then, he's been searching for a way to get rid of me."

"He is full of hate," she said softly.

Luke muttered, "I don't want to be like him."

"You are not, Luke. You are not at all like him."

He turned his face to her, and his eyes were full of misery. "But he fills me with hate, too," he said. "He makes me want to hurt him, to see him suffer as my mother suffers." He looked away again. The muscles of his jaw tensed, over and over.

"Luke, I could—perhaps I could speak to Mreen. She knows what Axl is like."

"You told her what we heard."

"No, no, I did not! She already knew."

He straightened, and looked at her closely. "Why? How did she know?"

Emle shrugged a little. "The Cantrix's Gift is a strange one," she said. "She knew before we arrived that the *hrussmaster* did not like the Gifted."

"His brother was Gifted," he said. "And was favored by their father."

"Ah." Emle sighed. "My brothers resented me as well, Luke. They were happy to see me off to Conservatory. To have the honor of the Gift in the family, but not the burden."

Luke shook his head. "I don't understand."

And then the memory flooded back to Emle, as vivid and real as if it had happened only moments before. Whether it was Luke's easy company, the breeze from the Summer Sea, or simply that it was time, at last, to deal with it, she did not know. But she recalled, in a moment of clarity as vivid as the

144

rising of the sun, what had happened. She gasped, and pressed her palms to her cheeks.

Luke looked at her curiously. "What is it?"

"Oh," she whispered. "Oh. I have just remembered."

"What?"

"Why my brothers—why my whole family, really—were glad to see the back of me! Oh, Spirit, Luke, I have not been able to recall this for two whole summers! Ten years!"

He hesitated, watching her. "You don't have to tell me," he said softly. "But it can't be so bad. Two summers—you were younger than Gwin."

"I was four years old. And it was bad enough." Emle dropped her hands, and twisted them together before her. Luke was right. She had been too young to understand what had happened. And there had been no one to explain it to her.

Emle tried to muster a laugh, but it died in her throat. "It is a foolish tale." She sighed, and stared out over the water. "My brothers were always fighting, wrestling, shouting, hitting each other. My mother could not control them, and my father—" Emle broke off. Thinking of her father brought a swell of sorrow. "He was a felter, and he often worked all day and into the night. He was a gentle man, and I think my brothers were beyond his understanding." She paused, and then said in a rush, "Two of them were playing with one of my father's knives, a sharp one used to cut yarn for the felting. They were playing some silly game, throwing the knife at things, and they threw it at my doll."

She managed a wry shrug, and was grateful for Luke's silence. She pulled at a strand of hair as she talked.

"They knew I loved that doll," she said quietly. "My father made it for me, dressed it in cloth he made himself, carved its face and little feet. That was why they did it. Because my father could do nothing for them, but for me . . ." She sighed. "They set my doll on a chair, and threw the knife at it. Perhaps they meant only to tease me, but the knife flew right by its head, and stuck in the wall. I was crying, and they were laughing. One of them pulled the knife out of the wall, and the other one held me by my arms, and they threw the knife again."

Again she broke off. It had been a terrible day, full of screams and recriminations and then, at the end, the discovery. "It was such a childish thing."

"Cruel of them," Luke said.

"My brothers were not so kind as you, Luke," she said. "I believed they meant to destroy my doll, the gift from my father, and so . . . when the knife flew toward it a second time, I . . . I did not know I was doing it, even. I was as shocked as anyone . . . but I deflected the knife. With my psi, that I did not know I possessed."

"Ah."

"Yes. I deflected the knife, and it struck my brother, the one standing near the doll. It pierced his boot and lodged in his foot. It bled so much that my mother had to call the Cantor to come and stanch it. There was blood everywhere. My mother was screaming and my brothers were all shouting, and the one who was hurt was crying and pointing at me."

"Your brothers blamed you?"

"They blamed me because the Cantor told the Magister what had happened, and he was angry at my family for not knowing. It was the Cantor who realized my Gift turned the blade. He was proud that Perl had produced a Gifted child. But my brothers never forgave me."

"That still hurts you."

"Yes, but . . ." The Visitor slipped beneath the horizon as Emle paused. "I was so little. I knew nothing about the Gift. I heard people's thoughts, but I thought everyone did that." She hugged herself, shivering. "And then my father—he took my doll, and threw it in the waste drop."

Luke shook his head in sympathy. "I couldn't bear to see Gwin hurt that way."

"You," Emle said, glad to turn the subject away from herself, "are a wonderful brother."

He rewarded her with that rare smile that lighted his eyes and softened the stern lines of his face.

She looked out over the darkening sea. "It grows dark," she said. "And cold."

"Yes, and I have work to do," he said. "Axl left on a trip this morning."

"I will walk back with you."

They walked together, side by side. Emle watched Luke, and saw how easily he moved, how surely he placed his feet, how he carried his head. He was, indeed, much changed. Grown up, she supposed. She wondered what would happen to him now.

WHEN MREEN AND Brnwen came into the *ubanyix* later that day, Emle was already there. She had washed her hair, and was simply floating in the big tub, letting the warm water push her this way and that, idly trailing her fingers through the scattered flower petals floating in it. She sat up, ready to leave the tub to the two of them, but Mreen waved her hand. *Please, Emle*, she sent. *Do stay and enjoy your bath. My stepmother tells me she has hardly spoken to you.*

Emle moved to the bench, and settled on it, dragging her fingers through her wet hair to push it away from her face. Mreen and Brnwen moved to one side of the *ubanyix* to slip off their clothes, and Emle saw that Gwin had come with them. Her narrow face was more relaxed than Emle had ever seen it, and her dark eyes glowed.

*Does Gwin's family know she is with you?* Emle sent to Mreen.

Mreen nodded, dropped her tunic and trousers in a careless pile, and walked to the tub. Her halo of light made her bare skin glow like a snowfield beneath the stars. *Her mother does. Her stepfather, apparently, left the House this morning.*

Emle glanced at Gwin, and saw that her eyes were following the two of them as they sent to each other. She raised one eyebrow, and the little girl grinned, and then ducked her head.

*I knew that,* Emle sent. *I forgot.*

It was Mreen's turn to raise her brows, but she made no comment. She signed something to Brnwen, and Brnwen smiled at Emle as she stepped down into the water. "Oh, this is ever so nice and warm. You must have warmed it, Singer? Thank you."

"Oh, no," Emle said quickly. "It must have been Mreen. Or Josu."

Brnwen splashed her face with scented water. "Well, it's

lovely. I could stay here until the evening meal."

Mreen signed to her, and Brnwen laughed. "Yes, I do feel lazy. There is still no end of work to be done at home." She turned again to Emle. "Though we have now had a proper Cantoris for three summers, the House was crumbling about our heads when Kai and I first arrived. Mreen was just a babe. And our Magister Pol, though he's old now, is as stubborn as ever. He will accept no help from Lamdon, since he will pay them no allegiance, and so the rebuilding goes slowly."

Gwin squatted beside the tub, watching the three of them. Emle and Brnwen chatted, and Mreen occasionally signed something to her stepmother, or sent some remark to Emle. Gwin's dark eyes flicked from face to face, following Mreen's signs, Emle's and Brnwen's spoken conversation. But her lips curved whenever the Gifted sent to each other.

Gently, the way older students at Conservatory sent to the younger ones, Mreen sent, *Gwin? Can you hear us?*

Light blazed in the little girl's eyes. A jumble came from her, unintelligible, indistinct, but definitely a stream of psi, and she nodded with vigor.

Mreen sent, *Very good, Gwin. We will practice together, and you can practice with Singer Emle, too.*

The little girl grinned hugely, and sent another flood of confused images. She settled down, cross-legged, beside the scrolled edge of the tub, ready for more. Emle laughed. *Later, Gwin. We will practice later.* And aloud to Brnwen, "Gwin is Gifted, you see."

Brnwen laughed. "Oh, I know that, Singer. I have a good bit of experience in recognizing it!" She put out her hand and touched her stepdaughter's wet, curly hair, then caressed her cheek. "I know what the Gift looks like."

Mreen laughed her soundless laugh, and Emle marveled at the easy way they had together.

Brnwen had taken on a new mate, a tiny motherless babe, and a House that was falling apart, all at the same time. She was a simple Housewoman, but she had created something marvelous, something lasting. She smiled when she found Emle's gaze fixed upon her. "What is it, dear?" she asked softly. "What are you thinking?"

Emle blurted, "That I wish you had been my mother!" and then wished she could slide beneath the water to hide her embarrassment.

But Brnwen neither laughed nor frowned. She put out her hand, and took Emle's. "Ah," she said. "Cantor Theo would say, 'To a *hruss*, the next meadow is always the best one.' But the Spirit made me to be a mother. It has always made me happy. And I wish all children could have happy homes." She released Emle's hand, and gave her arm a pat. "You two, as Cantrixes, will not know what it is to be a mother, so you must trust what I say. Your mother loved you, Singer Emle, I'm certain of it. She probably did the best she was capable of. It's hard to be a parent, and to allow your child to walk her own path." Her voice broke as she said, "And the more you love your child, the harder it is."

WHEN THEY HAD dried themselves, dressed in fresh linens, and rebound their wet hair, Brnwen kissed Mreen and went in search of Kai and Theo. The time for their return to Observatory was growing near. Emle followed Mreen up the stairs, carrying their soiled clothes over her arm to give to Lispeth. Mreen opened the door to her apartment. Lispeth whirled when they came in, clutching her dustcloth to her chest.

Mreen signed something, but Lispeth stood staring at the floor.

"Lispeth," Emle said. "You know what the Cantrix wants. I showed you the sign."

Lispeth cast a fearful glance at Mreen. "I can't remember them," she said. "I'm sorry, but I just can't! It's hard." Mreen turned her back on Lispeth to stalk to the window. She stood with her arms folded, looking out. Lispeth backed away, making a wide circle around Emle. "Can't you just tell me, Singer, what it is she wants?"

Emle repeated the sign, the touch of two fingers against the back of her opposite hand. "Cantrix Mreen needs paper," she said. She made the sign again. "Paper. Her parents will be leaving tomorrow, and she wants to send a letter with them to her sister."

Lispeth nodded, and reached for the latch of the door.

"But, Lispeth," Emle said, in as stern a voice as she could muster. "I will not always be here to tell you the Cantrix's meaning. You must learn her signs."

The only answer was the firm click of the door as the girl made her escape.

Emle stared at the door in exasperation. *I do not know what else I can do with her,* she sent to Mreen.

Mreen turned slowly from the window. *It does not matter,* she sent.

Emle spread her hands. *But it does! How are you to manage?*

Mreen shook her head. *I do not know. But it is not my chief concern.* Her eyes had gone dark, and her halo glimmered with shadows.

Emle watched her, forgetting Lispeth for the moment. *What is it? Is it because your family is leaving?*

Mreen nodded. *That, of course.* She turned back to the window, and pressed her forehead against the limeglass. *And you will leave, too, Emle. You will return to Conservatory, and I will be alone.* Mreen sighed, so deeply Emle could hear it all the way across the room.

Emle pressed her fingers to her lips, thinking. *I will speak to the Housekeeper,* she sent finally. *She must give you a different Housewoman, someone not so . . .*

*Timid?* Mreen finished for her, with a ghost of a mental laugh.

*Or stupid,* Emle sent, and they both laughed.

*Do not tell Gerta that Lispeth is stupid. That would be cruel.*

Emle hastened to say, *It would not be true, either. You are right, she is timid. But she can read, which will be useful to you. And she is really quite pleasant, even lively, when she is . . . I mean, when we are alone.*

*You mean, when she is not with me!* Mreen sent emphatically.

*Yes.* Emle gave Mreen a wry glance, and then slipped out of the apartment, starting down to the lower level to find the Housekeeper. On the landing she passed Lispeth, with a neat packet of paper in her hands.

Emle thought of what Brnwen had said earlier in the

*ubanyix*. Perhaps each person could do only the most they were capable of. And surely someone, in a House of three hundred people, would be willing to learn Mreen's ways. Or perhaps she, Emle, would be asked to stay.

She descended the staircase slowly, thinking. She didn't want to stay here at Tarus, though she had grown fond of Mreen. She wanted to return to Conservatory, to walk again in those halls filled with music and silent conversation, to see the plain walls and unadorned rooms. She wanted to study. And still, despite her struggles, she wanted to Sing.

# Fourteen

IT WAS BRNWEN who insisted, the next morning, that Emle sit with them at the morning meal. When Emle demurred, Brnwen said warmly, "You're not intruding at all, Singer Emle. And you should get to know Cantor Theo. We're all devoted to him at Observatory."

Mreen, hearing this, sent to Emle, *Please do join us, Emle. Then when I want to talk about my family and Cantor Theo, you will understand.*

And so Emle sat across from Theo, with Mreen at her left, for a long, pleasant hour. The light through the limeglass windows had begun to change, to slant in a different way, and they all knew that meant that the peak of the short summer had passed. The gaiety in the great room seemed all the more intense because of it, as if everyone embraced the moment with all their energy.

At one side of the room, Emle caught Luke's eye and smiled. He sat, as usual, with Erlys and Gwin, but they were a more cheerful group this morning, with Axl away. Gwin stared at the upper table where Emle sat, and Emle imagined she was trying to hear whatever thoughts they sent. Emle sent, *Your turn will come, Gwin.*

Gwin's forehead creased as she tried to understand, and her mouth tightened. Luke, unaware, lifted one hand to Emle before she turned back to hear something Theo was saying.

Theo, according to Mreen, was the same age as Magister Kenth, but he was so full of life and good cheer that he seemed much younger. Though his once-blond hair was now gray, his queue curled thickly on his shoulders. His eyes were almost as blue as Emle's own. He leaned across the table, smiling at her.

*Singer,* he sent. *You must be very shy.*

*Oh, no!* she sent. *No one seems to think so.*

*But we have hardly spoken.*

*I did not want to intrude,* she answered him.

*That was thoughtful of you. But I am always eager to meet one of Sira's students.* He grinned, and his eyes crinkled at the corners. *You must tell me some gossip about her. Your Magistrix and I are old friends, you know.*

The twinkle in his eyes made her laugh, and she sent back, *So I have heard, Cantor. There are many stories whispered in the dormitory about Magistrix Sira, but we never know which are true.*

He laughed, too. *Probably less than half, Singer Emle! Tell me a few.*

She tipped her head to one side. *Well—they say the Magistrix once worked as an itinerant Singer.*

He leaned back against his chair. *That story is true, Emle. I did, too. I began that way, in a time when I could not send or hear thoughts, or perform the quirunha.*

Emle considered for a moment, and then she looked up at him from beneath her lashes, and sent mischievously, *If you will tell me how she came by her scarred eyebrow, I will be the most popular student in the second level.*

He touched his temple with one finger. *I think I will let her tell you that story herself.*

*I beg your pardon?*

*Your Magistrix will be here today.*

Emle straightened as if someone had pinched her. *Today? Are you certain?*

*So I am, young Emle. Now do not turn all pale with fear. She is not so terrible. And I hope that when she comes, you will sing. I am told your voice is beautiful.*

Emle bit her lip. *Of course I will sing for you. As an entertainment, at least.*

*Only as entertainment?*

She firmed her lips so they would not tremble. *My Gift is incomplete, Cantor Theo. When I try to make* quiru . . . She lifted her hands, and tried to keep her expression light. *Something goes awry.*

He regarded her for a long moment. His smile was gone, but his blue gaze was sympathetic. Finally he braced his chin on his knuckles, and sent gently, *They say, here on the coast of the Frozen Sea, that if one wave does not wash up the* carwhal, *another might.*

She frowned, puzzled. *I have no idea what that means—but you live up to your reputation!*

He chuckled. *You mean, as an old itinerant with too many proverbs?*

She was laughing again. *Yes, exactly that! Except not the old part.* She bowed where she sat. *So Cantrix Mreen has told me.*

*Yes,* he sent. *I suppose she has. But Emle, it means that you should never cease trying. It has not been so long since I learned my skills that I cannot remember how difficult it all was. Persevere, Singer.*

She smiled, comforted by his goodwill and easy humor. *I will,* she promised.

*And I expect a song tonight!*

She laughed again. *I would not dream of failing you,* she sent. He winked at her, and turned aside to speak to Mreen.

MREEN HAD WOKEN early, and lay in her bed, gazing out the window at the summer-bright sky. She had stretched out her psi, searching, listening for Sira. It was rumored that Magistrix Sira, in her youth, had broken another Singer's mind with her psi. Mreen had no doubt it was possible, but there were too many wild stories about the great Magistrix. They could not all be true. But on this day, at least, Sira's legendary psi reached across the miles to assure Mreen that she would arrive soon.

Mreen hurried to tell Cantor Theo, and she saw how his eyes softened. He responded only, *It will be wonderful to see her again,* but she thought he glowed almost as brightly as she herself did.

By the time the Magistrix of Conservatory rode into the courtyard, Tarus had turned itself out in a style worthy of the Magister of Lamdon himself. The stone steps were swept and shining, the courtyard as clean as the very floors of the kitchens. Kenth and his mate, the Housekeeper and all her staff, and of

course Mreen and Josu and Emle and Theo, assembled themselves outside the doors. All together, they made a rainbow of
bright and dark tunics.

The sun rode high over the mountain peaks to the east,
and the Visitor poised on the horizon, ready to dip below the
distant line of the sea, when the riders appeared from the
turning in the cliff path, and rode through the stone arch into
the courtyard.

It was a surprisingly small group. Sira, Mreen supposed,
had acted as Singer. Her Housewoman, Ita, had come along, as
well as Gram and Jane, Conservatory's oldest and most trusted
riders. There was no one else. The stableman, Luke, followed
them through the arch, and stood ready to assist the riders.

In moments they were ranged before the welcoming
party, the Magistrix in the middle, Ita quick to slide out of
her saddle and ready, Mreen was sure, to begin her complaints at the difficulties of riding *hruss* and sleeping in the
open. Sira dismounted before either of the riders could offer
assistance. She bowed to the assembly as a whole, and they
bowed in return, and then, instead of speaking to Magister
Kenth, or even sending to the Gifted, she strode to the lower
steps, and held out her hands to Brnwen and Kai.

Mreen dropped her eyes. She knew she should shield
herself, but this was, in the end, all about her. And about her
mother.

Brnwen and Kai hurried to greet the friend and supporter they had not seen in two summers. Sira held Brnwen's
hands in hers, and then took Kai's. The feelings between
them were almost visible in the still air. And Mreen knew the

unspoken name that hung between them, the memory the three of them shared, which she could not. Isbel. Laughing, dimpled Isbel, who had been a Cantrix and had borne a child.

Mreen had known this since she was tiny, but not until she went to Conservatory had she understood how great an offense her mother had committed. And there had been nothing to help her understand how it had happened, how she, Mreen, had come to be.

She felt Emle's eyes on her, brows raised, lips a little open. Sweet Emle, who despite her own troubles had stood beside her these past months as her companion, her supporter—her friend.

*Are you all right, Mreen?*

Mreen gave her a tremulous smile, and a tiny nod. *Yes. Yes, of course I am.*

And now Sira turned, her face set in its usual firm lines. She came up the steps to Cantor Theo, and they, too, touched hands.

Mreen couldn't help herself. She listened.

*My dear friend,* Sira sent to Theo. *You are always so much in my thoughts, it seems we have never been apart.*

*Sira,* he responded, *the sight of you brings true summer to my heart.*

At that Mreen withdrew. What was between the two of them, Sira and Theo, was too personal, and too intense. She shielded her mind.


THE EVENING MEAL became a high summer festival. Magister Kenth had also known Sira in the old days, and he spared no effort or expense of his House to celebrate her return. The softwood burned heartily all day in the big ovens, and the cooks turned out the softest bread, the richest fish chowder, and the tastiest vegetables Emle had ever eaten. The Housemembers caught the air of rejoicing, and there was laughter and much moving back and forth between tables all during the evening meal.

Emle regretted what nervousness did to her appetite. She had promised Cantor Theo a song, and she meant to keep her word. She had begged a little help from Mreen with the modulation from *Lidya* to *Mu-Lidya*, and practiced most of the afternoon on Mreen's *filhata*. Mreen had declared her new song lovely, and made Emle promise to teach it to her. Throughout the meal, Emle went over and over the words in her mind, and her fingers danced on the tabletop as she ran through the chord progressions, the little thematic motifs she had added. Once she caught Cantor Theo watching her, and at his nod she blushed.

*You have not forgotten, Singer?* he sent.

*No, Cantor Theo,* she responded. Again her fingers played her tune on the ironwood tabletop.

And so, after the meal was cleared away, and Magister Kenth had made a short speech with many references to Sira's fame and achievements, Theo stood, smiling down at Sira, and then at the assembled Housemembers.

"It is very good to be among you again," he said. "To eat the finest fish on the Continent, to see one of my first students now installed as your Cantrix, and to be reunited with old friends." He gestured to Emle. "And the youngest

Singer in your House has promised us an entertainment."

Spirits were high in the great room, and as Emle rose to retrieve Mreen's *filhata* from a window seat, the assembly burst into applause. She felt a spasm of nerves in her middle, and she took her time unwrapping the *filhata*'s leather covering, folding back the tooled panels, checking the tuning, taking breaths as steadily as she could. Still she felt shaky and exposed. She was painfully aware of where the Magistrix was sitting, her long legs crossed at the ankle, her fingers linked before her on the table.

Emle turned where she was, and settled herself into the window seat, the *filhata* across her knees. She paused for just a moment, her fingers poised above the strings, her mind on the first words. When she looked up, she saw Luke's dark face turned toward her, his eyes bright with anticipation, and with friendship. Suddenly she felt better.

She took a good, deep breath, and played the first notes. She had composed a winding melody in *Lidya*, with the second stanza in *Mu-Lidya*, so that the song had a mournful, longing quality. She let her voice be pliant, the phrases long, the words clearly enunciated. The range was not wide, but the turns of melody felt pleasing in her throat, in the resonance of the room. She sang:

*The waters of the Summer Sea*
*Wash the beach with sun-warmed waves.*
*Kikyu float like bubbles of foam,*
*Like softwood leaves in a mountain stream.*

And then, in *Mu-Lidya*:

> *Come with me, my summer love,*
> *Let us float away,*
> *Like bubbles, or like leaves,*
> *Let us sail away on the Summer Sea*
> *To the land of legend,*
> *Where the two suns shine.*

Emle played a last flourish in *Mu-Lidya*, letting the sense of longing, of nostalgia, flow out with the final chord. She waited a moment, allowing the sound to die away before she laid the flat of her hand against the strings.

Applause broke out again before she looked up, and it lasted a satisfyingly long time. She smiled at Theo, and at Mreen, and bowed to Magistrix Sira. But when she looked for Luke to smile at him, too, he had disappeared.

# Fifteen

ALL THE GIFTED gathered in Magister Kenth's apartment the next morning, with Magistrix Sira at the head of the long table, Cantor Theo at the foot. The younger Singers found seats around the table. Sira invited Kenth to remain, saying, "We know we can trust you, Magister. You understand better than most the troubles we face."

Emle sensed complex emotions from Kenth, guilt, regret, worry. He and the Magistrix behaved as if they shared some deep secret. Something fascinating was always happening around Sira.

Cantor Theo could hardly be more different from Sira. Even now, as they prepared for what promised to be a meeting of some gravity, he teased Mreen to make her dimples flash, and he sent to Emle, as she seated herself, *I looked out over your Summer Sea this morning. If only I had such a kikyu, I would have been off over the waves!*

She pressed her lips together to keep from laughing. *I think not, Cantor,* she sent demurely. *When we have such a delightful gathering as this to enjoy?*

He chuckled, and winked at her before he turned to face down the length of the table. Emle lowered her eyelids, but watched Sira and Theo regarding each other. A smile pulled at the corners of Sira's narrow lips, in a way the students of Conservatory rarely saw. She cared for Theo, Emle thought, and he for her, yet they had put duty to the Gift above their feelings.

"I think you all know," Sira said, speaking aloud out of consideration for Kenth, "that the Magistral Committee has precipitated a crisis."

"You mean because of the new provision?" Kenth asked heavily. It did not seem possible that he and Theo had attained the same number of summers. Kenth seemed infinitely older.

"So I do," Sira said. She smoothed her scarred eyebrow with one long forefinger. "After these past ten years of struggling to nourish the appearance of the Gift, to reward its presence with celebration and respect, now the Committee is trying to buy it. This provision will negate all our efforts."

"Buy it?" asked Josu. He frowned, and leaned his slight body forward. "How can they buy the Gift?"

"They cannot, of course," Sira answered. "But by offering an honorarium—"

"Call it what it is, Sira." Theo's face was grim. "It is a bounty."

"Indeed." Sira lowered her hand to the table. "It is meant to frighten the families of Gifted children into turning them over to Conservatory, as if we were some sort of dictatorship. Or prison. The fee is paid, and in bits of metal, to whomever finds a Gifted child."

"Or exposes one?" Kenth said.

Sira's dark eyes turned to him. "Exactly so. Exposes one. That is the word to use, because it implies a world in which the Gift hides itself again. And my entire Magistership of Conservatory has been dedicated to just the opposite, to the belief that the Gift will burst forth in abundance, when families—and their Gifted children—have choices."

Emle glanced across the table. Mreen's glow had dimmed. She kept her eyes on her entwined fingers, and though Emle waited, she did not look up.

"We have just such an abundance at Observatory," Theo said.

"How many are now in your school, Theo?"

"We have seven," he said. "Trisa, of course, has been Cantrix these five years. And next year we will have two more, ready to step into Cantorises anywhere on the Continent."

"If Lamdon will accept them," Sira said with some bitterness. "Seven, can you imagine? From one House, and a small one at that."

"The number proves you right, Sira," Theo said. He leaned forward to include everyone at the table. "These families, if they so choose, can have their Gifted children trained right there, at Observatory. Or, if they wish, they can send them to Conservatory."

*As they did with me,* Mreen sent suddenly, almost explosively. Emle was so startled that she forgot to translate for Kenth.

Sira did it for her. "You see, Magister, Mreen was brought up at Observatory, although she was born elsewhere."

Emle cast Mreen another surreptitious glance, but Mreen still stared at her fingers.

"Mreen's parents, and Theo and I, felt that because of the nature of her Gift and its scope, she would do better at Conservatory. I believe we have been proved right in that as well."

"We at Tarus are grateful to have her," Kenth said. Every eye turned to Mreen then, and she lifted her head.

*Emle,* she sent. *Tell the Magister I am honored.*

Emle did. The conversation went on, around and around and around the problem.

"Can you simply refuse to comply?" Kenth asked at last.

Sira sighed, and sat up straight, stretching her back. "The Committee installed its envoy right in Conservatory. We can refuse to support their policy, but we can hardly turn away a Gifted child who comes to our door."

"And have any come?" Theo asked.

Every head turned to Sira for the answer. Slowly she nodded, and the lines in her face deepened, drawing her mouth down, dragging at her eyes. "Three," she said. "And one of them, Magister Kenth, came from your own House. He came from Tarus."


THE MEETING CONCLUDED with nothing resolved. Mreen watched Sira and Theo leave the room together. They rarely touched, and yet the bond between the two of them was almost tangible. She had known since her infancy, of course, how Sira and Theo cared for each other. Yet they had never violated the trust placed in them by the Gift. They had found a way to deal with the paradox.

Mreen stumbled out of the Magister's apartment by herself, not seeing where she put her feet, hardly knowing where she was going. Watching Theo and Sira together brought all her buried feelings to the surface. She kept them pressed down most of the time, using her music, her practice, her work to cover them. But seeing Kai and Brnwen again had laid all her emotions bare. She felt she could hardly live with the shame that was hers, left to her by the mother she never knew.

She found her way to the back staircase and descended slowly, aimlessly. She wanted only to be alone with her dark thoughts. She loved Kai, her father, but she could no longer pretend she did not know his part in Isbel's disgrace.

She paused on the landing, where a small window faced due south. If she stood very close, she could see past the dun mounds of the waste drop to the cliff edge and the sea beyond. The light was changing, the Visitor's position lower on the horizon, the green of the waters darkening. She yearned to be outside, to breathe the salt air, to let the fresh wind blow away her worries. But it was almost time for Cantoris hours, and then the *quirunha*. These things never changed, no matter the season, no matter the day. The Gift's hand on her felt heavy.

She rested her hands on the sill and stared at the shifting sea. The Summer Sea, Emle had named it. But soon, all too soon, it would freeze again. Mreen's heart felt as if it were already frozen.

She leaned closer to the limeglass. There was something at the cliff's edge, beyond the waste drop—no, some*one*. A small figure, poised in that narrow strip between the path and the precipice, where the hoists for the *kikyu* were built into the rocks. The hoists were empty now, the *kikyu* anchored in the bay, or out at sea.

The children of Tarus were forbidden to play there, where the ropes and pulleys and piles of equipment waited to trip a careless foot, where the protective wall opened to give access to the stairs carved into the cliff. Yet, this was surely a child! And even now, Mreen watched the little one lean out, as if to look down on the water, bracing one hand on a hoist.

Mreen knew, despite the distance, who it was, though she had no idea why she would be there, what she might be looking for. She whirled, and rushed headlong down the final flight of stairs. She dashed down the corridor toward the back of the House, where she had never been. There had to be a door leading out to the waste drop, a path through the refuse. It was little Gwin who teetered there, on the narrow timber of the hoist, high above the water and the rocky verge.

The gloom of the lower corridor surprised Mreen. The upper levels were always bright, especially during the day, with great windows that opened to the south and the north. But in this corridor there was only the *quiru* light to brighten the dimness, and the unfamiliar smell of oil lamps coming from the apartments. Mreen fumbled her way along, searching for an exit. As she went, she sent carefully, *Emle! Emle, where are you?*

She didn't dare broadcast a general plea for help. Josu might hear, or Theo or Sira. When she received no answer, she sent a little more strongly, *Emle? Are you there?* But wherever Emle was, whatever she was doing, she wasn't hearing Mreen's narrow call.

Near the end of the corridor a Houseman emerged from one of the apartments. His eyes widened at the sight of her. He bowed deeply and backed away as she approached as if her nimbus might burn him.

She signed at him frantically, asking for help, but he only stared at her. She wondered if he even understood that the patterns her fingers made meant something. Perhaps he thought she had something wrong with her hands, or a nervous habit! No comprehension dawned in his face.

Beyond him she saw a door that looked as if it led outside. She tried to ask him, pointing at it, making the sign for outdoors, but he only bowed again, his head ducking almost to his knees in his haste to show his respect. She gave up, and simply ran to the door and unlatched it.

She sent thanks to the Spirit as she pushed open the door and stepped over the threshold into the crisp morning breeze.

The soil in the waste drop had been meticulously turned and turned since the thaw had begun. There was not the rank smell Mreen had expected, nor was it unsightly. Even now, a Houseman labored at one end with a shovel. Mreen turned the other way, and found a narrow path leading between the spaded mounds. It was dirty but dry, and she raced along it without regard for the soles of her soft boots. As she ran, she broadcast much more strongly, *Emle! I need you!*

At last, there was a reply. *Mreen? Everyone is waiting for you in the Cantoris. Where are you?*

Now Mreen could focus her psi, send to Emle without alerting the other Gifted ones in the House. *Please, Emle, come to the cliff, where they raise the* kikyu. *There is a door—at the back of the House—*

*But the* quirunha—

*Please, Emle. Do not argue.*

*Mreen, what has happened?*

Mreen dared not send Gwin's name, and her breath caught when she realized she could no longer see her. *Just come. Oh, Emle—hurry!*

EMLE STOOD UP from her seat in the Cantoris and hurried down the aisle. She sensed the surprise around her, Sira and Theo at one side of the big room, Josu waiting, embarrassed and a little worried, on the dais. The House-members stared at her as she hurried past, and then turned their faces forward, to Cantor Josu, hoping for an explanation. Emle didn't know what was happening, but the urgency in Mreen's sending made her feet fly.

Like Mreen, she had never used the corridor that led to the waste drop. She found it now, beneath the stairs, branching off at an angle to the one that led to the stables. Mreen sent nothing further, and Emle thought she must be occupied with something, something important. More important than the *quirunha!* The idea was frightening. She ran, her breathing noisy in her ears. It took only moments before she found the door at the end, and the path through the waste drop. She spotted Mreen in the distance, at the cliff edge, bending forward beneath one of the empty hoists. Emle ran faster.

As she came near enough for Mreen to hear her footsteps, Mreen's hand came up, the palm turned outward. Emle halted, wondering, alarmed, and took more cautious steps toward the cliff. Now she heard Mreen's sending, but it was not for her.

*Gwin. Take my hand.* Mreen was broadcasting, as clearly as if it were painted on a wall, the image of herself with Gwin's hand in hers. *Gwin! My hand!*

Emle crept forward, and knelt on the cold rocks. She leaned gingerly over the rim to see what had happened. Her whole body went cold at the sight.

Gwin's bright red tunic shone like some seacoast flower against the gray cliff. She clung to a promontory of rock just below the path, her feet on the narrowest of stone steps. The little girl's eyes were squeezed tightly shut. Emle clutched cold stone with her hands. *O Spirit! What happened?*

*She slipped. She should not have been playing here alone.* Mreen cast a quick glance at Emle over her shoulder. *Talk to her, tell her to take my hand. She does not understand me.*

Emle cast a glance down the sloping precipice, and then tore her eyes away. There was abundant reason to be frightened. "Gwin," Emle called, striving to make her voice steady. "Gwin, it is Emle. Singer Emle. Just put up your hand for Cantrix Mreen."

A whimper reached them, barely audible beneath the constant hiss of the waves against the verge far below. "Gwin!" she said. "Mreen will take your hand, and I will hold Mreen's. In a few moments you will be safe."

*She is too frightened,* Mreen sent. *I will have to go down to her.*

*No! Let me go instead,* Emle sent. The idea of a full Cantrix risking herself in such a way was too much. *I am more dispensable!*

*Nonsense.* Mreen put her leg cautiously over the edge, and her foot found the first slippery step.

*Mreen*—Emle began, but Mreen's shielding went up as surely as if she had shut a door in Emle's face.

She watched helplessly, gripping the stone rim as if she could hold the child in place with the strength of her own hands. Mreen carefully lowered herself down the awful staircase, one step at a time, until she stood beside the little girl. There was barely room for the two of them, and when Gwin released her hold on the outcropping, and threw her arms around Mreen's waist, Mreen tottered for a terrible moment, then balanced herself with a hand against the naked rock.

"Mreen," Emle said aloud. "Send her up ahead of you. I will take her hand, and then hold yours."

Mreen looked up at her. Her hair whipped about her face, and the child clung to her with all her strength. *Tell her,* Mreen sent.

"Gwin," Emle called. "Mreen will be below, and I will take your hand up here. You have to climb back up."

There was no answer from the little girl except a tightening of her grip on Mreen.

"Gwin, the steps are too narrow. Mreen cannot carry you."

Again, Mreen sent a strong image, this time with Emle holding Gwin's hands, and the little girl climbing safely up the steps. "You received that, did you not, Gwin?" Emle asked.

A jumble of thoughts spilled from the child's mind, but they were a little brighter now, a little more focused. "All right," Emle said. "Now. Let go of Mreen, and she will help you reach my hands."

Gusts of wind spattered all three of them with spray as Gwin negotiated the steps. There were only four, but they were so steep, and so slick with salt water, that she slipped twice. Emle lay flat on her stomach, with only her shoulders and head over the edge, and stretched her arms as far as she could. Her shoulders burned, and the stone bit into her chest, but in a few agonizing moments, she had the child's hands, and was guiding her up and over the lip of stone to safety. She turned back to Mreen, and Mreen gratefully accepted her help as she climbed.

When all three were safely on the path, Emle crouched beside Gwin, holding her almost as tightly as the child had gripped Mreen a short time before. "Gwin, what were you doing out here? Where is your mama?"

And the child sent an image clearer than any she had managed before. Both Emle and Mreen saw Axl arriving home, coming into the apartment. There was some sort of dispute, ending with Luke stalking out of the apartment, and Axl taking Erlys into an inner room, leaving Gwin outside the closed door.

"And Luke?" Emle asked.

Gwin gave a little shuddering sigh, and buried her face against Emle's shoulder. "I do not know where he is," she whispered. "I was looking for him."

# Sixteen

LUKE HAD STORMED away from the House in a rage, so full of hatred he thought he would catch fire and burn. Axl had surprised them in the apartment after the morning meal. Luke was about to return to the stables to finish repairing a saddle rack, a chore he had been at work on before most Housemembers had risen from their beds. Axl gave him no chance to explain.

"Worthless layabout!" he shouted. "I leave you a few simple tasks, and what do I find? The tack room in a mess, tools everywhere, saddles lying in the dust—"

"Axl, wait," Erlys had said, and tried to take his arm. "Luke wasn't—"

Axl shoved her aside without even looking at her. She crashed against the table in the common room with a yelp of pain, and began to cry. Gwin froze against a far wall, her eyes fixed on her feet.

Axl cocked a fist. "You want more of this, Luke?"

"So I do," Luke snapped. "If there is no other way."

"No, Luke," Erlys pleaded. "Not again. Please, both of you."

Axl lowered his fist. "You're upsetting your mother."

Luke gave a short, mirthless laugh.

Axl's answering smile was equally without humor. He leaned over the table, bracing himself. "I've spoken to Kenth already. Luke leaves for Arren at the end of the summer to repeat his apprenticeship. But in the meantime"—he straightened, and pointed at his stepson—"I'll thank you to do the work you're given, or take an even worse reputation with you than you've already earned."

"Not fair," Luke said. He began to tremble with the familiar fury. He took a step around the table, ready for another confrontation. Eager for it.

"Not fair?" Axl jeered. "A whining, lazy . . ."

Luke took another step, and was gratified to see Axl jerk back, out of reach. "I'll go to the Magister myself. Tell him everything that goes on here—"

"Luke, no!" Erlys moaned. "Stop, I can't bear it. . . ."

Luke stopped, and Axl's eyes gleamed with triumph. Gwin edged along the wall, her arms wrapped around herself, her face closed tight. Luke shook with the heavy pounding of his heart.

"Erlys," he said. "Take Gwin to the ambry with you. Now."

Erlys began to move, but Axl seized her arm, and she cried out. "Your fault," he hissed at her, and she began to sob again. "Stop that mewling!" he roared, and drew back his hand.

Luke reached him before the blow could fall. He seized Axl's upraised arm from behind. Axl, off balance, careened into him, his heavier weight sending Luke sprawling on his back, on the floor. Unbelieving, he saw Axl pull back his foot, ready to kick with his heavy riding boot.

Gwin threw herself bodily onto Luke, burying her face in the hollow of his neck. Erlys screamed. Luke, with Gwin in his arms, rolled to one side, and Axl's vicious kick missed its mark, catching the leg of a stool, overturning it so that it crashed into a bureau. Everything on top of the bureau clattered to the floor. Erlys sobbed through it all.

Luke scrambled up, setting his little sister on her feet behind him, and stared across the mess at his mother where she cowered in the bedroom door. "How can you let this go on?" he asked. "How can it be worth it?"

"Luke," she wailed, tears running down her face, her lips swollen and trembling. "You don't understand . . . you don't know how it is . . . two children, and no mate. . . ."

Axl roared at him, "Out! You clumsy half-wit, out!"

Luke hesitated for one hot moment, yearning to smash something, to see something shatter under his fist, to vent his fury in destruction. If he did that, he was no better than Axl himself. He took a deep, shuddering breath.

Without looking back at his mother, or his eerily quiet sister, he spun away, slammed out of the apartment, and bolted down the corridor and out of the House.


HE HAD RUN through the stables, ignoring the inquiring whickers of the *hruss*. He pounded along the cliff path, past the bluff where the hoists for *kikyu* were set into the rock, where the perilous staircase led down to the rocky slice of beach below. All the *kikyu* were at sea, making the most of the waning days of summer. He ran on to the point where the path faded, on through the stands of irontrees that leaned away from the sea, permanently bent by the ocean winds. He ran until his legs burned and his breath labored, until he spent his fury and frustration. He came to rest, at last, on a rocky promontory. He threw himself down, and lay on his back on a stony patch of ground, waiting for his heartbeat to slow and his panting to ease. After a time, he sat up, and stared out over the featureless water, wondering what was to become of him.

The Visitor already sat low above the sea. Summer would end soon, and he would be packed off to Arren in disgrace. His little sister would retreat more and more into herself, would grow more silent every day. She was burying her Gift to protect her mother—a mother who refused to protect herself, and in so doing, made herself powerless to protect her children.

Luke was shocked to find himself weeping, his tears as silent as Gwin's. He rubbed them away, grateful there was no one to see.

When the light began to fade, he took a last look at the empty ocean, and then stood to begin the long walk back to the House. He would finish the saddle rack, clean the stalls, and spread fresh straw. Erlys would be tremulous and fluttery at the evening meal, trying to placate everyone. Gwin would be still. Axl would smile, and nod to the other Housemembers, the perfect father, mate, and Houseman. It was all a great farce, a pretense. If it were not for Gwin, he thought, he would escape this very night. He would steal a *hruss*—no, he would take his own stallion that he had brought to Tarus's stables—he would take Brother, the poorest saddle, the oldest saddlepack, and the thinnest of bedfurs, and he would ride off through the mountains, find a place in some other House where Axl could not poison minds against him.

But he could never abandon Gwin. Not until he was forced to leave.

# Seventeen

SIRA HAD BEEN waiting when Mreen and Emle had
returned through the lower corridor, leading Gwin by the
hand, all of them flushed and windblown. The look in Sira's
eyes told Mreen there was no need to explain why she had
missed the *quirunha*. She signed to Emle to return Gwin to
her mother and then come to her apartment. She and Sira
climbed the stairs together to wait for Emle to join them.

Emle appeared a short time later, saying, "I told Lispeth
to bring a pot of tea. I thought we would need it."

Sira nodded her thanks. "That was thoughtful, Emle."
She had taken a chair by the window, as she did whenever she
had the chance. Mreen thought she yearned for the out-of-
doors, for the days when she and Theo had ridden the passes of the Continent together. Sira made a peak with her long
fingers, and gazed at them. *You knew she was Gifted.*

Mreen saw Emle's startled glance, and sent, *The Magistrix
followed us. With her psi.*

Emle sank slowly into a chair near the wall. Near her
shoulder, Mreen's *filhata* hung from its wall peg.

Mreen sat opposite Sira, her hands linked in her lap, and waited for Sira's judgment.

*Her family is not pleased about her Gift?* Sira asked.

Mreen shook her head. *I do not know the family well,* she sent. *But Emle and I are aware that her father—that is, her stepfather—abhors the Gifted. All of them. Us.*

Sira fixed Emle with her gaze. *Do you know why?*

*I think so, Magistrix,* Emle sent. *Gwin's brother tells me that Axl—their stepfather—*

*Who is master of* hruss *here,* Mreen put in.

Emle nodded. *Luke says that Axl had a Gifted brother who was favored by his parents.*

*And he transferred his resentment to us?* Sira lifted her scarred eyebrow.

Mreen sighed. *It seems excessive, does it not?*

*So it does. Surely he has not expressed his aversion to you, Mreen.*

*No. Not directly.*

*Then how did you know he felt this way?*

*Magistrix—* Mreen began, and then stopped. She glanced at Emle, and then began again.

*At first it was inadvertent.* She swallowed, and didn't know whether to be abashed or to laugh.

Sira waited.

*On our journey here, I picked up something of his, a trifle. As I held it—I heard a child weeping. And then, when we had been here some weeks, I became aware of tension whenever the* hrussmaster *was in the House. I asked Emle to bring me a bit of leather thong from the stables, something he had handled. I learned nothing more, but again I heard a child crying. Not the same child. A different one.*

Sira frowned. *None of this is specific.*

Mreen sensed Emle's discomfort. Emle was twisting a lock of hair around one finger, over and over, and staring at her feet. *Emle?*

Emle looked up, startled.

*Can you tell the Magistrix something further about the* hrussmaster?

Emle dropped the lock of hair. *I—Yes. It is not much, but . . .*

*Emle,* Sira sent calmly. *Rules are being broken here, it is true. But we would not be the first to make compromises. If there is anything that can help us understand why this little one wishes her Gift to be secret, please tell us.*

Emle nodded slowly. *Yes, of course, Magistrix. And Mreen, I did not tell you only because Luke was already so ashamed.*

Mreen knew something of shame, but this was not the time to say so. She sent only, *It is all right, Emle. Can you tell me now?*

Emle drew a deep breath. *I have become friendly with Luke—Gwin's brother. He is Axl's apprentice in the stables. He brought wild* hruss *down from the mountains, with two foals, and I asked to see them. While we were at the paddock, Axl came to the stables with the Magister and—* Her cheeks glowed like a dawn sky, and she dropped her eyes again. *We hid ourselves,* she sent in a rush. *Behind an ironwood bough.*

*Why would you hide, Emle?*

*The* hrussmaster *is cruel to Luke, Magistrix. He shames him in front of other people, so that Luke hardly shows his face in the great room. And—Axl lied to Magister Kenth about the* hruss. *He took credit for adding them to Tarus's stables, when it was Luke who found them, and led them down from the mountain.* She looked up, her eyes sparkling with anger. *It is so unfair! Poor Luke thought I would think he had made up his story about finding the* hruss, *about persuading the young stallion—who is so beautiful, Mreen, you must see him—*

Sira interrupted. *Emle.*

Emle twisted her fingers. *I am sorry. But Luke has no one to protect him. The* hrussmaster—

*But, Emle how did you know the* hrussmaster *lied and not the apprentice?*

Emle responded with spirit. *I am sorry, Magistrix Sira. I listened to his mind.*

*And what did you hear?*

Emle shrugged a little, and unwound her fingers, which had gone white around the knuckles. *He has no Gift at all. His thoughts were like the mud of the paddock in the first thaw of summer. But he lies all the time, that much I understood.*

Mreen added, *Emle is right. She is not the only one who has tried to take the measure of this man.* She paused. *I believe him to be dangerous. But I cannot say in what way.*

*He would not be the first to have an aversion to the Gift,* Sira sent mildly.

*Somehow it is all connected,* Emle sent, surprisingly. *The new provision, the weeping children Mreen hears, Axl's dislike of us.*

*Indeed, Emle. You are wise in saying so. I have often said that the Gift is like the ironwood forests. All the trees are connected by their system of suckers, so that when one tree is damaged, the entire forest feels it.* Sira's eyes sought the window again. *And if a new sucker is cut, the treeling cannot grow.*

After a moment, Mreen sent, *You are thinking of Gifted children, then?*

182

*So I am.*

*And so Gwin hides her Gift, and grows more and more silent each day,* Emle sent.

*The sacrifices the Gift demands are too great to be forced on its bearers,* Sira sent wearily. She rubbed her eyelids with her fingers. *How long will it be until Nevya understands?*

LUKE PAUSED AT the paddock before he went into the stables. Brother trotted to meet him, lowering his fine head for Luke to rub his ears. Luke leaned against him for a moment, his fingers buried in Brother's thick black mane. The *hruss* smelled of wind and sunshine and good clean animal scent. Luke closed his eyes, and let Brother comfort him for a long moment before he turned to his waiting tasks.

He found that Axl had finished the saddle rack in his absence. He would pay for that, too, he supposed. He set about feeding the *hruss* in the boxes, mucking out their stalls. He knew it was time for the evening meal, but he had no wish to sit in Axl's presence. He bent to his work, thinking that perhaps he would put a saddle on Brother, try a bit of a ride in the paddock. He had already ridden both the wild mares. Soon they would be as tame as if they had been foaled and raised in the stables.

When the stalls were clean, he went out to the paddock with a halter in his hands. The stallion whickered at the sight of him. Luke gave him a little grain, and then slipped the halter over his head and led him into the passageway. He tied the halter rope to a peg and brought a saddle out of the tack room. He was just settling it over the stallion's withers when the inner door opened and Erlys came in, a napkin-covered dish in her hands, Gwin at her heels.

"Luke," Erlys said, as if nothing had happened earlier. "You weren't at the evening meal."

"Not hungry." Luke pulled up the saddle cinch. The *hruss* tossed his head and rumbled in his throat, but he didn't pull away. Luke gave him a moment, stroking his neck, then checked to see that the cinch remained secure. He loosened the halter, and slipped a hackamore over the stallion's head, holding his drooping ears out of the way as he adjusted buckles and straps.

His mother set the plate down on a shelf. "Where were you today? Gwin has been looking for you."

Luke glanced down at his sister. Her little mouth was pressed tight, as if to hold back any stray words that might try to escape. Her eyelids were swollen. "Gwinlet?" Luke said. "Are you all right?"

Silently, she nodded.

"Come and eat something, son," Erlys pleaded. "Please."

Luke smoothed the *hruss*'s mane and turned the stirrups in his hands. "In a minute."

"We'll sit with you," Erlys said hopefully. "Have a little time together."

Luke and Gwin exchanged another glance, and Luke lifted one shoulder in a shrug. "All right." He picked up the plate, and led the way to the tack room. They sat on the bench, Gwin on one side of Luke, Erlys on the other.

His meal was half-finished when Gwin suddenly stood up. She stared at the inner door, and then half-turned, as if she were considering bolting from the tack room.

"What is it, Gwinlet?"

She whispered, "He is coming."

Erlys said, "Who's coming?"

Luke cast his mother a look of pure disgust, and put his plate aside. "Who do you think, Erlys?" he demanded. "And how do you think she knows? Can't you see what's happening?"

Erlys's eyes filled with ready tears, and her lips trembled. "What do you mean, Luke? What's happening?"

Luke felt the familiar anger begin, and he turned away from his mother, struggling to control it. It made his voice shake. "Erlys, I'm sorry," he said. "Gwin, come on. I'll take you outside."

Erlys stood up, too, her hands clenched before her. "I don't understand. What are you talking about?"

Luke took Gwin's hand, and she clung to it with a force that surprised him. "Axl's coming," Luke said. "It's better if I'm not here. If he asks, tell him I'll unsaddle the stallion later." He cast a quick glance around the tack room to see that there was nothing for Axl to complain of, and then he led Gwin down the passageway and out the door into the cool evening.

They walked around the paddock, and through the archway to the front doors of the House. A few Housemembers still sat in the courtyard, bundled in furs, treasuring the evenings they could spend outside before the deep cold returned and drove them into the warmth of the *quiru*.

Luke and Gwin stopped for a moment, too, to look up at the stars. She pressed close to him.

"Luke," she whispered.

"Yes, Gwinlet."

"Take me with you. When you go to Arren, take me with you."

MREEN HAD STEADFASTLY refused to count the days that Kai and Brnwen and Theo had been at Tarus, or the hours she had left to spend with them. But the day after her adventure with Gwin and Emle, she knew by the emotions running high around her that it must be the last day. When she stepped into the Cantoris to play the *quirunha* with Josu, it was Theo who waited for her on the dais. Josu, smiling, sat next to Emle and Sira on the foremost bench. It was his *filhata* in Theo's hands.

Even as Mreen gave Theo a brilliant smile, a hard ache began in the center of her body. It would be, she thought, the hardest and yet the proudest *quirunha* of her life.

She bowed to Theo. *Maestro,* she sent.

He returned her bow. *Cantrix,* he responded. *You know I have not earned that title.*

*But you are my Maestro,* she sent, as she took her seat and began to tune her instrument. *Though it has been a long time since I struggled with modulations under your grim eye!*

*It was not my eye that was grim,* he sent, with a mental chuckle. *But Sira's.*

Mreen lifted her eyes to where Sira sat with the other Singers. Her eyes glittered darkly, and Mreen knew without doubt that the next day would be one of farewells.

Theo stated a melody, his eyes on Mreen. She gave a small nod. At this one moment, she was glad to have no voice. She doubted she could have spoken, much less sung, through the ache in her throat.

Theo had chosen *Iridu*, the most difficult mode. His tempo was brisk, the notes tripping neatly from his fingers, forcing her to concentrate. She knew he had done it with intention. Theo began to sing, and she followed his psi out into the Cantoris, feeling Sira join them, and Josu. Emle followed at a distance, like a shadow. Theo's harmonies shifted swiftly, and his wordless tune was jaunty, spontaneous, as full of humor and strength as the man himself.

She gave herself over to it, exulting in the precision of her fingers on the strings, the effortless ensemble with Theo, the honor of being joined with Sira. Tarus would glow with abundant energy when they were finished. She would always remember this *quirunha*.

The House *quiru* brightened as swiftly as if the two suns had come to shine directly over the tiled roof. Mreen regretted its coming to an end. She opened her eyes, and lifted her head.

Sira and Theo were gazing at each other, Theo with a grin, Sira's eyes hooded. And Emle—Mreen was startled to see that Emle's cheeks were wet with tears, and her lips trembled.

Privately, she sent to her, *Emle, dear. What is the matter?*

*It was so beautiful,* Emle responded. *It was perfect.*

*Yes. Such things do not come often.*

Josu stood to begin the closing chant. Mreen stepped off the dais and took Emle's arm to walk up the aisle and out of

187

the Cantoris. In the great room, Kai and Brnwen claimed her, and she had to release Emle, but not before she pressed her cheek to Emle's damp one. She went off to spend the last precious hours with her family, but even through her own sorrow she was aware of Emle's yearning, like a hungry ghost flitting in corners, hovering beneath the high ceilings, searching for answers.

EMLE ROSE EARLY the next morning, and slipped downstairs to the *ubanyix* with her *filla* in her hand. This would be a good day, she thought, to be able to warm the water, to save Mreen the task when her mind and heart were so full. The dawn was a gray specter beyond the windows. Full daylight arrived later and later as the brief summer waned. The *ubanyix* was deserted, though the Housekeeper had left everything in readiness for the travelers to bathe before their departure.

She would, she decided, clear her mind completely. She would make it as blank as an empty snowfield. She would close off her memories, and the awful images that came with them. She would try to forget they were there.

She pulled her *filla* from her tunic, and standing alone in the dimness, she played a melody in *Doryu*. Her tone was a little muffled by the low ceiling of the *ubanyix*, but her intonation was precise, her quarter-tone embellishments soft but clear. She waited until the second statement of the tune before she began to reach out toward the water with her psi, at the same time avoiding that dark corner of her mind. It was a surprisingly difficult task. Her music went on, but her psi struggled, divided in two, its power diverted by her double challenge.

She played through to the end of the little piece, but she knew, even before she finished, that it would not work. Reluctantly, she opened her eyes and surveyed the *ubanyix*. If the air was any brighter at all, she could not tell. She didn't trouble to test the water. She sank onto the carved ironwood bench, and rested her head in her hands.

*Emle.*

She lifted her head, and saw that Sira had come into the *ubanyix*. Emle stood and bowed. *Magistrix.*

*Forgive me,* Sira sent. She walked around the room to where Emle stood, and Emle saw that Sira, too, had her *filla* in her hand. *But I heard you playing that lovely little* Doryu *air.*

Emle waved a despairing hand at the unwarmed water. *It was useless.*

*Emle——I did not intend to intrude, but I sensed something different. Will you tell me what you were trying to do?*

Emle leaned against the wall, and turned her *filla* in her fingers. *I did something terrible,* she sent. *When I was little, before I understood my Gift.* She stared at her feet, her shoulders sagging. *The Gift is dangerous when the wrong person bears it, Magistrix Sira. And it seems I am the wrong person.*

*I do not believe that.*

*But it is true. There is something wrong with me.*

Sira gestured to the bench. *Come,* she sent. *Tell me what you did that was so terrible.*

Emle waited until Sira had settled herself on the bench

before she sat down. She tucked her *filla* into her tunic and then stared at her empty hands. *I hurt my brother,* she began, and then, in a rush, told the entire story.

When she had finished, she lifted her gaze to Sira's face. The Magistrix's features were still, as they usually were, her eyes calm. A moment passed in silence before Sira sent, *You know, Emle, I did something much worse. I was an adult, already a full Cantrix, and I used my psi to break the mind of another person.*

Emle almost gasped, but caught herself just in time. So the story was a true one!

*What is worse,* Sira added, *far worse, is that I did it on purpose.* She rose, and went to stand beside the tub, bringing her *filla* to her lips as she moved. She played a brief, intense bit of music in *Doryu,* so short and sharp it could hardly be called a tune. Steam rose from the water almost immediately, ephemeral gray ribbons rippling up to the timbered ceiling. The air brightened, too, lighting every corner of the *ubanyix,* gleaming on the piles of clean towels.

Emle sighed. Sira was certainly the greatest Singer on the Continent.

Sira tucked her *filla* into its pocket and came back to sit beside Emle. She laid her long-fingered hand on Emle's, and looked directly into her eyes. *I refused a Cantoris for a very long time after that, Emle,* she sent. *Like you, I was terrified of what my Gift could do. But learning to harness its strength, to employ it for the good of our people, is what being a Singer—especially a Cantrix—is all about.*

*I want to do that, Magistrix,* Emle sent. *I want it more than anything. But I do not know if I can.*

Sira touched Emle's cheek. *You are young,* Sira sent. *The Gift is laid upon us when we are too young to know what we want.* She pulled her hand back, and stood up. *It is a choice we make, every day, one we go on making our whole lives. Only you can know if it is the right choice for you.*

Emle came to her feet, and bowed to Sira. *I fear the Gift is wasted on me.*

*The Gift is never wasted,* Sira responded. *It only remains for you to discover what you are meant to do with it.*

Emle looked away when she answered. *I thought I was meant to Sing.*

*Perhaps you are.*

*I do not see how.*

Footsteps and voices sounded in the corridor outside the *ubanyix.* The early risers in the House were coming to bathe.

Sira sent, *I know only this, Emle. You must face your fears, and deal with your memories. You cannot run from them, or bury them. They are a part of you.*

Emle bowed again, just as the door opened and three Housewomen came in together. *Thank you for your kindness, Magistrix.*

*Have courage, Emle. You will find your path.*

Emle forced her brightest smile to her lips. *By the will of the Spirit!*

Sira nodded approval. *You have strength you do not recognize yet, Emle. I will be waiting for you.*

# Eighteen

ONLY DAYS HAD passed, but Luke knew the cold season was coming by the thickening of the *hruss'* coats. The soft undercoat was growing so heavy that he could hardly drag the currycomb through it. Brother grew restive in his stall, and paced the paddock when he was outside the stables, tossing his head and gazing up at the mountains.

"You want to visit your old meadow, don't you, my friend?" he said, tugging the *hruss's* silky ears. "But you know your mares won't leave now. They're with foal again, and they like their comfort."

The stallion whickered, and pulled his head away to push at the gate with his forehead, straining the latch.

"Yes," Luke said. He patted the *hruss's* withers and glanced over his shoulder at the stables. "I'd let you go, gladly, and have no doubt you'd be back. But Axl would have my hide. I'm trying not to be sent away any sooner than I must." He gave the stallion one last rub. "Tomorrow, we'll have a ride, my friend. See how you like having a great creature like myself in your saddle."

The stallion gave up pushing at the gate, and nosed Luke's chest.

He laughed. "I'll take that as agreement." He checked the latch to be certain it would hold, and after a last look around the paddock, he went inside the stables, closing both the top and bottom halves of the door against the increasing chill. The Visitor had barely skipped along the horizon today. Tomorrow it might not show its face at all.

The last of Tarus's summer guests had departed days before, returning to their own homes to prepare for the coming cold season. Tarus's Housemembers who had been visiting friends and family returned, laden with gifts and letters and news from Filus and Bariken and distant Manrus, at the edge of the Great Glacier. Axl had made a short journey to Arren, to arrange for the sale of Luke's *hruss*, and had returned looking pleased with himself. An itinerant Singer named Lev, a small, secretive man, was with him, for it was no longer safe to travel without a Singer.

Gwin was waiting in the passageway. Luke smoothed her hair. "Gwinlet. Did you come to help me sweep up?"

She only nodded. It seemed to Luke she spoke fewer words every day. If Erlys noticed, she gave no sign. Her girlish laugh scraped Luke's nerves until he could hardly bear to be in the apartment, especially when Axl was at home. He had not sat in the great room for a meal since his stepfather's return. He handed Gwin a broom, and turned away to hide his worried frown.

They worked together in silence for a few minutes, until Luke heard the clatter of Gwin's broom. He whirled, and saw that she had dropped it, and disappeared.

"Gwin?" he called. He strode to the door, and put his head out into the passageway. "Gwinlet? Where are you? Is something—"

Axl was there with Lev. Luke stiffened as Axl's eyes swept the stable. The straw in the passageway was freshly laid, the tack room floor clean, the saddles and hackamores and halters neatly hung.

"Where's the young stallion?" Axl asked. "Lev wants to try him out tomorrow."

"Paddock," Luke said, gesturing with his head toward the outer door. "But he's not ready."

Axl seized the opportunity, and spun on his heel to face Luke. "Not ready? What have you been doing with him, then?"

Luke's stomach tightened. "Taking it slow," he said. "Don't want to ruin him."

"Ruin him?" Axl laughed, a scornful sound that made several of the stabled *hruss* scrape their hooves against the floor. "Coddle him, you mean! He's not a pet, Luke, and you're far too old to be playing around as if he were. By the Ship, put a saddle on him and be done with it!"

"Saddled him today," Luke growled. He folded his arms and leaned against the doorjamb, trying to quell the anger burning his chest. "I'll ride him tomorrow."

The Singer, his back to Luke, murmured something to Axl, and both men laughed. "Never mind," Axl said to Luke. "You've had weeks. I'll take care of it now."

Luke watched helplessly as the two men opened the door to the paddock and went through. Gwin slipped out of her hiding place behind a stack of grain sacks and came to him, pressing herself against his leg. "Can you not stop them?" she whispered.

Luke spoke through a tense jaw. "No," he said.

"He knows you like Brother," Gwin said, so faintly he could hardly hear her.

"I know, Gwinlet. I know."

Luke went to the work table and picked up a frayed halter. He hung it over his shoulder to carry to the apartment, and then he held out his hand to Gwin. "Come on, little one. Let's go find your mama."

When they emerged from the tack room, they found Axl and Lev talking together in the passageway. The men glanced up as they passed, and Gwin clung so tightly to Luke's hand he thought her fingermarks must be pressed permanently into his palm. As the door swung closed behind them, Gwin whispered, "I do not like that Singer."

"You don't? I thought you liked all the Gifted."

She lifted her eyes to his. "He watches me."

"What do you mean, watches? He hasn't tried to touch you?"

"No. But he watches me. In the great room. In the Cantoris." They reached their apartment, and Luke reached for the latch, but Gwin tugged him back. "Do not tell Mama," she pleaded.

"I won't," he promised. He opened the door, and stood back to let Gwin precede him.

It would do no good to tell Erlys in any case, he thought. She wouldn't listen.

⌒

VERY EARLY THE next morning, Luke opened the half-door to carry his saddle and tack out to the paddock. He paused a moment, the saddle braced on his hip, and looked south over the sea. The waters were a dull green, the sky heavy with gray clouds. The disc of the Visitor was still there behind them, low on the horizon, made vague by the overcast.

He coaxed Brother to the fence so he could slip a halter on his head, and he spent a moment stroking him, letting him lip a bit of grain from his palm. "I mean to be first," he murmured. "No matter what." The stallion made a rumbling sound in his throat, and pushed at Luke's hand, looking for more. "Not now, my friend," Luke said. "But if you have it in you to behave quietly, I'll give you an extra measure later."

He opened the gate, and led the *hruss* through. The foals, grown tall and leggy, came to the fence and stood watching, their ears flicking forward and back. Luke patted each one as he passed. "Your turn is coming, little ones."

He looped the halter lead over the hitchpost and spent another few moments rubbing the stallion down with the blanket, then settling the saddle slowly on his back, drawing up the cinches. He talked to him all the while, reassuring him, letting him know where he was as he moved to his hindquarters, around to the other side, and back again. The stallion was already accustomed to this activity, and he stood quietly, turning his head to follow Luke's movements.

When Luke was satisfied the tack was properly adjusted, he stood back and found that the Singer Lev was standing in the passageway between the boxes, looking out over the open half-door.

"You're taking your time about it," Lev said.

Luke glanced at him, and then back at the stallion. "Best way," he said shortly. "No point scaring the poor beast."

"He grew up wild, Axl tells me."

"So he did."

"You haven't been on him yet?"

Luke shook his head. "No. This is it."

Lev looked over his shoulder, no doubt making certain Axl had not come into the stables. "I don't mind your trying him first," he said lightly, as if intending to be generous.

Luke felt his lip curl. The man was afraid. Afraid of the *hruss*, and afraid of Axl.

Luke could have reassured him, at least about the stallion. In his years at Tarus he had trained half a dozen *hruss* to the saddle without ever being thrown. Axl had no patience for the task, and had let him do it his way, taking time over each step, winning each beast's trust and confidence.

But he had the urge to let this unpleasant Singer sweat. He said, staring at his boots as if he were exactly the half-wit Axl claimed him to be, "*Hrussmaster* said to let you be first."

"Well," Lev said. He looked over his shoulder again. "Well. Yes, but . . . since Axl isn't here yet . . ."

"I'm his apprentice. Have to do as I'm bid." Luke took the hackamore rein in his hand, and led the stallion to the stable door. "Here you go," he said, holding out the rein to Lev. He twitched it, just a little, and Brother obligingly tossed his head. It was impressive, Luke thought. Brother was taller than any other *hruss* in the stables, with a deep chest and strong shoulders.

Lev took a hasty step backward. "Listen, Houseman," he said. "I have a bit of metal in my pocket. It's yours if you'll do this for me." At Luke's curious glance, he added, with a forced laugh, "I like my mounts old and comfortable."

Luke gazed at him a moment through narrowed eyes. Gwin was right not to trust this man, he thought. He was a liar and a coward. Fit company for Axl.

Disdaining the shining bit of metal Lev held out in his fingers, Luke turned the *hruss*'s head and led him away toward the cliff path. He could feel the Singer's gaze on his back as he eased himself into the saddle, letting the stallion stand still for a long moment. It took time for a *hruss* to get accustomed to a new weight on its back, the change in his balance. When it seemed Brother was comfortable, Luke urged him gently across the stableyard and away from the House. He resisted the urge to cast Lev a scornful glance over his shoulder.

Soon even the cliff path would be filled with snow, but for now it was smooth ground, worn level by the feet of countless *hruss*, the runners of *pukuru*, the feet of walkers strolling beside the stone wall. Brother adopted the easy swinging walk that was the natural gait of *hruss*. Despite Lev's fears, a *hruss* almost never bucked. Their broad backs tended to be inflexible once they matured. Luke believed the Spirit created *hruss* to be the perfect mount—sweet-natured, curious, hungry for human company, comfortable to ride.

He spent a few minutes experimenting with the rein, finding out how much he could coax Brother to do, but careful not to frustrate or tire him. When he thought it was enough, he gently turned him back toward the House, using his knee against his neck, praising and reassuring him at every step. Willingly, the stallion swung back down the road, and Luke sat back, easy in the saddle, wishing he could take Brother with him to Arren.

When he rode back into the stableyard, Axl, dressed in his riding furs, was waiting for him beside the mounting post. Luke kept a wary eye on his stepfather as he dismounted.

"Your trick didn't work, Luke," Axl said. "I'm still taking the stallion."

"Trick?"

"Don't play the fool with me, son. I know you frightened Lev off the *hruss*. And got him to give you metal besides."

Luke slung one arm protectively over Brother's neck. "I didn't take any metal."

"Don't worry. I took it for you." Axl held up the bit between his thumb and forefinger, and then slid it into his own pocket. "You wouldn't know what to do with it anyway."

Luke had no choice but to hand over the reins when Axl reached for them. "Thanks," Axl said. "All warmed up for me."

Luke chewed on his lip as Axl adjusted the stirrups and checked the cinches. He knew all too well how rough his stepfather could be with *hruss*. Finally, he said, "It's new to him. Could you just—just take it slowly? He hasn't learned the rein yet. . . ."

Axl snorted. "Telling me how to ride *hruss*?" he said. "You really are a fool, Luke."

He swung up on Brother's back in an abrupt motion, making the stirrups creak and the saddle pull to the left. The stallion grunted in surprise at Axl's weight, and danced sideways.

"Easy, easy," Luke said, not sure whether he was speaking to the *hruss* or to Axl.

Axl laughed. "That's the way you think life should be, don't you, son? Easy." He wrenched the *hruss*'s neck around to the right with a heavy hand on the rein, and smacked his flanks with his boot heels. The stallion quivered all over, and danced in a circle, tossing his head. His nostrils flared as he fought the rein. His eyes rolled, searching for Luke.

"Axl . . ." Luke began, taking a step forward, and then stopped. He wanted to say that the *hruss* didn't know what Axl wanted, couldn't understand the pulled rein, the boot heels in his ribs, but he knew it was useless. The more care he showed for the beast, the worse Axl's treatment would be.

Axl forced the *hruss*'s head to face away from the stables, out toward the stand of softwood. He used the end of the rein to smack his rump, and the stallion bolted, his broad feet driving against the hard-packed dirt of the stableyard as he lumbered away. Axl jounced in the saddle, almost falling, before he got a tight hold on the pommel.

Luke watched his beautiful *hruss* pound away down the cliff path, his head pulled too high by Axl's heavy hand, his gait roughened by Axl's unbalanced weight.

"Sorry, friend," Luke whispered. "I should have left you and your band in the meadow." With a heavy heart, he turned back to the day's chores. "Should have stayed there myself."

# Nineteen

"LISPETH," EMLE SAID, with something like desperation. "Watch my fingers, please. The signs are not hard. Even Gwin has learned them!"

Lispeth had lovely eyes, with long lashes as pale as her sun-bright hair, but now they filled with tears. "I can't do it, Singer Emle! I just can't! When she looks at me and she doesn't say a word . . . I just crumple up inside."

"Cantrix Mreen only looks that way because she is frustrated." Emle leaned closer to Lispeth, and touched her hand lightly. Lispeth wiped her eyes with the corner of her scarlet tunic. "Imagine what it might be like, Lispeth, if you could not speak to me, tell me what was bothering you or what you needed. How would you feel?"

"I don't know," Lispeth said. "I'm only a Housewoman, Singer, born and bred here at Tarus. What do I know of the ways of the Gifted?"

Emle sat back, and found herself pressing her fingertips together, in the way Magistrix Sira had when she was thinking.

"Why did you agree to become the Cantrix's Housewoman, Lispeth? Surely others wanted the assignment?"

The girl looked up at that. "Oh, yes," she said. "I begged Gerta to teach me to read so I could do something important." She gave a deep sigh. "And I wanted to help Cantrix Mreen, truly. . . ."

"But then . . . what is the matter?"

Lispeth's eyes swam again. "When she stood on the steps, that first day . . . and that light around her . . . she made those signs with her hands, and they go so fast! And then she looks angry. . . ." She buried her face in her hands. "I suppose Gerta will assign someone else!"

"Perhaps," Emle said gently. "But you are hardworking and responsible and smart, everything the Cantrix needs in a Housewoman. Come now, suppose we try again? I will make it as simple as possible." Lispeth lifted her tear-stained face, and Emle held up one hand, and arranged her fingers, the middle one extended, the thumb at an angle. "You see, this means 'want.'" She made another shape, finger and thumb pinched together. "And this means 'tea,' or 'cup of tea.' If she wishes a cup of water, she will separate her finger and thumb a bit. It is not difficult if you think of it as a language. You learn the parts separately, and when you know them well, they will not appear to flow by so fast, but seem as clear to you as speaking words."

Lispeth drew a shaky breath, and put up her own hand, to try the shapes.

"Good!" Emle said. "Now, you have just asked me for tea."

"But the Cantrix will never make the words slowly enough for me," Lispeth said sadly. Still, she made the signs again, and then again. "What is the one that means '*filla*'? And 'strings'?"

"Those are different." Emle showed Lispeth, carefully. The sign for '*filla*' was simple, curving all four fingers with the palm turned upward, as if the *filla* were already in the hand. "And this means 'strings,'" she said, drawing her thumb and fourth finger down an imaginary line. Of course, if the signs were combined they had other, more complex meanings. But Emle would save those for a later time, when Lispeth had gained some confidence.

Before Lispeth went next door to collect Mreen's clothes for washing and to see that her apartment was tidy, she had mastered a vocabulary of twelve signs. It was, at least, a beginning, Emle thought. But she would have to suggest that when Mreen signed to her Housewoman, she made the signs more slowly, each one distinct from the next. Would Mreen frown at her—look angry, just as Lispeth had said—or dimple and agree she should have guessed that for herself?

Emle sighed. She would simply have to make Mreen understand, for her own sake. It would hardly help to choose a new Housewoman, and start all over.

Emle closed the door to her apartment and turned to the staircase. There was still an hour before the evening meal. She meant to visit the stables, to see how the foals were coming along. She had not seen Luke in several days.

She was dismayed to find him almost as withdrawn as he had been on their first meeting. He answered her greetings with a monotone grunt and refused to look at her. She could have turned away from the rebuff, but she knew his nature now. She planted her feet squarely in the passageway, her hands on her hips. "Luke," she said. "I know something is wrong. Put down your pitchfork and talk to me."

He stopped in his work, his barrow half full of dirt and straw. He leaned the handle of the tool against the stable wall, and straightened. "Sorry," he said. "You may be the only friend I have in this House."

"I doubt that," she said. "But tell me. What is the matter?"

"Axl took him," Luke said. His eyes, when he finally raised them, were shadowed, the planes of his face tightened, sharpening his cheekbones. "Took Brother out, yanking on his head, kicking his ribs like they were slats of wood. He'll come back, saying the *hruss* is no good. And it may be true. After such a ride, he could be ruined. And then Axl will say it was me who spoiled him."

"Oh, I am so sorry," Emle breathed. "Poor Brother."

"And he's sending me away," Luke blurted, every word dripping misery. "Packing me off to Arren to repeat my apprenticeship, when I've almost finished it already."

Emle caught her breath, and pressed her palms together. "But, Luke! How can he do that? Can you not ask the Magister . . ."

He gave her a bleak look, and picked up the pitchfork again. "He deceives the Magister, as you heard. And who is to defend me?" He dug the fork into a layer of straw, and said bitterly, "Certainly not my mother!"

"I will do it for you, Luke. I will tell Magister Kenth the truth."

Luke didn't look up. He hoisted the forkful of straw and offal and loaded it into the barrow. "Can't let you do that," he finally said. "He will blame Erlys, and Gwin will suffer, too." He dropped one more forkload into the barrow, and then hefted the handles. Emle saw how his muscles bunched beneath his tunic, how his shoulders had broadened. In the short time she had been at Tarus, he had grown to be a man. He trundled the barrow to the door, and maneuvered it neatly over the sill. She followed, and stood watching as he emptied it into the waste drop.

The Visitor had shown only the upper edge of its dim face on this day. The sea was choppy and dark, shaded by gathering clouds. The evening was already drawing in.

"It is almost over," Emle said sadly. "The summer is gone."

"So it is," he answered. He brought the barrow back, and turned it upside down against the outer wall. A cold salt breeze stirred the tops of the ironwood trees and Emle's bound hair. Luke stood beside her, warm from his labors, smelling nicely of *hruss* and leather and sweat. Together they watched the first flickering of stars over the water.

"I suppose I must leave soon, too," Emle murmured. "To return to Conservatory."

"Aren't you glad to be going back?"

"I am, in a way," she said. "But I am sorry to leave Cantrix Mreen and . . ." She glanced at him from beneath her eyelashes. "And my new friends," she finished. "You, and Gwin, and Cantor Josu."

"Nevya is a hard place," he said. "We may never meet again."

"If the Spirit wills it, we might."

He looked away from her, out into the night. "I feel abandoned by the Spirit."

Emle followed his gaze to the ocean, dark now, with sparks here and there of reflected stars. "I know that feeling," she said slowly. "My Gift will not repair itself, no matter how hard I try. I do not know what will become of me."

He turned toward her, with deliberation. "You would make someone a wonderful mate."

She gaped at him, her mouth open, speechless for long moments. Finally she managed to croak, "You must not say such things."

He shrugged. "It's not so terrible. Many girls mate."

"Not Gifted ones!"

His jaw tensed, and his cheeks flushed. "Itinerant Singers do. And they have children."

"But, Luke, they don't raise House-sized *quirunha* and maintain them, day in and day out, for a lifetime. The work takes all our strength, and all our focus. We learn very early at Conservatory that mating dilutes the Gift, often with tragic consequences."

Luke turned his head away, and gave a short, humorless laugh. "Well," he said gruffly, "I thought it wouldn't hurt to ask."

Emle took a step backward, almost stumbling. "Luke," she breathed. "Were you . . . did you mean to ask . . . *me?*"

He didn't look at her. "No, no, of course not. I would never do that. I knew what your answer would be."

Emle could think of no response, nothing that would express how honored she was, and how confused. As she searched for words, hoofbeats sounded in the stableyard. Luke went outside to meet his stepfather, and Emle stood in the passageway, listening. When she heard Axl's harsh voice begin a listing of Luke's faults, she retreated into the House, her heart aching.

AFTER THE EVENING meal, Mreen sent a terse message to Emle. *Please come to my apartment*, she sent. *There has been a message from Conservatory.*

Emle climbed the stairs slowly, knowing what the message must be, both looking forward to it and dreading it. Housemembers smiled at her, or nodded greetings, but she couldn't answer. She tried to phrase things she must say to Mreen, to list the things that must be finished, but she could hardly concentrate. Poor Luke!

Mreen looked up as she came in. She was seated at the table beneath the window, holding a thick packet of paper in her hand. *Emle? What is the matter?*

Emle crossed the room, and stood beside the table, twisting her fingers together. *I . . . I do not know if anything is really the matter—or if I have made some terrible mistake.*

Mreen laid the packet of paper aside. It bore the signet of Conservatory marked in blue ink. *Sit down*, Mreen sent. *Tell me what has happened.*

Emle settled slowly into the chair opposite, staring at the packet without really seeing it. She was seeing Luke's bleak expression instead, the line of his jaw as he turned away from her. *Oh, Mreen!* she sent in a rush. *I think perhaps I have misled Luke, and I feel terrible about it!*

*Misled him? Surely you have not.*

*Not on purpose, no, of course not. But he has asked—he just—he said*—Emle buried her face in her hands. Her cheeks burned against her cold fingers. She felt Mreen's fingers, gently pulling her hands down, cradling them on the tabletop.

*Emle, I know you would never hurt anyone if you could help it. Now, please. Tell me what Luke said. We will talk it out together.*

Emle, sighing, told Mreen every word of her conversation with Luke. It was not, after all, a very long recitation. Little had been said. Far more had been left unsaid, and that made her feel even worse.

*He is my friend,* she sent at last. *Of course I care about him, and I like being with him, and his* hruss. *And his stepfather is just awful to him! But I never intended that he should think—or feel . . . If I were not a Singer, if I did not long to be a Cantrix, like you—it would be different! But it is who I am. I thought he knew.*

Mreen's eyes darkened as Emle spoke. She released her hands, and shifted in her chair to gaze out the window. The day was already gone, the sky black, sparsely brightened by stars. Mreen's nimbus darkened, too, with telltale shadows flitting here and there.

*Are you angry with me?* Emle asked anxiously.

Mreen shook her head. *No, Emle. You have done nothing wrong. It is a misunderstanding, perhaps, or it is just that Luke is a young man, ready to take the next step in building his life. You are still a girl.*

*But . . .* Emle bit her lip. *But something in this makes you sad?*

Mreen stood up, pushing her chair away from the table, and moved to her bureau, where the little tooled leather panel rested on its easel. The thong Emle had borrowed from the tack room curled around its base. Mreen picked up the panel and brought it back to the table, setting it between them. *All my life*, she sent, *I have seen my mother only through my Gift.*

What did Mreen's mother have to do with Luke?

Mreen sat down again, and trailed her fingers across the panel. *Even now I see her,* she sent. *She was beautiful, very much as you are beautiful, although of course she had my hair, and my eyes.* Mreen rested her palm on the bit of split leather. *But all my life I have wondered what weakness of hers, what terrible mistake, led to my birth.*

*Your birth could never be called a mistake,* Emle sent.

*My mother was a Cantrix,* Mreen responded, with a blunt force that made Emle wince. *She was Cantrix Isbel v'Amric, and she conceived a child. Me.*

Emle lowered her eyes. This story was also true, then.

*Magistrix Sira loved my mother. She was her very best friend, and Sira has told me how lonely my mother was, how desperate for a friend. Her senior was a terrible man, cruel and cold, and Isbel had no one. . . .* Mreen picked up the leather panel. *Still, I have never understood how it came about that my father and my mother could allow such a thing to happen.* She broke off, and held the little bit of tooled leather to her breast.

Emle waited, her pulse beating in her throat. Mreen's nimbus darkened more, fading to a dull glow. A tear made a slender, shining track down one cheek.

*I have been ashamed of my mother. All these years.* Mreen wiped the tear with one finger. *And now you will return to Conservatory, and I will be as alone as my mother.*

*You will not make the same mistake,* Emle sent cautiously.

Mreen fixed her with a fierce gaze. *No! No, I will not! But I do not have an awful senior to work with, and I have had you to help me become accustomed to my new House.* Her gaze sought the stars beyond her window. *I should not have been ashamed for my mother. I should have been sad. I should have thanked the unknowable Spirit for the circumstances of my birth! It is myself I should be ashamed of.*

Emle said aloud, "Your mother would not want that."

*You are right, Emle. You so often are.* Mreen stood to return the panel to its easel. *But you see how easy it is for a person to turn to another for understanding, when life is difficult.* She faced Emle, leaning her back against the heavy bureau. *And Luke's life is very difficult, I think.*

*You do not think this was my fault.*

*Luke's feelings cannot be your fault.* She paused. *Yet they have helped me begin to understand my mother's feelings.*

Emle sighed again. *Poor Isbel,* she sent.

Mreen crossed the room and resumed her seat. She picked up the packet from Conservatory and opened it. *I wish I had known her,* she responded. *Theo tells me she was a collector of stories, and that she loved to laugh. She had, he said—*She passed her hand over her eyes again, but no more tears escaped her. Instead, she gave Emle a trembling smile. *Theo says I have her dimples.*

*Then she must have been very beautiful indeed,* Emle sent warmly.

Mreen's smile steadied. She withdrew a folded sheet of paper from the packet, and held it out.

Emle took it, but she didn't look at it. *Does your father speak of your mother?*

*No.* Mreen shook her head. *It is too painful for him.*

*And Brnwen?*

Mreen smiled. *Brnwen was just a Housewoman, and my mother was a full Cantrix. Brnwen did not know Isbel at all.*

Emle thought of beautiful Isbel, four summers past, singing in a Cantoris, laughing with Theo, meeting the young Kai v'Amric. It was, she thought, a sad, romantic story. *Do you think I should speak to Luke?*

*So I do,* Mreen sent gently. *As a friend.*

Emle nodded, and opened the letter from Conservatory that would summon her home.

# Twenty

THE VISITOR DID not rise the next morning.

Luke was in the paddock early, dressed in his furs, trying to calm Brother. He used no halter or tack, but stood with one hand lightly on Brother's withers, stroking his neck with the other hand and murmuring to him. The stallion rolled his eyes and laid his ears back. Long minutes passed before he calmed. When Brother finally bent his neck to push his head into Luke's chest, Luke tugged at his ears and whispered, "I'm sorry, my friend. I'm so sorry."

All night he had tormented himself with worry over the *hruss*, and with chagrin at what he had said to Emle. He lay awake for hours, cursing himself, listening to Gwin's light breathing from her cubby and the low-voiced conversation of his mother and Axl in their room. He longed to take Brother and run. If it had all happened at midsummer, he might have done it.

But now—he looked out past the bay, and saw that though the sun was fully up, the Visitor was nowhere to be seen, not even its edge visible. The summer was over, the cold season begun. No one would be traveling anywhere without a Singer.

He looked at the gate to the paddock, wondering what would happen if he opened the gate, let Brother walk through. He glanced back at the stables, but Axl had not yet made an appearance. No doubt he was still being flattered and cajoled by Erlys at the morning meal.

On an impulse, he coaxed the stallion nearer the gate. Keeping an eye on the mares and their half-grown foals, he opened the latch, and swung the gate wide. "Go, Brother," he whispered. "Just go. Back to the mountains!"

The stallion trotted through the open gate and across the stableyard, his head held high, his black mane lifting in the wind. He stopped at the cliff path, whirled, and fixed Luke with an expectant gaze.

Luke latched the paddock gate again, and stood with his back against it. "Better hurry," he said. "Before he gets here." He gave a bitter laugh. "Believe me, my friend, I'll pay for this. But it will be worth it to think of you free in the mountains."

Still the *hruss* didn't move. Luke waved an arm, stamped a foot. "Go! Go back where you came from!"

But Brother took a step back across the stableyard. He whickered anxiously.

Luke sighed. They were so trusting, these beasts, and so easily attached themselves to human beings, even cruel and hardhanded ones like Axl. He had never heard of one that had been domesticated returning to the wild.

Brother took another step toward him.

"You won't go, then?" Luke murmured. "And I suppose if I tried to drive you off, you'd be back in an hour."

Brother nuzzled his shoulder. Luke turned to the south. Soon the bay would be glazed with ice, the sea glittering with shards of it as far as the eye could see. He muttered, "If I were you, Brother, I'd take to my heels, and never see this House again."

A door opened and closed inside the stables, and the stallion jerked away from Luke as if the last few minutes of peace had never been. Axl had done a thorough job of terrifying him. "*Hrussmaster* indeed," Luke hissed through his teeth. "As poor a master of *hruss* as there has ever been." Brother tossed his head with a nervous snort. Luke straightened his shoulders, and wheeled to face his stepfather.

But it was Emle, her long-fingered hands resting on the bottom of the half-door, her neatly bound hair appearing darker in the dim morning light. "Luke," she called softly. "How is he today?"

For a moment Luke couldn't speak. The sight of her lifted his spirits and dashed them at the same time. He swallowed, and managed to say, "Confused, mostly." He took a handful of Brother's mane to lead him easily back to the paddock. He opened the gate and the stallion trotted through, crossing to the mares, whuffing deep in his throat.

Luke closed the gate behind him, and went to meet Emle. "I tried to let him go," he told her. "But he won't leave."

She waited as he shrugged out of his furs. The *hruss* in the boxes hung their heads out into the passageway, watching the humans.

"I came to tell you," Emle said, when he turned to face her, "that a message has come from Conservatory. They are sending a party of riders for me."

"You knew this was coming."

"Yes. But I will be sorry to leave. And I wanted to explain . . ."

He held up a hand. "There's nothing to explain. I'm sorry about—about what I said yesterday. It just—sort of—popped out of my mouth."

"No, Luke, do not say so. It was the most wonderful thing anyone has ever said to me."

Luke felt as if his heart would leap out of his chest. He turned his head, afraid she would read the strength of his feelings in his eyes.

She went on, "I want you to know . . . if I were not a Singer, even a bad one . . . if I were to mate, to have children . . . no one could please me more than you."

He turned back to face her. "You don't have to say that, Emle."

"I know. But it is true." She gave a light, musical laugh. "It took me until this morning to find words to explain myself!"

He drew a deep breath, and found to his surprise that he was smiling. "Six Stars," he exclaimed. "Finding the right words is hard!"

"So it is," she said, nodding, looking as relieved as he felt. "So it is."

THE MOOD WAS subdued at the evening meal. No one spoke of the disappearance of the Visitor, and there was an air of resignation and melancholy in the great room. Emle sat at the lower table with Lispeth, practicing finger signs, and she felt Mreen's gaze on them more than once. Emle had spoken truly. She looked forward to returning to her studies, but she also had begun to feel at home here at Tarus, and she knew she would miss Mreen, and Josu. And Luke.

He sat with his family at a table near the door. Both he and Gwin kept their heads down, not speaking, barely eating. Erlys fluttered over them, handing them things, pressing them to eat more, to drink more. Axl ignored all three. He leaned close to his companion, the itinerant Singer, their heads close together as they talked.

"He is so handsome, don't you think?" Lispeth whispered.

Emle glanced at her, startled. "Who? The *hrussmaster*?"

"O Spirit, no, Singer. Not him. He's too old!" Lispeth laughed, and smoothed her bright hair. "No, I mean the stableman. The tall quiet one, with the black hair."

Emle followed her gaze. "Luke," she said quietly. "That is Luke."

"Do you know him, then? Will you introduce me?"

Emle turned to Lispeth, considering this new possibility. "So I will," she said slowly. She started to smile. "I will introduce you to him, Lispeth, when you learn ten more signs . . . and use them with Cantrix Mreen!"

Lispeth looked across the room at Luke, and then up to Mreen where she sat at the high table with the Magister and his mate. She gave a dramatic sigh. "I suppose I must, then."

"It will be all right, Lispeth. You will come to understand the Cantrix. I have explained your difficulties to her."

"I hope you're right. I'll try."

"Good." Emle grinned at her. "Ten new signs!"

Lispeth's laugh bubbled up again, and her eyes brightened. "You promise to introduce me to the stableman?"

Emle thought of Lispeth fluttering her eyelashes at quiet Luke, and she laughed, too. "Promise."

Together they watched as Luke and Gwin stood, and walked together out of the great room. Luke looked very tall next to his tiny sister.

Lispeth propped her chin on her hand, and said, "Ten new signs! We'd best hurry, Singer. I hear you're leaving soon."

"Yes," Emle said, sobering. "Yes, I think we had better hurry."

The party from Conservatory was expected at any moment. The Housekeeper had told Emle to prepare, and had already presented her with a stack of fresh linens and two or three small gifts to carry with her to Sira and to Magret. Emle's eyes strayed again and again to the courtyard beyond the tall windows, watching for the riders. This was the way of the Continent. When she said good-bye to Mreen—and to Luke—no one could say when, or if, they might meet again.


MREEN WATCHED EMLE laughing with Lispeth, thinking what a pretty sight they made, the fair and the dark heads bent close together, their faces merry.

Change was at hand. Emle would depart tomorrow, or the next day. Mreen already sensed the deep cold closing in around the House, edging up from the Frozen Sea, inching down from the Great Glacier. The gathering of softwood had begun, the sawyers cutting and stacking the firewood in great piles that reached up to the second level of the House, and making other stacks in the timberlands. The softwood had to last a very long time, through all the cold seasons. Mreen realized that she knew nothing of how it was conserved, or even how much of it was required to prepare a meal such as the one she had just eaten. There was a great deal she did not know about the House and its people. And who would tell her?

The Housemembers were rising from the meal now, the kitchen workers coming in to gather the bowls and spoons and baskets. Lispeth and Emle stood up, and Lispeth turned her face up to the high table. Mreen tried to smile at her Housewoman across the heads of the Housemembers. Lispeth, hesitantly, smiled back.

It was a small thing, really the smallest possible detail, but a hopeful one. Mreen bid her senior a polite good-night and made her way out of the great room. As she passed the far table where the *hrussmaster* sat with his mate, she felt his hostile gaze on her back, but she ignored him.

She cast her mind out to find where the little one might be, and she detected the small, bright spot of psi, far off in the stables. Mreen nodded to herself as she climbed the stairs alone. Gwin was with her big brother, safe and sound. And until she decided for herself to reveal her Gift, Mreen intended to simply watch over her from a distance. Sira had agreed with this plan, and Mreen, herself so much a child of the Gift, had no wish to make it a punishment for Gwin.

In Gwin's own time, they had decided, she and Sira. At a time of the child's own choosing.

Mreen went into her apartment and sat with her mother's brushes in her lap, stroking the old *caeru* bristles with her fingers, gazing out into the night. The stars were dimmed by the light of the *quiru*. The high snowfields, widening each day, glimmered in the distance. The summer was over. And Mreen knew she must find a way to be content in her new life, to reach out to those around her, even in her silence.

When Lispeth knocked on her door, and came in bearing a fresh pitcher of water for the night, Mreen rose and faced her. She made a sign against her breast, a flutter of all four fingers—*I am sorry*—and then repeated it, slowly, as clearly as she could.

Lispeth's pale cheeks colored, and she shook her head vigorously. After she set the pitcher down, she crossed the room, coming to stand just outside Mreen's halo of light. "It's not you, Cantrix Mreen. It's me. I'm too slow."

Mreen shook her head in turn, and signed again. —*People fear me.*—

Lispeth gave a little duck of the head, and said frankly, "I was afraid."

Mreen signed, —*It is my light.*—

"Yes. We're not used to it, you see."

—*I know.*—

"But I'm not afraid now. And I'm trying to learn the signs, really I am."

—*I have no other way to speak to you.*—

Mreen signed the thought twice before Lispeth nodded

in understanding. "I know it's cumbersome, but you could write things down, sometimes. If I don't understand." And she added, softly, "I suppose it is hard for you, Cantrix. Lonely."

—*Yes.*—

Lispeth hesitated a moment, and then, a little awkwardly, but intelligibly, she signed, —*I am here to help.*—

Mreen beamed at her, and the Housewoman smiled back.

When Lispeth had gone, a basket of soiled clothes under her arm, Mreen turned back to the window. She stared at her reflection in the limeglass. Her halo frothed and bubbled around her, a sure sign of hope.

# Twenty-One

THE NEXT DAY dawned dark and gloomy, with a scent in the air of an early snowfall. Luke, as usual, went early to the stables, and was surprised to find that Axl and Lev had already departed. Axl, despite his complaints about the new stallion, had taken Brother.

Luke stared at the empty paddock, his heart as heavy as the gravid storm clouds gathering over the bay. He knew Axl had done it deliberately. He blamed himself. He had allowed his stepfather to see that the *hruss* mattered to him.

He turned to his work, trying not to think of Axl thumping at Brother's ribs with his boots, confusing him with his heavy hand on the reins. Perhaps Axl would sell the stallion to Arren. Surely Arren's *hrussmaster* would treat him better. It was a small hope, but it was all he had.

Luke opened the loose boxes and turned the *hruss* out into the paddock so he could clean. He found the halter he had used on Brother tossed carelessly over one of the gates, and as he picked it up, he remembered with a pang Brother's proud head, the flex of his muscles as he moved, the feel of his velvety muzzle against Luke's palm.

He was just beginning on the first stall when he heard Erlys's voice in the corridor, calling Gwin's name. Luke straightened and leaned the pitchfork against the wall. His throat dried, and his heart began to pound as he backed out of the stall. Erlys came through, looking anxiously from right to left, her hair not yet bound, her tunic askew.

"Erlys," Luke said, his voice cracking. "What is it?"

"It's Gwin!" she cried. "Isn't she here? I can't find her!"

"I thought she was with you. In the great room."

"Was she in her bed when you woke? Have you seen her?"

"Axl left early. Didn't Gwin come to your bed?"

"No! I thought she was with you!" Erlys's cheeks paled, and she stumbled backward, clutching at her throat. "O Spirit! Where could she be?"

Luke grabbed his furs from their peg by the stable door. "Check the Cantoris," he said. "And then the *ubanyix*. And the linen ambry, and the nursery gardens. I'll look outside." Erlys, not moving, began to whimper.

Every Housemember knew that outside meant the cliff, the precipice every child was warned against. Luke would scan the path, peer into the shadows beneath the ironwoods, brace himself to look over the very edge of the cliff, hoping against hope to see nothing but the sharp rocks of the shore.

Erlys sobbed into her hands, her unbound hair hanging over her face. Luke hesitated one moment, and then spun on his heel, pulling on his furs as he ran. He had to know the worst first.

There was no one about at this early hour. The House-members would just be gathering in the great room for the morning meal. He looked to his left and right, but there was no one on the path, or under the trees. He hurried to the stone wall and bent cautiously forward to look down on the verge beneath. The rocks were dark with spray. The *kikyu* hung in their harnesses from the hoists, safe from the ice growing in the bay. There was no sign of Gwin, or of anyone. The sea wind lifted the hem of Luke's furs, and his ungloved fingers stung with cold.

He made a slow progress along the cliff, scanning every inch of the stony ground at its foot. By the time he had completed his circuit, the sun had risen behind the heavy clouds, casting long, shifting shadows on the surface of the sea. He turned from the cliff, and scanned the area around the House. The sawyers had begun their work on the great pile of felled softwood trees, littering the ground with clear green leaves. Two Housewomen, in heavy furs, emerged from the back door carrying pots to empty into the waste drop. One of the cooks was collecting softwood from the last of the previous summer's pile. But he saw no small child, not in the courtyard or the stableyard or hiding beneath an ironwood sucker.

When there was no place left to look, Luke strode back to the stables. He found Erlys still huddled in the passageway, sobbing. He stood above her. "Erlys. Stop crying, and tell me. Tell me everything."

Before she could answer, he heard Emle's clear voice. "Luke? Luke! Do you know where Gwin is? Cantrix Mreen and I—"

She stood in the open door from the House, staring at Erlys, lifting her wide eyes to Luke's face. "O Spirit," she said softly. "He has taken her."

NO PARENT, EMLE thought, could look more stricken than Luke did at the knowledge that his little sister was missing. Gently but firmly, he led Erlys to the bench in the tack room. He knelt before her, holding both her hands in his, and said, "Erlys. This is no time for tears. You must tell us what happened."

He spoke to his mother as if she were a child, but it seemed right that he did. Her face was red and blotched, her voice broken with childish weeping as she choked out a few painful words.

Luke looked up at Emle, and the grimness of his expression made him seem far older than his four summers. "Did you know, Emle?" he asked. "Did you know Gwin was Gifted?"

Emle pressed her hands together. "We did, Luke," she said. "I am sorry I could not tell you. We felt it was up to Gwin when she told her family."

Luke came to his feet. His back was straight, his chin set in a firm line. "I already knew," he said. "And it seems my mother's mate discovered it, too."

Erlys broke out in fresh sobs. "He promised!" she wailed. "When he found out, I begged him to say nothing, and he promised!"

Emle put a hand on her shoulder, but she spoke to Luke. "We heard her, Mreen and I."

"Heard her?"

"Her psi, Luke. When children first come into their Gift, their psi is unpredictable, sometimes very strong, before they learn to control it. We have heard Gwin before, when . . ." Emle paused, fearful of offending. "When you and your stepfather . . ."

He gave a sharp, short nod. Erlys sobbed louder, her shoulder shaking beneath Emle's hand. "Housewoman," Emle said. "Your tears will do no good. You must go to Magister Kenth and tell him what has happened."

"No," Erlys moaned. "No, I can't. Axl will . . . he will . . ."

"He already has," Luke said bitterly. He turned away, toward the door. "You should have gone to the Magister before this, Erlys," he said over his shoulder. "Now I'm going to do it."

Emle left Erlys to her tears, and hurried to catch up with Luke. "He is the one, then," she said, almost trotting to keep up. "Axl is the one stealing Gifted children from their families, taking them to Conservatory."

"I should have guessed," Luke said. "And I should have seen that he was watching her, he and that Singer."

"The itinerant? Lev?"

"They left early today, supposedly to take *hruss* to Arren to sell. Erlys thought Gwin was with me, and I thought Gwin was with her. I never suspected . . ." He struck one fist into the other palm.

"Luke. You have no blame in this. You are not Gwin's parent."

He stopped, and turned to face her. His face was so full of suffering that she wished she could throw her arms around him, share it with him. "Emle, I am all the parent she has. Erlys stopped being Gwin's mother a long time ago."

Emle thought of Erlys weeping in the stables. She heard anew the distant cries of the frightened child in her mind. She winced, and shielded herself. "I fear you are right, Luke. I am sorry."

And then Mreen's powerful sending pierced her shielding. *Emle? Have you found her?*

*No.* Emle followed Luke as he turned to go up the staircase to the Magister's apartment on the upper level. *Luke believes Axl has taken her.*

*Can you meet me in the Magister's apartment?*

*We are already on our way.*

"MAGISTER, HAS THE itinerant from Conservatory arrived yet?"

"No. We have no itinerant Singer in the House. Lev was the last."

Luke sat stiffly at the Magister's long table, his arms folded, his face tight with tension. "I have to go after her," he said.

"There is this new provision of the Magistral Committee . . ." Kenth began.

Mreen shook her head. Her eyes were shadowed, and Emle knew she was aware, constantly, of Gwin's distress. *Tell him, Emle, that Sira intends—*

*Yes. Mreen, shield yourself.* Emle leaned forward. "Magister Kenth, Magistrix Sira told us she will defy the provision. If

Gifted children come, as some have done, she has to accept them. But she will not be party to forcing children to come to Conservatory."

Kenth took a sorrowful look around the table at the Gifted. "You knew," he said flatly. "You all knew we had a Gifted child here."

"I did not," Josu said. "But," he added stoutly, "I support Magistrix Sira's position. We cannot force people into the Cantoris."

"Where is Gwin's mother?" Kenth asked.

"I sent Lispeth to her," Emle said. "Lispeth will know how to comfort her, as much as is possible. But I think we must consider Luke to be the guardian of his sister."

Kenth frowned deeply. "I don't know what is to be done here. Magistrix Sira told me a child had been brought to Conservatory from Tarus, but I knew nothing of that child, either."

*An itinerant's child,* Mreen sent. Emle repeated the words aloud.

"That makes sense," Josu said quietly. "There is a great deal of pressure on itinerants."

"Axl," Luke said bitterly, "is very good at applying pressure."

Kenth looked even more grieved. "But what can we do? Without an itinerant Singer—we can hardly spare our Cantors—"

*We could spare one,* Mreen sent.

Josu's eyes widened, and he stared at her. *Oh, no! We would not dare to leave one of us alone. . . . What if something happened?*

*You could create the* quirunha *by yourself,* Mreen sent.

*No,* he responded. His lips trembled. *No, Cantrix Mreen, I cannot. I have never done so.*

For a long moment nothing happened at all. Kenth and Luke looked uncomfortable, as the unGifted often did when the Gifted were communicating. Mreen and Josu stared at each other, Mreen's face determined, Josu's filled with anxiety.

Emle leaned into their line of sight. *Mreen has created a* quirunha *by herself. I was present when she did it.*

Mreen's features did not move, but her halo shifted and glimmered about her. Josu stared at her, and then turned to Emle. "When?" he asked aloud. "When did she make a House-sized *quiru* entirely on her own?"

"Conservatory," Emle said. She included Kenth and Luke in her glance as she explained. "Magistrix Sira felt she should do it alone, to prove that she was fully qualified, though she could not Sing. And it was the swiftest, strongest *quirunha* any of us had ever seen."

"Excuse me," Magister Kenth said. "Are you suggesting that one of you should go after the girl? And leave the other alone in the Cantoris? I can't allow that! It puts my House at risk!"

*Emle.* Mreen's eyes burned with green fire. *We cannot let Gwin go this way, dragged to Conservatory against her will! It could ruin her forever.* She fixed her gaze on Kenth's face, and it seemed to Emle that even without the Gift, he must understand her meaning. *Tell him it will be for a short time.*

Emle relayed this to Kenth, with urgency. Still he shook his head, doubtful.

*Tell him he has my word, upon my own Gift,* Mreen sent firmly.

When Emle had repeated this aloud, Mreen stood up. *Josu, there is no time to lose. They are already a half day's ride away. You must prepare.*

Josu's hands on the table had begun to tremble. *Mreen, I— I cannot! I am afraid of—of hruss, and of travel, and—*

Emle stood up, too, and she gave Josu her bravest smile. "Cantor Josu, I will be with you. So will Luke."

"But who will speak for the Cantrix?" Kenth blurted.

Mreen's nimbus glittered with a hard light as she sent, *Lispeth must do it. Fetch her for me, Emle.*

EMLE RELAXED HER shielding for just a moment as she hastily stuffed things into a saddlepack—a change of linens, a brush and an extra binding for her hair, a cloth for washing. She lowered her shields to listen for Gwin's anguished and increasingly hopeless cries. They were growing faint. Emle wondered how much the honorarium must be, that Axl would abduct his own mate's daughter to win it. But it was, she supposed, retribution as well as profit. It was the way Axl could hurt Luke most.

When she reached the stables, Luke had three *hruss* already saddled, with bedfurs tied behind each cantle. He took her pack and tied that on behind the rolled bedfurs, adding a packet of food as well. Each saddle was as heavily laden as her own. "Not taking a pack animal," he said. "Slow us down."

Emle touched her *filla* beneath her furs. No Singer, how-ever flawed her Gift, liked to be without it. "Do you know what we will do when we find them?" she asked. Josu came through the door from the House and stood in the passageway with his furs over one arm, and a bulging saddlepack dangling from the other hand.

"I am simply going to take her back," Luke said. "Axl can't refuse me."

"But what if he does?" Emle asked. "He is a violent man."

"I won't let that stop me." Luke pulled back his furs, and Emle saw that at one hip he had slung a long, wicked-looking hunting knife. It filled her with horror. Her worst memory flashed through her mind, the knife slashing skin and bone, the red stream of blood spilling over the stone floor. "Oh, no," she breathed. "Surely there is another way?"

Luke's voice was as hard as the set of his shoulders. "I hope so," he said. "But I have to be prepared." The change in him took her breath away. Where was the sullen, remote youth she had first met? He had been replaced by a tall, grim stranger whose every movement had purpose. Luke put out his long arm to take Josu's pack.

Josu dropped the pack from nerveless fingers, and gave a little gasp. "How can this be, Houseman?" he said faintly. "We are all too young—we have no experience—"

Luke's jaw clenched and unclenched as he lifted the pack from the straw-strewn floor. "Youth has nothing to do with it, Cantor," he said flatly. "I have experience enough. You'll have to trust me." He squinted up into the lowering clouds. "It may snow. We must go quickly. With every hour that passes, they are farther from us."

He led the *hruss* out, one at a time. As he helped Josu into his saddle, Emle looked hard at the stirrup on her beast's left side, and decided she could do it herself. By the time Luke came to help her, she had already figured out how to pull herself up. She fitted her right foot into the opposite stirrup, and pulled her hood forward to block the damp sea wind from her ears and her neck. Luke nodded approval as he swung up onto his own mount. "Can you manage your reins, too?"

"So I can," she said, hoping she sounded confident. She lifted her reins, and felt the *hruss* turn its attention to her.

Luke took Josu's reins, and they started off at the brisk, swinging walk that was the favored gait of *hruss*. Emle rode behind Josu, noting with sympathy how he clung to his pommel and jounced against the high cantle of the saddle. She was luckier. She fell easily into the rhythm of her *hruss*'s gait. In truth, it needed no guidance to follow the two beasts ahead of it. She let the reins lie loosely across its neck, and glanced back at the House as they rode out of the stableyard. Erlys stood in the shadows of the stables, watching them leave, and Emle recognized Lispeth's tall slender figure behind her. Emle lifted her hand, and Lispeth answered the gesture. Erlys only stared, her eyes round and dark in her white face.

Emle turned forward again, minding her reins, her *hruss*'s head, her stirrups. Lispeth would have to deal with Erlys, and also with Mreen. There was no help for it.

The soundless wail spun through her head again and made her stomach clench. She sent, as strongly as she could, *We are coming, Gwin. Your brother is coming. Try not to be afraid.* But she had no indication that the child could hear her.

# Twenty-Two

LUKE DIDN'T LOOK back as the traveling party left Tarus's stableyard. He felt the need for hurry in his very bones, knowing that if Axl and Lev reached Conservatory with Gwin, he would not be able to bring her home again. The deed would be done. His little sister would be delivered, paid for, irretrievable. It wouldn't matter that, in the end, she was destined for Conservatory. What mattered was Axl's victory over her, his ability to control her life. Luke was not so worried about Gwin's Gift as the Singers were; he was worried about the hurt she must be suffering. He couldn't bear to think of how her stepfather's—and her mother's—betrayal might have shattered her spirit.

Luke pushed the pace on the narrow cliff path, hurrying east, knowing there was at least a day's ride to complete before they could turn into the Southern Pass, which would lead them to Conservatory. The other direction lay almost due west, circling the Continent along the seashore, all the way to Filus. He remembered that long journey from Filus,

when Gwin was still a toddler, and his own heart still sore
from losing his father. He remembered watching his mother
in wonderment as she tended to her new mate, fussing with
her hair and her clothes, displaying the gifts Axl had given
her. Luke had not felt angry then, only uncomfortable and
bewildered. Before that time, Erlys had been only his mother.
He had been forced, when she accepted Axl v'Tarus, to see
her as a woman, and he resented it.

When the path widened, Luke drew up the reins of Josu's
mount so the *hruss* could walk side by side. "Cantor Josu? Are
you comfortable?"

Josu clung to the pommel of his saddle with both hands,
and his face was creased with effort. "I fear I am no rider," he
panted. "I bounce and slide as if my saddle were made of ice."

"If you could sit a little straighter," Luke offered. "Lean
into your stirrups a bit, and keep your weight back in the
saddle. . . ."

Josu leaned back against the high cantle, loosening his
grip on the pommel, and then yelped as he slid sideways.
"Oh, no, Houseman. I must hold on, or I will fall!"

Behind Josu, Luke saw with gratitude that Emle rode as
if she had been born to it, her hands easy on the reins, her
body swaying with the gait of her mount. She needed no
instruction. He brought his attention back to the struggling
Josu.

"Try just one hand on the pommel, then," he said. "And
feel the beast's gait beneath you. I do think the Spirit made
*hruss* to fit us."

"I suppose you are right," Josu said breathlessly. "I only

wish the Spirit had made me more fit for *hruss*. And given me more courage!"

"You're here, Cantor Josu," Luke answered. "That is courage enough."

A LIGHT SNOW began to fall at mid-afternoon, dusting the boulders and the treetops, powdering the *hruss'* manes and tails. They had left the protective wall behind them hours before, and the abyss yawned to their left. The breeze from the sea was sharp and cold, and all of them kept their furs pulled tightly about them.

Luke kept an eye out for landmarks. He had never traveled so far on this road, but he knew its pattern, knew the jumble of boulders that marked the turn toward the Pass, the three entwined irontrees that would mean they had reached it. His father's maps lay rolled in his bureau drawer, a slender legacy. Luke had brought the one that would guide them to Conservatory, but he had no need to take it out of his saddlepack. He remembered every mark on it with perfect clarity, and had long ago memorized the symbols that indicated the Houses.

They ate a belated meal in their saddles. Gerta had packed dried *caeru* meat and fish, dried fruit, and a loaf of bread. Luke suggested they eat the bread while it was fresh, and save the fruit for the next day. They passed it back and forth between them. Josu ate little, fearful of freeing his hands, but Luke couldn't see how to help him. He could hardly feed the Cantor, as if he were a child. He told himself he would make certain Josu ate a good meal when they camped for the night.

They pressed steadily on. Snow fell in fits and starts. By the time the light began to fade, the snow was falling faster, catching on their eyelashes and their furs. Reluctantly, Luke called a halt.

"Cantor, I think we should make camp here," he said, pointing to a space sheltered by two ancient ironwood trees with thick suckers that coiled above the ground to form a natural windbreak. Josu didn't answer, and Luke hurried to help him down from his saddle. The Singer's face was pale, and his hands trembled as he pulled out his *filla*.

And then Emle was at his side. "I will help the Cantor, Luke," she said with confidence. She put her hand under Josu's arm, and led him to a flat boulder where he could sit and draw breath for a moment. Luke turned back to the *hruss*, to pull off their saddles, fill their feedbags with grain, and hobble them loosely, though the likelihood of them straying from the *quiru* was faint. He turned to the campsite with an armload of softwood, and heard Josu's melody, the sound of his *filla* distressingly thin. Perhaps, Luke thought, it was muffled by the thickening snow.

It was a relief to see the light bloom, its brightness pushing back the twilight, its warmth melting the new blanket of snow that clung to the rocky ground. The *hruss* lifted their heads and flicked their ears, almost as grateful as the humans for the envelope of warmth.

When Josu had finished, Emle left him sitting on the boulder, and came to help Luke with the cookfire. He glanced up to thank her, and saw that her face was drawn as if with pain. "Are you all right, Emle?"

She nodded. "I am, but I hear her, Luke."

He found the flint and stone in his saddlepack, and straightened. "It will be a long night," he said. His jaw ached, and he realized he must have had it clenched all through the day's ride.

"Yes. I will keep trying to reach her, though with this noise . . ." She closed her eyes.

He knew she meant the noise of Gwin's psi, the mental keening that it was not in his power to hear. He hurried to put flint to stone. The fire would comfort them in the wide darkness. As he knelt, he prayed to the Spirit to bring the same comfort to Gwin, to give her courage and patience. As the fire began to crackle and pop, a cheerful sound that mocked his misery, he looked up at Emle. "Are we closer?" he asked softly. "Will we catch them?"

Her eyes were haunted. "It seems so," she said. "I cannot shield my mind from her. I think that means we are close."

Josu, huddled on the stone, nodded. "I hear it, too. You must strengthen your shielding, Emle, or you will get no rest."

She bowed to him, and murmured, "Yes, Cantor Josu. Thank you."

Luke remembered with surprise that Josu was Emle's senior. Here, away from the House, it had seemed to be the other way around.

Luke turned away from the fire and stood looking out into the darkness. The snow fell faster and faster, shrouding the stars. He peered to the northwest, where the Pass wound between the Marik Mountains. Where was she? Were they keeping her warm, giving her food? And how long until they could catch them?

EMLE ROLLED HERSELF in her bedfurs after seeing that Josu was safely in his. She had strengthened her shielding, but she still heard echoes of Gwin. She hoped the child would sleep eventually, so that she could, too. But she had another concern, one she dared not give voice to.

When Josu had begun the *quiru*, he had faltered. Luke, she knew, had been busy with the *hruss* and had not seen. But she had, and it shook her to her very bones.

The *quiru* had trembled as it rose, shrinking, swelling, falling back, and only after long moments of playing had its column of light and warmth steadied. It was his fear, she knew, his dread of another day in the saddle, his discomfort at being out of doors. Josu had spent all his life behind the safety of thick stone walls, and he was terrified.

There was reason to fear. The Continent abounded with dangers, from the occasional marauding *urbear* or *tkir* to the risk of a *hruss* falling, or a bone breaking. But the deep cold was the greatest fear of every Nevyan. And if Josu's Gift failed them, they would all freeze.

She watched from the warmth of her bedfurs as Luke set their camp in order for the night. He banked the fire and checked the *hruss'* hobbles before he unrolled his own furs. He took off his boots, and slipped into his bed. He turned on his side, away from the fire, to settle down into the nest of thick *caeru* fur.

Emle pulled her own bedfurs close under her chin. She closed her eyes, offering prayers to the Spirit that on the morrow, they would catch up with Axl and Lev and their captive. She also prayed that Josu would be stronger, but a tiny voice in her mind warned her that the opposite was possible, that Josu would weaken under the pressure of responsibility, of threats real or imagined. Their precipitous departure, their long, relentless ride today, and the one that faced them tomorrow—these were very real challenges.

It was a shock to find themselves in a snowy campsite instead of safely in their beds at Tarus, watched over by their Housemen and -women, the Magister, the double security of two Singers in the Cantoris. Why was it, Emle wondered, that she faced these dangers with more equanimity than Josu? Why did Luke appear to grow stronger and more capable with every new crisis? There was no answer. The unknowable Spirit had made them that way.

Long into the night, Gwin's cries faded from her mind, and she knew the little girl must have fallen asleep at last, no doubt utterly spent by the events of the day. Emle was, too, and she slid into sleep with a long sigh of pure exhaustion.

It seemed she woke only moments later, hearing Luke's voice in her ear. "Emle," he said quietly. "Emle, can you wake up? And wake the Cantor? Dawn will soon be here. We can gain a little on them if we leave now."

She sat up, clutching her bedfurs with both hands. For a moment, she couldn't think where she was, and it was so dark—it was never this dark in the House—and then she remembered. They were on the cliff path, riding toward the Southern Pass. Josu's *quiru* had already begun to fade, and the snowfall masked everything beyond it, the rocks, the iron-wood suckers, the tapering tips of branches. Stars still glittered overhead, but they had begun to fade, too. The eastern sky was gray with dawn light. She reached for her boots, seeing that Luke had already packed up everything except a single pot, which rested now on the rekindled fire.

"You should have wakened me earlier," she whispered. "I could have helped you."

"You will be helping me if you can wake Cantor Josu without frightening him," Luke said with a grimace.

To her surprise, on this dark and alarming morning, she found herself suppressing a giggle. She cast out with her mind for Gwin, but she heard nothing. That seemed a good sign. Perhaps Axl and Lev would sleep long this morning, and let Gwin sleep, too. Luke and Josu and she could overtake them all the sooner.

She resolutely refused to think about what would happen when they did.


LUKE LED HIS group at a hard pace all morning, urging the *hruss* to their swiftest walk, watching Josu over his shoulder until his neck ached. At midday it was clear they would have to give the Cantor a rest. He slumped over his saddle, clinging to the pommel with both hands, his legs at awkward angles in the stirrups. Then a *ferrel* cried high above their heads, and Josu startled. He lost his balance and his grip. Slowly, inexorably, he slid out of his saddle and fell to the ground, landing hard on his left hip with a cry of pain.

Luke stopped the *hruss* and leaped down. Josu moaned as he boosted him back into the saddle.

Luke soon found a reasonable place to build a small cook-fire, and gently helped Josu off his mount. Emle was there the moment Josu was on his feet, leading him about to stretch his legs a bit. Luke rummaged in his saddlepack for softwood, the cooking pot, and three bowls and spoons. When he turned to the food, he found that Emle had already retrieved some dried fish and a handful of vegetables, and was holding out her hand for the pot.

"At least there is snow to melt," she said.

"Thank you," Luke said. "I hate stopping. Didn't know what else to do."

She filled the pot with snow and brought it to him. He struck the flint and brought a little blaze to a few twigs of kindling, then crossed the fire with three short softwood pieces. He glanced up at Emle and saw that the look of pain was in her eyes again.

"You are hearing Gwin," he said.

"So I am," she said tiredly.

"And yet she has grown so silent at home that it is rare to hear her speak."

"Yes, we saw that," Emle answered. Her eyelids looked slightly swollen, as if she had not slept well. He supposed she had not; neither had he. "She was working hard at hiding her Gift."

"I didn't know it was that hard."

Emle rubbed her eyes with her fingers. "It is a very difficult thing, Luke. Especially for a child, whose Gift is new and undisciplined. It is like trying to carry water in a cracked jug. It spills out at every step, and the little Gifted one has no idea how to stop it."

Luke set the fish to boil, and glanced back at Josu. The Cantor was sitting on a boulder, his back against a tree, his eyes closed. His lips were pale as ice.

Emle asked, very softly, "How many days to Conservatory from Tarus?"

"About four days' ride," Luke said. He glanced up into the sky. "Longer if it continues to snow."

"We will not find them today, I fear."

"No." Luke looked at Josu again, who gave no sign of hearing. "I was afraid he would fall again," he said. "He's not strong."

"Tomorrow, then."

"If the Spirit wills," Luke said, and he heard the bitterness in his own tone. He touched the knife at his belt. That, too, had been his father's.

That night they made their camp in the Southern Pass. Luke saw how slow Josu's *quiru* was to rise, how it trembled in the light breeze, and how Emle stayed close to him, closing her own eyes as he worked. When she opened her eyes, she looked doubtfully at the slender column of light. It barely reached out to the *hruss*, and it seemed to Luke that it was rather pale, a ghost of a *quiru*.

Josu hardly touched the *keftet* Luke had prepared over the cookfire, and he lay down in his furs, groaning over his sore thighs and aching shoulders. Luke knew Emle was watching him, too, and he gritted his teeth. There was nothing to be done about it now. They were here, and it made no more sense to turn back than to press on. But if Josu collapsed . . . they would all be finished.

Surreptitiously, Luke watched Emle's profile as she sat cross-legged on her bedfurs, the firelight gleaming on her smooth cheeks, picking out the gold in her hair. It could not happen, he told himself. He could not be responsible for anything happening to Emle. They would ride harder tomorrow, tie Josu into his saddle if need be. Once they had Gwin, perhaps Lev could be persuaded to return with them to Tarus. Luke would promise him something, some barter, or even some of Axl's metal, if he could steal it. . . .

Axl, of course, would never allow it. Axl had ruined their family, wasted Luke's apprenticeship, and now threatened their very lives. Luke clenched his fists as he stared through the weak glow of the *quiru*, yearning toward the reaches of the Pass, his body tense with the need to hurry.

I'm coming, Gwinlet, he thought. He wished that, like the Gifted, he could send his assurances to her. I'm coming. Hold on.

# Twenty-Three

MREEN SAT ALONE in her apartment, watching the snow fall on the mountains to the north. She had followed the travelers as far as she could with her mind until she lost them this afternoon. She had been unable to hear Gwin since the night before. Still she sat, concentrating, hoping for some word, some flash of intuition that would tell her what was happening.

Darkness crept in from the sea, creating long fingers of shadow. The *quiru*, which she had created alone, almost without effort, shone with generous light and warmth, spilling out over the courtyard, over the stables—where two Housemen had volunteered to fill in for Luke during his absence— over the nursery gardens, even over the waste drop. Mreen held her mother's brushes in her lap now and caressed their carved ironwood handles. She had felt, during her solitary *quirunha* this afternoon, as if Isbel were at her shoulder. When the *quirunha* ended, Mreen found, to her surprise, that her eyes were wet. Only Lispeth seemed to notice.

A tap on her door signaled her Housewoman's arrival. Mreen turned to see Lispeth come in with a tray. She ducked her head in a sort of bow as she set the tray on the table.

Mreen laid the brushes aside and lifted one hand in greeting: a touch to her breast, the palm turning outward. Lispeth, removing the cover from the cup and crossing the room with it, gave her a shy smile. "Hello, Cantrix," she said. Her voice, Mreen thought, was nice—rather low, with a warm timbre to it. "I thought you would like some tea before bed. And the cook gave me a bit of warm nutbread for you."

Mreen took the tea, but signaled, —Not hungry.—

Lispeth bit her lip as she studied Mreen's fingers. "You don't—oh! You're not hungry."

Mreen flashed her another sign, but Lispeth colored and shook her head. "I'm sorry, Cantrix. I don't understand."

Mreen set the teacup down on the windowsill, and tried again, slowly, separating each part. —Would you like to eat the nutbread?—

Lispeth's cheeks flamed even brighter, but she smiled. "Oh! Yes, I understand. I will eat it, Cantrix, so the cook will not be disappointed!" She laughed, the first time she had laughed in Mreen's presence. "I'm so tall, you see, it seems I never have enough to eat."

Mreen smiled, too, and patted her own waistline.

"It's true, Cantrix, you are much smaller than I am. And I've watched you—you hardly eat anything." Lispeth picked up the plate of nutbread. "Can I do anything else for you tonight?"

Mreen shook her head, and signaled, carefully, —Thank you. Good night.—

Lispeth, at the door, managed a quite credible bow. "You're welcome. Sleep well."

And then she was gone, and Mreen, with the comforting warmth of the teacup in her hand, resumed her solitary watch.

On their second morning in Ogre Pass, Luke rigged a sort of harness for Cantor Josu, to assure that he could not fall from his *hruss*. Josu accepted it, keeping his gaze averted.

*Are you all right, Cantor Josu?* Emle asked him.

Still he did not look up. *I hurt all over, Emle,* he sent, and there was a plaintiveness to his sending. A . . . a weakness, there was no other word for it.

*I am sorry,* she responded. *We are not much used to riding.*

*I am a terrible rider,* he answered. *On my journey from Conservatory to Tarus . . . I was the despair of all the riders. And I am worse now, I fear.*

Emle looked up and around at the swaying snow-dusted treetops, the mountain peaks that were the first to glow with sunlight. She inhaled the fresh cold air, her nostrils flaring as if she were one of the *hruss* foals. She felt Luke's eyes on her, and she wheeled to look at him.

"You love this," he murmured. "As much as I do."

She nodded, and turned to mount. "I would love it, if I were not so worried."

They rode out, with Josu's mount close behind Luke's. Emle, again, came last, keeping a careful eye on Josu. Unlike the Cantor, she felt no soreness at all. The *hruss*'s gait seemed as natural to her as walking. Emle had to press down a feeling of impatience with Josu's complaints. Surely, if he would only try . . .

But, she told herself, that was his nature. He could not help it.

She closed her eyes and listened for the spark of psi that would mean Gwin was awake, and that her captors were on the move again.

EMLE HAD NOT slept well for a second night, and by midday the rhythmic swing of the *hruss* beneath the saddle lulled her into a sort of half-sleep. Her eyes were open, her body responding to every dip and curve, but her mind drifted, accustomed by now to the little bright spot of psi she followed with her mind. She found, as the hours passed, that though she was anxious, she became used to that as well.

The Pass wound to the north, the scenery changing little as they followed its narrow, stony floor. And so, as the afternoon wore away into early evening, Emle startled awake when she realized that Gwin's psi was suddenly very easy to hear. The little girl no longer wailed and wept in her mind, but only mourned, in a steady, slow way that Emle supposed meant she had given up hope. But, seemingly all at once, Emle heard her with no effort at all.

She called out, careful to pitch her voice low. "Luke! We are almost upon them!"

He reined in his *hruss* and turned in the saddle to look at her. Between them Josu sat slump-shouldered and knock-kneed, braced by the harness Luke had devised for him.

Emle, meeting Luke's eyes, touched her temple, using one of Mreen's finger signs. "I hear Gwin so clearly," she said. "I think they must be very close. And"—she closed her eyes to concentrate—"they have stopped."

She saw how Luke touched the knife at his belt, much as she so often touched her *filla* beneath her tunic, and she shivered. The moment was at hand.

A feeling of dread overwhelmed her, momentarily stealing her breath. How could they have believed they could do this? Their hasty planning now seemed utterly inadequate, dream-spinning, wishful and dangerous thinking. Axl was a hardened, determined man, and he had Lev to stand at his back. Emle's legs shook with fear as she slid to the ground and stepped forward to help Luke unstrap Josu from his saddle. They helped the Cantor down, and he staggered, clutching at Emle for support.

Luke's lips thinned to a hard line. "I'll make a fire," he said. "I hope Josu can create a *quiru*, while I go up ahead on foot."

"I will make the fire," Emle offered. "I watched you do it."

He pulled out several sticks of softwood and a bit of kindling, and handed her the precious flint and stone. "*Quiru* first," he said shortly.

"Yes. Of course." She put her hand under Josu's arm, and helped him to a flat rock. He sat, and took his *filla* out with shaking fingers. She knelt beside him as Luke turned to stride up the road. She called cautiously, "Luke? Be careful."

He didn't look back. "I will."

Emle watched him disappear over a rise in the road, his

boots scattering the dry snow. *Cantor Josu,* she sent. *Play very softly.*

He didn't answer, but he did begin a quiet, halting melody in *Iridu.* Emle closed her eyes, prepared to follow him. With alarm, she noticed the faltering tempo, the uneven tone of Josu's playing, and when she opened her eyes, she saw that the air around them flickered here and there, but the *quiru* did not bloom.

Josu tried *Aiodu,* a short melodic fragment that he repeated over and over, without grace or embellishment. His tone was thin and harsh, but the light around them brightened a bit and—Emle was relieved to see—steadied. It would not, she knew perfectly well, be enough to keep them warm through the night, but it was a start.

She bent over the little pile of wood Luke had left, brushing away the snow beneath and arranging the makings as she had seen him do, with a few stems of dry straw as tinder on the bottom, the kindling arranged loosely on top of the tinder, and the softwood sticks propped on one another to allow air to circulate. She took the flint in one hand and the stone in the other, and took a deep breath. This would be the hard part.

The stone was hard and smooth, the flint angled at one side. She gripped them over the wood, and struck them together. A spark flew, but it fell wide, into the thin layer of snow. She tried again, and this time the spark fell onto the wood, but nothing happened. She found she was holding her breath, and her arms ached from the effort. She took another breath, and shook out the tightness in her wrists. They needed this fire. Only if it caught did she think Josu would relax enough to create a real *quiru*.

She struck again, holding the flint close to the tinder, and was rewarded by seeing a thin curl of smoke rise from the straw. She struck the flint again, more confident now, using a fluid, quick motion. One more time, and all the straw was burning. The kindling caught, and then the dry softwood. She blew a little on one corner, where the flames seemed slow to rise. A moment later, cheerful small flames were snapping into the gathering evening.

Relieved, Emle looked up, and saw how dark the sky was growing. *Cantor Josu,* she sent urgently. *You must try again.*

As Josu put his *filla* to his lips, she stood to peer anxiously out into the gloom, searching for Luke's tall figure. He had to return soon, or be caught in the cold. Josu's melody wound around her, *Aiodu* again, steadier this time, his tone more focused. She closed her eyes, and reached out her psi to support him. Even if her psi was flawed, she could lend a bit of energy, a bit of strength. . . . And she realized she could not hear Gwin, that the little glowing locus of her psi had disappeared.

When she opened her eyes once again, the *quiru* was noticeably brighter. She could feel its warmth on her cheeks and hands. She looked up, beyond the light, and saw Luke hurrying toward them through the twilight.

Emle left the *quiru*, and ran to meet him. Already the air had grown frigid, chilling every bit of her exposed skin. "Luke!" she whispered as she drew close. "Did you see them? Is she there? Is she all right?"

He looked down at her, his eyes narrowed in his grim face.

His voice, when he spoke, was tight with fury. "They cut her hair."

She stumbled on a rock beneath her feet. "What? Why would they—"

"They cut her hair to make her look like an itinerant's child," he said bitterly. He strode toward the *quiru*, and she had to run to catch up.

When they reached the *quiru*, Luke stood over the fire, his hands clenched into fists. "They're camped not far ahead, where a little grove of softwood has grown up between the ironwoods. Gwin is already in her bedfurs, beside the fire. Axl"—he spoke the name as if it tasted foul in his mouth—"Axl and Lev are drinking, joking—in no hurry. I suppose they think we just gave her up! That we wouldn't come after her!"

Emle put a hand on his arm. It was hard as stone beneath her fingers. "They knew there was no other itinerant in the House. They would never dream that Cantor Josu would come out with us."

"Her hair . . ." he muttered.

"It will grow."

He lifted his eyes from the flames to meet her gaze. "I know it will grow, Emle," he said bleakly. "It's just part of—of everything they've done. As if she were just—a possession. A"—he looked away again, as if he could hardly bring himself to say the words—"a commodity, like *hruss*, like *caeru* meat. . . ."

"Luke," Emle said. "Come, let us make a bit of food and sit and think of what to do. Do not torture yourself. By the will of the Spirit, we will have her with us by this time tomorrow."

He didn't answer, but he turned to the saddlepacks and began to take out the packets of food, the cooking pot, and the bowls. He tossed more softwood on the fire and went to collect snow in the pot.

Josu sent, *Emle, what will happen now?*

She had no idea what to tell him.

# Twenty-four

"YOU DON'T HAVE to come with me," Luke said.

He and Emle faced each other across the fire. He was dressed and ready to face Axl and Lev. The hunting knife swung at his belt, and he wore his furs unfastened.

The sun had not yet risen. Luke had slept little, and he thought Emle had also been wakeful. Josu was still wrapped in his bedfurs, but Emle had heard Luke up and about, and now she, too, was dressed.

"I cannot wait here," she said.

Even in this tense moment, she made his heart beat faster. What a *hrussmaster*'s mate she would make! Spirited, strong, quick to adapt to whatever situation presented itself . . .

But this was no time for such thoughts. "Thank you," Luke said simply, and his hand dropped to the knife as he turned to go.

"Luke—Luke, do not take the knife. I have such a bad feeling about it."

He looked at her over his shoulder. "You hate all knives, Emle."

"It is true," she admitted. She fastened her own furs, and came around the fire to join him. Her eyes shone with firelight. "But this one—today—I fear it will bring on something terrible."

"Axl wears a knife," he said flatly. "And he's capable of using it."

"Not on you, surely, Luke!"

Luke looked away from her, out into the gray light of early dawn. "I need to go now, Emle. I want to surprise them."

She drew a noisy breath, and then said, "Very well. I am ready."

"Shall we wake Josu?"

"He will be stronger if he rests. I will send to him, when he is awake."

The snow beneath their boots was icy and slick, the air sharp in their lungs. The wind covered the sounds of their passage. They climbed the rise and then followed the road down the next slope. They kept to one side, threading their way around roots and stones. Once, some small creature, a *wezel* perhaps, or even a hardy *caeru* on an early hunt, skittered away from them across the floor of the Pass.

The first rays of the sun touched the mountain peaks above their heads. Cautiously, they approached the stand of softwood trees that hid Axl's camp. Luke lifted a hand in warning. He led the way to the shelter of a broad ironwood trunk, and peered around the tree. Emle pressed close, trying to see past him.

Three sets of bedfurs were arranged around a banked campfire in a shallow depression. Four *hruss* stood dozing just inside the circle of Lev's *quiru*, their heads down, waiting patiently for the day. A fifth held his head high, his ears flicked forward, his black mane shining dully in the dim light.

Brother.

The stallion's nostrils flared and he whuffed, deep in his throat.

Someone was awake in those huddled bedfurs. The smallest mound stirred, and a tiny white hand appeared, cautiously pulling the furs away from her shorn head.

Luke backed around the tree again, pulling Emle with him. "Can you send to her?" he whispered. "Can you call her up here, to us? Without waking them?"

Emle closed her eyes and concentrated. A furrow appeared between her brows. The sun rose steadily and slowly in the east as she tried to reach Gwin. Luke held his breath.

Emle, eyes still closed, murmured, "She hears me. I do not know if she understands."

"She understands," he whispered back. "She's coming."

Cautiously, Emle opened her eyes, and leaned past Luke to look down from their little ridge. It seemed he was right. Gwin was putting her legs out of her bedfurs, one at a time, slowly. Just as cautiously, she put her feet in her boots and pulled her furs around her. She moved gingerly, teetering on her toes around the fire, scurrying through the hobbled *hruss*. Then she stopped, her shorn head lifted. Looking for them.

"She can't see us," Luke said. He stepped forward, around the tree, and raised his arm to get Gwin's attention.

Brother's ears lifted at the movement, and he gave the long, strong call of the stallion.

The other mounds stirred. First Lev's gray, cropped head appeared. He stared blearily around in the gray light. Then, abruptly, Axl sat up, his blond hair ruffled. He squinted at Brother, and then across at Gwin's empty bedfurs. He gave some wordless exclamation, and both men scrambled out of the bedfurs, reaching for their boots.

"Tell her to run!" Luke said urgently. "Will she understand?"

*Gwin*, Emle sent, as strongly as she knew how. *Hurry! Up here, hurry! They are awake.*

Gwin left the shelter of the *hruss* herd and began to run up the hill to Luke's and Emle's sheltering tree. In only seconds, Axl spotted her and began to shout. He was still struggling with his boots, but he came after her, one foot still bare. "Stop, damn you!" he shouted. "Where do you think you're going?"

And then Axl spotted Luke at the top of the hill, his back braced against the broad ironwood trunk. Axl froze in midstride, shocked into silence for a long moment. He put his bare foot down in the snow, and a slow, humorless grin spread over his features.

"It's you," he said. They were close enough that he had no need to raise his voice.

Luke answered, "So it is."

"What in the name of the Six Stars do you think you're doing?"

"Taking my sister home," Luke grated. "Come on, Gwinlet, you're almost here. Come on!" The little girl, puffing, slogged up the slope toward Luke.

"She's going where she belongs," Axl said. "She's going to

Conservatory. Just as the Magistral Committee has ordered."

"Not without her mother's permission," Luke hissed.

"Her mother will do what I tell her" was Axl's response.

"Gwin doesn't want to go yet, and you're not going to force her."

"I'll report all of this to the committee, Luke. You have no right—"

Emle stepped out then from the shelter of the tree. "I represent Conservatory in this matter, Hrussmaster," she said as coolly as if such confrontations were an everyday matter for her. And as if what she said were true. "Conservatory wishes the child to come in her own time."

"I doubt," Axl smirked, "that a young lady with a useless Gift would be allowed to speak for Conservatory."

Luke lost his temper. Gwin reached them and he thrust her behind him, into Emle's waiting arms. "Take her to the camp," Luke muttered, and then he stepped forward, down the hill, moving straight toward his stepfather. In the campsite, Lev had hastily rolled his furs and was strapping them on one of the *hruss*.

"Luke, no. Let it pass!" Emle pleaded. She took Gwin's cold, small hand in hers. "We have her now, let us go."

"He will never allow it."

Axl had his boots on now, and he was moving, too. His smile was gone, his face darkening, growing ugly with anger. "You half-wit," he snarled. "How dare you interfere with the way I do my work!"

"Work?" Luke snapped. He stopped where he was. "When have you done any real work, Hrussmaster? You think collecting bounties on the heads of children is proper work?"

Emle saw, with a tremor in her heart, that Axl's knife, like Luke's, was slung at his belt.

"Bounty?" Axl shouted. "There's a reason they call it an honorarium, you fool! And Nevya needs these children!"

"None of what you've done is for Nevya. It's for you, to satisfy your greed. And to prove you can make Erlys do whatever you want."

Emle watched, holding her breath, as Axl kept coming up the slope. Luke braced himself where he was.

LUKE SUPPOSED THAT the two of them, he and Axl, had been headed for this moment from the beginning. In a way, it was a relief to have reached it. He felt the weight of the knife against his thigh, beneath his furs. He left it there and waited to find out what Axl would do.

There was a clatter of hoofs on stone as the itinerant Singer made his escape. Lev obviously wanted no part of this situation.

"Emle," Luke said. "Take Gwin back to the camp. Build up the fire and stay there."

His eyes were on Axl, on the wicked knife that gleamed at his waist. He felt no emotion at all, neither fear nor regret— nor even, now, anger.

"So how did you manage this, you great fool?" Axl hissed. "Get one of those mewling Cantors to come with you? That coward Josu, or that other one—the dummy?"

"Doesn't matter. I'm here. Taking Gwin home."

"I don't think so, son." Axl walked slowly and deliberately up the hill, his hand poised over the knife hilt. "No, I think she's going where she belongs, and I'll take her there."

"You may not have noticed," Luke said, "but your Singer's gone."

Axl paused in mid-step and glanced behind him at his abandoned camp. When he turned back, his face had grown hard as stone. "I see," he said. "Well. I'll just have to take yours."

"We have what we came for, Axl. We're going back to Tarus." Luke hesitated only briefly, and then, deliberately, he turned his back.

"Luke."

Luke wheeled back to face Axl.

"You wouldn't leave me out here to freeze," Axl growled. "You're too soft for that." His hand hovered above his knife.

"You choose," Luke said. "Catch up with your Singer, or come with us. We're going."

For answer, Axl drew the blade. The sun was well up now, and the blade of the knife glittered with morning light. The thin dusting of snow had started to melt, but more clouds threatened from the north.

"Put it away, Axl," Luke said evenly. "You have nothing to gain."

Axl took another long step up the slope, the knife in his hand, the blade pointing down. "I'm still master here, son." Deftly, he flipped the knife in his hand. The tip pointed at Luke's breast, and he felt a spot flame there, beneath his furs, as if it invited that wicked sharpness to invade his flesh and bone. "Now I'm coming up there, and your Singer and the girl are coming with me." His lip curled. "But I'll let you join us. Erlys wouldn't like it if I left you."

Luke shook his head. He eyed Axl for another moment and then turned again to resume his walk up the slope.

Axl growled, "Stop right there." Luke glanced over his shoulder. Axl brandished the knife and showed his teeth in a mirthless grimace. "I'll use it, son," he said in a flat, cold tone. "There's no one to stop me."

"You'd never get away with it."

Axl laughed, a sound that chilled Luke's blood. "You have no idea what I've gotten away with, Luke."

Luke took another step.

"You'd better listen," Axl said. "What do you think happened to the itinerant whose boy is studying now at Conservatory?"

"I assume you paid him," Luke said, but he stopped.

"Her," Axl said softly. "And she wouldn't take my payment."

For a moment Luke could hardly breathe. He turned, very slowly, and stared at Axl. "You killed the child's mother?"

"I had to get rid of her. She was coming after me, just like you."

Luke's lip curled with utter and complete revulsion. He pulled back his furs to show Axl his own knife. "You can't get rid of me," he rasped. "And the Continent would be better off without the likes of you."

"Tell it to the Magistral Committee," Axl said. He lifted his arm, and with a much-practiced motion, he threw his knife at Luke.

# Twenty-five

EMLE LED GWIN hurriedly down the far side of the slope toward the camp, where Josu was now sitting up, looking around him with some alarm. When he saw Gwin, his face lighted.

*Emle! You found her!*

*Luke found her.* They reached the camp, and Emle said, "Gwin, get into my bedfurs, here." She helped the little girl to slide between the layers and then pulled them up to her chin. "You must stay here, Gwin. Promise me! No matter what happens, stay here until I come for you."

"Luke . . ." Gwin began, her voice as fragile as a breath, her lips barely moving.

Emle bit her lip. It rarely did any good to lie to one of the Gifted in anything important. "Gwin," she said. "I am going back to Luke now. But I cannot do that if you will not promise."

Josu surprised her by saying, "I will see that she stays, Emle. Do what you must."

Emle cast him a look of gratitude. "Luke wanted me to build up the fire. Will you do that, Cantor Josu?"

He said, "I can try."

Emle hesitated only a moment more, and then turned to dash back up the hill. As she reached the top, a terrible apprehension gripped her. She reached the ironwood tree and slowly, slowly, crept around the trunk.

The thick bark of the ironwood scraped her back and caught at her hair. She heard voices, Luke's, and then Axl's, and they sounded curiously flat to her, uninflected. She peered cautiously past the drooping branches of the tree. Then, on an instinct, she stepped free of the screening branches, the needles scraping her cheeks and forehead, into clear view of Luke. He had turned his back to Axl. Axl was, at just that instant, throwing his hunting knife.

The knife spun, once, twice, in the clear morning air. The haft revolved neatly, the blade catching the light along its high trajectory. It made no deviation from its path as it drove straight and swift toward its target.

Emle fell to her knees. Her eyes were open, following the arc of the knife. Her stomach turned with it, but her mind was still. There was no time to doubt her Gift. Even as Luke poised to dodge out of the knife's path, even as Emle's knees bent and the ground rushed up against them, her psi lashed out, faster than any physical object could move.

It was so simple. You flexed your mind, as you would any muscle. You gathered the strength of your psi, in the most natural way possible, gathered and then spent it, in a manner easier than tossing a stone or flinging a handful of snow.

Emle's psi batted away the knife, just as it had so long ago, only this time she was not protecting a toy. The force of her thought drove the hunting knife downward, a hand's breadth from Luke's feet. She heard the crack of its point breaking in the stony ground.

There was no time to feel triumph in the successful use of her Gift. Axl shouted something wordless, and lunged up the short rise, using his greater weight to throw Luke, who was already off balance, hard to the ground beneath the iron-wood tree. Emle did not know if she cried out in reality, or only in her mind, as the two men, the burly older one and the tall, slender young one, rolled from side to side, both struggling to take control of the knife that still hung in its leather sheath at Luke's belt.

Luke made no sound, not even a grunt, though the hasp of the knife must have dug into his hip as he fought. She became aware of Josu calling to her, *Emle? Emle? What is happening?* and that Gwin also cried out for her brother. Emle spared one quick glimpse over her shoulder, and saw that they had kept their promise. They knelt beside the rekindled cookfire, Josu with a protective arm around Gwin, Gwin staring up at the top of the rise as if her life depended on it.

Emle struggled to her feet, and stood poised to do what-ever she could to protect Luke from Axl's fury. For a moment it seemed Luke would prevail, as he gained the advantage on Axl, rolling on top of him, striving to pin his hands. But Axl was too heavy, and too strong. With a great heave, he threw Luke to one side, and leaped on him. Emle heard the air rush out of Luke's lungs.

This time she did cry aloud, deliberately. "No!" she screamed, and Axl looked up, startled, distracted for one precious moment.

By the time Axl registered her presence, sneering in disdain, and then turning back to his quarry, Luke had regained his breath. They wrestled, each with a hand on the grip of Luke's knife, the only sound their grunts and panting. Emle braced herself, focusing on the knife, on Luke's every movement, waiting to do what might need doing.

Axl freed one meaty fist enough to strike Luke directly on the point of the chin, and as Luke's head popped back from the blow, struck him again. A heartbeat later, Axl had the knife in his hand, and Emle watched, horrified, as the *hrussmaster* raised his arm, the knife poised just over Luke's exposed throat.

Now she did remember, in a rush, the blood and the shouts and the mess of her childhood. And she could not, she would not, allow that to happen again.

She had no time to think, or to decide to deflect the knife to the left or the right. Luke thrashed from side to side, trying to avoid the inevitable, and she could just as easily drive the knife into his throat as miss it. She closed her eyes and delved into Axl's mind.

She saw Luke through Axl's eyes, saw the tender skin of his throat, the grimace as he tried to squirm out of Axl's reach. And then Emle flooded Axl's mind with all the psi she could muster. She meant to interfere with his sight, to disturb his aim, but she had no opportunity to refine her effort, to define her target. The psi rolled through Axl's mind like an avalanche, blotting out his will and his breath as well as his sight.

With a choked gurgle, the *hrussmaster* fell to one side. The knife, Luke's knife, dropped harmlessly to the ground.


WHEN LUKE AND Emle appeared at the crest of the hill, leading Axl between them, Josu and Gwin stared up in astonishment. Axl stumbled, his hands groping the air before him, and Luke and Emle had to guide him around the obstacles in his way, support him across the uneven ground.

Josu stood up, the cookfire cold at his feet. "I could not make the fire burn," he said. And then, staring at Axl, "What has happened to him?"

Gwin huddled on Emle's bedfurs, her arms wrapped around her knees, her eyes on Axl. "He is blind," she said. "He cannot see anything."

Axl's eyes were open. He turned his head, following their voices, and his parted lips were slack and wet. He made no sound. Emle, too, was silent. Luke settled Axl on a boulder, saying harshly, "Stay there. I'm going back for the *hruss* and the equipment."

Axl slumped on the makeshift seat as if he were made of melting snow. His head hung forward, and a string of saliva dripped down his chin.

Emle, who had bent to embrace Gwin, rose to follow Luke. Josu said anxiously, "Singer Emle, please. Do not leave me here with him." He gestured to Axl. "I do not know what . . ."

She shook her head. "I do not know, either. But he cannot harm any of us now."

Josu whispered then, "Will he see again?"

Emle only shrugged, and crossed to where Luke waited. As they walked back up the slope, he watched her face, searching for some clue to her feelings. There was nothing.

When they reached the other campsite, she set about rolling Axl's bedfurs. There were two cups and bowls, which she picked up and stowed. Luke's head and jaw ached from Axl's blows. He stole a moment to caress Brother's strong neck, to let the *hruss* nuzzle his chest. He leaned against Brother, and found that his hands were shaking. And no wonder, he thought.

He steadied himself to put the saddle on the stallion, to strap the saddlepack on the pack beast. He took a last look around the campsite, and then turned to Emle. She was gazing up the hill at the spot where Luke and Axl had struggled, and where her psi . . .

"Emle," Luke said.

She turned to face him. Her eyes were very, very blue, the pupils enormous. Her lips were white.

"You saved my life," Luke told her.

"So I did," she answered quietly.

"And your psi, Emle . . ."

She took a step closer to him where he stood holding the reins of Brother and the pack beast. She pressed her forehead against Brother's silky mane, and closed her eyes. "It seems," she murmured, "that my Gift has its uses."

"You're unhappy."

She lifted her head and opened her eyes. Her pupils began to return to normal. A little color came to her lips. "Did you think I would be pleased?"

"But, Emle, your Gift!"

"It was so odd, Luke." She stroked Brother's neck. The stallion turned his head toward her, and Emle touched his muzzle. She said, "There was no time to think. It just—it just flowed out of me. I did not plan to hurt him."

"He was going to hurt me."

Emle straightened. "He was going to kill you."

"So he was."

"I could not let him do that." Emle took the reins of the pack *hruss* from Luke's hand. "But you know, Luke," she said, in a voice that trembled only slightly, "the Gift is meant to create, not destroy."

"Will Axl recover?"

"I cannot say."

"But Gwin—"

"Yes," she said, and led the way, the pack beast following obediently behind her as she set out to climb the slope once again. "All of this has been for Gwin, has it not? Perhaps the Gift was merely protecting itself, and I was its instrument."

WHEN THEY REACHED the campsite again, Emle saw that Axl sat a little straighter. His mouth was no longer slack, his hands no longer limp and useless. Even this slight recovery gave her a feeling of relief. His eyes still flicked from left to right, searching, she supposed, for a glimmer of light. Josu stood as far from Axl as he could without leaving the dying *quiru*. Gwin sat where they had left her, silent and watchful, on Emle's bedfurs.

*Has he spoken?* Emle asked Josu.

Josu cast Axl a fearful glance. He shook his head. *No. But when I came near, he reached out as if to seize me. He frightens me still.*

Luke squatted beside his little sister. "Gwinlet," he murmured. "Are you all right? Did they hurt you?"

"I am all right, Luke," she said. She, too, looked at Axl, her little face tight and angry. "He dared not hurt me, because I will be a Cantrix one day."

"So you will, Gwin," Emle said. "But you will go to Conservatory at the time of your own choosing." Axl's head swung toward her as she spoke. His lips parted, and his throat worked, but no sound came out. The sight of his struggles made her stomach crawl.

"But where will I go now?" the little girl asked mournfully. She looked up at her older brother. "And what about Mama?"

He patted her head, and straightened. "I don't know, Gwinlet. We'll figure something out with the Magister." He bent to stir up the fire, to feed it a few twigs. "First we eat, and then we begin our ride back to Tarus. We have a long day ahead of us."

Emle started across the campsite to roll her bedfurs. As she passed Axl, his hand grasped at her trousers and then her tunic. She whirled, shocked by the contact, sickened by the blank look in his eyes.

His lips distorted, and a harsh, guttural whisper was the only sound he could make. "What have you done to me?"

"I do not know," Emle said. "I only wanted to stop you from hurting Luke. From killing him."

Axl's hand fell uselessly to his thigh. His eyes flickered, rolling from left to right, up and down, seeking, finding nothing.

"Will I see again?"

Emle felt all eyes on them, and she freed herself from Axl's fingers with deliberate care. "I am sorry, Hrussmaster," she said in a level tone. "I simply do not know."

# Twenty-Six

FRESH SNOW BEGAN to fall just as the last of Josu's *quiru* evaporated in shreds like ground fog before the morning sun. The stony ground of the Pass had already begun to soften under a thickening blanket of white. Emle's boots slipped on the new snow as she swung herself up into the saddle. She collected her reins and looked ahead. The snow had already obliterated all but the largest landmarks.

Luke, astride Brother, with Gwin perched behind him on the saddle skirts, saw her glance. "Don't worry, Emle," he said quietly. "I know the road."

She smiled at him, the first smile of this long, frightening morning. "I have perfect faith in you, Hrussmaster," she said.

His lips curved, too. "I am no *hrussmaster* yet, Singer," he said.

She lifted her reins. "You will be, Luke," she said. "Without doubt. You will be."

They started out, Luke and Gwin in the lead, and Josu, as before, tied into his saddle, his *hruss* led by Luke. Behind

Josu, Axl rode, slumped over his pommel. None of them had considered leaving him to perish in the cold. It seemed obvious, even to Josu, that he would be no further threat. Luke tied the reins of Axl's *hruss* to Josu's saddle, forming a little line of linked beasts. Axl's long knife, with the broken point, was safely stowed in Luke's own saddlepack. Even if Axl had been able to get to it, his muscles seemed to obey his will only intermittently. His hands shook if he reached for something, and his step, as they lifted him onto the *hruss*, was unsteady. His eyes never ceased moving, searching for shape or shadow.

Emle came last. She closed her eyes, giving herself up to the rhythmic movement of the *hruss*, trying to come to some sort of understanding of what had happened. She felt a deep, grateful pride in having protected Luke. But Axl's slack face, his darting eyes, reminded her of the cost. She pitied him, though she knew now the true depth of his crimes.

For an hour or more, no one in the party spoke. The breathing of *hruss* and the soft hiss of falling snow were the only sounds in the wide wilderness of the Marik Mountains. Emle was warm inside her furs, and comfortable in her saddle, exhausted from tension. She lost track of the passage of time and caught herself nodding, drowsing as they rode.

She startled awake when Josu cried out with fear. A moment later Gwin's silent wail filled her mind, and her eyes flew open.

She saw to her horror that Axl had reached forward, beneath his *hruss*'s neck, to yank on the reins tied to Josu's saddle. He gave another powerful pull. The reins tore free, bringing with them the harness Luke had rigged to keep the

Cantor secure, and tilting Josu's saddle far to the right. Josu, with another cry, fell headlong from the *hruss* to land with a great thud on the snow-covered rocks.

"Luke!" Emle shouted.

He was already on his way back, Brother spinning about on his haunches faster than she would have thought possible. Luke leaped down beside Josu. Gwin clung awkwardly to the cantle of the saddle, her eyes wide.

Axl tugged at the reins of his *hruss*, forcing him out of the path, away from the other beasts. Emle, already half out of her saddle, saw him pass, and knew that though his muscles must have recovered some of their strength, he was still blind, his eyes staring at nothing, his fingers searching out the tangle of harness still tied to his reins. Emle heard the *hruss* nicker in protest at leaving its fellows, then grunt as Axl kicked its ribs with his boot heels.

"Where is he going?" she asked Luke.

"Don't know," Luke said, already on his knees beside Josu. "But he won't survive alone out here."

And then they both forgot about Axl as they lifted Josu's head and shoulders between them. Emle patted his hands, touched his temples. "Josu," she said urgently. "Cantor Josu. Are you all right?"

He didn't answer. Luke ran his hand over the back of the Cantor's head and lifted his palm to show the fresh red blood that streaked it. Josu's head lolled, and Luke hastily braced it again.

"Oh, Spirit!" Emle breathed. "Is it bad?"

"I don't know."

"Josu," Emle said again, and then she sent, *Cantor Josu. Can you hear me?*

Faintly, faintly, she heard his response. *My head—it hurts.*

*Yes, we know. Rest a moment.* Aloud, Emle said, "He is conscious, Luke. He sent to me, but weakly."

Luke looked at her across Josu's inert form, and she saw real fear in his eyes for the first time. She knew what it was, but she could not face it at this moment. She glanced over her shoulder for Axl. "Where has he gone?"

"*Hruss* will bring him back, if he lets it," Luke said shortly. "Let's see to the Cantor."

WHEN JOSU WAS made as comfortable as possible on his bedfurs, Luke built a fire, and laid out everyone else's furs as well. They were at least two days' ride from Tarus, but pressing on with an unconscious Singer would be pointless. Gwin watched him, perched on an ironwood sucker, her arms folded tightly around her small form. She understood, he could see, the danger they faced. If Josu didn't recover, and quickly . . .

Luke tried to push away his awareness of how weak Josu's *quiru* had already been. He kept himself busy, forcing himself not to track the path of the sun as it swung overhead, past the meridian, on toward the western horizon, where new snow glittered on the great peaks of the Mariks. The fire crackled to life. A weak, filtered sunshine warmed the back of Luke's neck.

He glanced at Josu's bedfurs, where Emle knelt beside the Cantor, rubbing his wrists, trying to get him to sip water from her own cup. "Is he any better?" Luke asked, coming to crouch beside her.

She looked up at him. Her face was pale, but her lips were firmly set. "No," she said bluntly. "He is not."

"Can you help him?"

It seemed that her face grew even paler, but her eyes held his with a steady courage that deepened his admiration for her. She reached beneath her furs and drew out her *filla*. The slender, polished cylinder fit her hand as if it had grown there. "I will try," she said softly.

He only nodded. Should she be unable to help Josu, all four of them would perish. There was no need to say it aloud.

Emle closed her eyes. Gwin came to stand beside her, and she closed her eyes, too. Luke could only watch, shut out by his lack of the Gift.

Little flurries of snowflakes fell onto their hasty campsite, powdering the bedfurs, hissing in the flames, dusting the *hruss'* ears and tails. Luke looked back up the Pass, where Axl had disappeared. Had Axl thought he could find Lev, or that Lev would be looking for him? Luke doubted that. Lev was a coward. And Lev alone, among them all, could be certain of survival. He was an itinerant Singer. He knew how to create camp *quiru*. Perhaps Axl, even in his damaged state, believed finding Lev was his only chance. Luke had to face the possibility that Axl was right. He and Emle, Gwin and Cantor Josu, were all in mortal danger.

Emle began to play her *filla*, a thin, delicate sound that brought an ache to Luke's chest. Her Gift might be flawed, he thought, but her music was lovely, beautiful almost beyond bearing. He saw that Gwin had tipped her face up, to let snowflakes fall on her cheeks and her closed eyelids. And Josu . . .

Josu groaned. His hands fluttered at his sides, and he raised them shakily to his head.

Luke sprang to his feet. Emle ended her melody and opened her eyes, raising them to Luke's face. Gwin squatted beside Josu and stroked his hands.

"Is he better?" Luke whispered.

"So he is," Emle answered softly. Her eyes darkened to the deep violet of the evening sky. "I did it, Luke. I stopped the bleeding. I have never been able to do that before."

Luke waited.

"He will not be able to make *quiru*, though," she said. She came to her feet, and straightened her shoulders. "I must do it. There is no one else."


EMLE PUT HER *filla* to her lips once again. Her breath felt cold as she drew it deep into her lungs.

She was almost painfully aware of them watching her, listening to her, Luke and Gwin and even Josu from where he lay on the bedfurs beside the little fire. She breathed again, and flexed her fingers, which were growing chill as the light waned. She could put it off no longer. They were counting on her, all of them. And this time, more than ever in her life, she could not fail. She sent a quick plea to the Spirit of Stars to sustain her, and then she began.

She played in *Aiodu*, for simplicity. Though she had not

consciously chosen the melody, it sprang from her memory, one of the earliest tunes she had learned at Conservatory, a straightforward, unadorned succession of notes. She stated it once, played the variation, and returned to the melody. As the notes wound above her, up into the snow-brushed branches of the ironwoods, out into the lacy curtains of snow that were growing thicker by the moment, she reached out with her psi. She stirred the smallest particles of the air as she might stir the slumbering ashes of a banked cookfire. The old fear was still there, but she had seen far worse things on this day, and faced far worse consequences than the screams of her mother and the shocked, pale face of her injured brother. There was no danger in using her psi. It was the right and proper exercise of the Gift that had been bestowed upon her. She neither forced it nor held it back. It spun itself out on the wings of her melody, not effortlessly but energetically, not blindly but deliberately. It was the result of instinct, but also the result of her training and her long, long practice.

And it did what it was meant to do. She felt the warmth of her *quiru* on her cheeks, on the backs of her hands. She heard Luke's sigh of relief, and she felt Gwin's shadowy psi with hers, rejoicing as the warmth bloomed around the campsite.

When she opened her eyes at last, she thought her joy and relief must make her glow like Cantrix Mreen herself.

Her *quiru* was small but vibrantly warm, a slender, brilliant flame in the gathering dusk. The falling snow melted as it struck the envelope of light, and the deepening snow beyond the *quiru* shone with reflected brilliance, glittering here and there as if stars had fallen among the snowflakes.

The *hruss* moved closer to the humans. Luke's dark eyes shone with reflected light, and Gwin, kneeling beside Josu, watched Emle with something like awe.

Josu's eyes fluttered open, and as they closed again he sent faintly, *Well done, Emle. Very well done.*

Luke built up the fire, and he and Gwin set about concocting a meal for them all. Emle sat on her bedfurs, giddy with exhaustion.

Just as the sun fell behind the mountain peaks to the west, hoofbeats sounded in the empty Pass. Axl's *hruss* hurried toward the beacon of light and warmth, toward the company of its fellows. Axl, swaying on the beast's back, was making no attempt to dissuade it. When it reached the *quiru*, it stopped abruptly, setting its feet hard into the thin layer of snow. Axl pitched forward over its neck, just catching himself on the pommel, and then slid slowly from the saddle. He clutched at the *hruss* for balance as he stood staring blindly into the warmth of the *quiru*.

"Are you there?" he croaked. "I can't see you. I can't see anything."

# Twenty-Seven

MREEN PACED HER room whenever she was free, listening with all her might for some word from Josu, or from Emle. Over the days of their absence, she had been torn by feelings of dread, anxiety, and, occasionally, flashes of optimism that made the return of her fear all the more painful to bear. On the fifth full day, she sat in a window seat in the great room, gazing out over the empty courtyard and the darkening sky above the Mariks, longing to see the traveling party return. She had offered the Spirit a hundred sacrifices to keep them safe, repented a thousand times letting them go.

"Cantrix Mreen." It was Lispeth, grown more and more confident in these past trying days. "You must come to bed, Cantrix," she said softly, but firmly. "You will wear yourself out. And the House is depending upon you."

Mreen tore her eyes from the empty view beyond the tall window, and faced Lispeth. She lifted her hand to her forehead, almost carelessly, signing, —*I know.*—

Lispeth responded with a quick sign of her own, passing her open hands before her closed eyelids. —*Sleep.*— She nodded toward the courtyard. "Everyone's watching for them, Cantrix. You'll know when they arrive."

Mreen stood, nodding to her Housewoman. She sketched three quick words as she turned toward the door, and then recalled her resolve to make her signs slowly and clearly. She looked back at Lispeth and found her smiling.

"Yes," Lispeth said, touching her forehead as Mreen had done. "It's hard to sleep." She pressed both palms together before her waist. —*Please.*— "At least lie down, Cantrix, and rest. Sleep may surprise you, as my mama always says."

Mreen, through her anxiety, had to smile. Lispeth was full, she had discovered, of her mother's wisdom. She touched her breastbone, and then extended her forefinger. —*I will.*—

Lispeth nodded satisfaction, and followed as Mreen moved toward the curving staircase.

They had not yet reached the turning of the stair when Mreen stopped as if she had run into a wall.

It was faint, but clear. It was Emle's clear, precise sending. *Mreen? We are but a few hours' ride from Tarus.*

Lispeth said, behind Mreen, "What is it? Is something wrong?"

Mreen held her hand up, signaling for Lispeth to wait. She sent strongly, *Emle, I am so glad to hear you. But it grows late, and dark. It will soon be cold, and the cliff path will be dangerous.*

*Yes, I know. But we are so close.*

*Who is with you?*

*Everyone except Lev,* Emle responded.

*I will brighten the* quiru, *Mreen sent.* Look for it.

When she lifted her head, she signed with careful clarity to Lispeth. —*Bring my* filhata *to the Cantoris. Then tell Magister Kenth they are returning. And tell Gwin's mother that her daughter is safe with Luke, Singer Emle, and Cantor Josu.*—

Lispeth surprised her by nodding vigorously, and touching her forehead without hesitation. The Housewoman dashed up the stairs, and Mreen hurried down to the Cantoris. She would make the House *quiru* as bright and broad as she could, a beacon to call them through the darkness, a brilliant warmth that the *hruss* would hurry toward. She could hardly wait to see Emle, to know that Josu was safe, to hear Gwin's story.

LUKE RODE AT the head of his party, but now he kept Axl's reins in his own hand, and had done so for the past two days. Axl had not spoken again. He huddled in his saddle, and seemed smaller, somehow, as if he had shrunk. His eyes still darted left and right, unceasingly. His face was no longer handsome, its heavy features sagging, the lips working as he peered into the darkness. Luke gritted his teeth, watching him, trying to push away the occasional stab of sympathy. He reminded himself of what Axl had done, and what he had meant to do. He glanced at Emle—Singer Emle, who rode close to Cantor Josu, his reins in her own hands—and remembered that only her strength and courage had stopped Axl from taking his, Luke's, life.

Still, the sight of a strong man broken disturbed him.

Luke didn't know if having such conflicting feelings meant he himself was a better man, or a weaker one. He shrugged the thought away. It had not been his doing, but Axl's own, that brought them to this point.

And Emle. He had watched her *quiru* spring up, strong and bright and warm, protecting all of them from the deep cold, and he had known that any slender chance of her being his mate had vanished. Hope had lingered, despite everything. But the choice—Emle's choice—to train her Gift, had saved them all. Had she been simply a Housewoman with a lovely voice, he and Gwin and Axl would lie frozen in the Southern Pass. She was everything he desired in a mate—intelligent, brave, honest, loyal. He would always care for her. But he must find those qualities in someone else.

He frowned at the darkening path as they worked their way along the cliff. He hoped he had not made a poor decision, allowing Emle to convince him to keep riding. He knew the dangers of this part of their journey. But Emle wanted Cantor Josu to be safe in the House, with Cantrix Mreen to treat his injury, as soon as possible. Even as he considered proposing another night's campsite to her, Gwin, clinging to him as she rode behind his cantle, exclaimed, "Luke! Look!"

He lifted his head, and saw Tarus's *quiru*, still hours ahead, suddenly blossom higher, wider than he would have thought possible.

He looked over his shoulder and caught Emle's eye. She smiled at him, and he nodded in return. That glow would reach down the coastline, brighten the most perilous parts of the cliff path, and light their way home.

MREEN EMERGED FROM the courtyard arch to find that a number of Housemembers had preceded her to the stableyard. They stepped back as she passed, bowing, several murmuring greetings. Lispeth, following close behind, chuckled softly. "They're impressed, Cantrix. They've never seen the *quiru* so large."

Someone whispered a question to Lispeth, and she turned back to Mreen. "Cantrix, do you know when the travelers will arrive?"

Mreen listened a moment, and then signed, *Emle thinks it will be about a half hour.*

Lispeth passed this along, and then said to Mreen, "When they arrive, Singer Emle owes me an introduction!"

Mreen laughed her silent laugh. She found a clear spot where she could lean against one of the paddock posts to wait. Magister Kenth came to join her, with his mate at his side. The Housekeeper came, too, fussing over the *ubanyix* and *ubanyor* being too cold for newly arrived travelers. Mreen signed to Lispeth that she would warm them as soon as she had seen her friends, and Lispeth carried the message to Gerta. Kenth had summoned two burly hunters to deal with any unpleasantness that might come with Axl's return. Mreen had had difficulty expressing to Lispeth that he would be mostly harmless. Lispeth frowned over this, trying to understand, and Mreen gave it up. In moments now, they would all see for themselves.

She pulled her furs close around her and watched the cliff road.

Luke came first, tall and erect on the beautiful stallion he had brought from the mountains the past summer. Mreen stared at him in wonder. His jaw was firm, his head high, his gaze confident. He did not smile, but he had, she thought, reason to be proud. His little sister rode safely behind him, perched on his saddle skirts.

Erlys gave a choked cry, and dashed forward from somewhere in the crowd of Housemembers, then stumbled to a halt when she saw Axl slumped over his horse's neck. He raised his head at the sound of her voice, and his eyes slid left and right, over and over. Erlys put a hand to her throat, standing as if carved of ice.

The two hunters stepped up to Axl's *hruss*, and set about loosing his bonds, pulling him down from the saddle. He growled something, and Erlys took a halting step backward.

Luke dismounted, and lifted Gwin down to the ground. The little girl's eyes fixed on her mother, but she made no sound. The hunters led Axl, stumbling and muttering to himself, in through the stable door, and Erlys followed, whimpering, wringing her hands together. Gwin watched her go.

Mreen stepped forward to take Gwin's hand in hers just as Emle and Josu rode into the stableyard. Several men hurried to take their *hruss*, to unfasten the harness that apparently held Josu in his saddle. Emle lifted her leg easily over her *hruss's* neck and slid to the ground with a lithe and practiced motion, as if she had done it all her life.

*Emle. Well done,* Mreen sent.

The younger girl gave her a brilliant smile, and then a deep bow. *Cantrix Mreen, I thank you. I have so much to tell you.*

*Is Josu all right?*

To Mreen's relief, Josu himself answered. He leaned on one of the Housemen, and his narrow face was pale, but his sending was clear. *I will be, Mreen,* he sent. *Thanks to Emle.*

Mreen, still holding Gwin's hand, bent to touch Emle's cheek with her own. *You will tell me everything,* she sent. *But first, I promised Gerta I would warm the* ubanyix *and the* ubanyor *so all you travelers can bathe.*

Emle returned her embrace. *There is no need for you to do that, Cantrix,* she sent firmly. *I am junior to you. I will do it myself.*

Before Mreen could react, Emle was gone, disappearing through the stable doors with a brisk step, and a merry grin tossed over her shoulder. Mreen's lips parted in amazement. *Gwin,* she sent. *It seems much has happened while you were gone.* She looked down, smiling.

But the little girl simply hung her head, staring at her feet.


LUKE DID NOT leave the stables until the last *hruss* was curried, cooled, and settled in the paddock with an extra measure of feed. He saw to every bit of tack. Two of the hunters stayed with him, helping him to set everything right. When they bid him good-night at last, they addressed him by name, and spoke with respect. Luke watched them disappear through the inner door to the House, marveling at how much had changed in the space of a few days.

He knew he should go to the apartment, explain to Erlys what had happened, but he stood for a long moment in the straw-strewn passageway, then spun on his heel to go back outside. Cantrix Mreen's enhanced *quiru* made the stableyard as bright as day, and almost as warm. Luke stood with one foot on the paddock fence to watch the *hruss* and try to sort out his thoughts.

Brother came to him, nosing his chest. Luke released an enormous sigh, and buried his fingers in Brother's silky dark mane. "We've had a great adventure, you and I, haven't we?" he said softly. Luke dug in his pocket, and found a bit of grain. The *hruss* lipped it from his palm and then stood, head over the fence, eyes half-closed, as Luke scratched between his drooping ears.

"You're not holding any of it against me, I see," Luke muttered.

Brother only tipped his head a little, to let Luke reach a deeper spot to scratch. Luke chuckled. "I don't know what will happen now," he said. "But at least you will be free of him. And so will I."

He gave the *hruss* a final pat. "I'll see you first thing in the morning, my friend. Just now——" He took a step away from the paddock fence, and he and the *hruss* gazed at each other. "Yes. Just now I really must see my mother, and make her understand. And, I guess, try to understand her." He sighed, and walked through the stable door, turning back to lock both bottom and top for the night.

Gwin awaited him beside the tack room. She was freshly bathed, dressed in a clean scarlet tunic, her cropped hair newly combed.

"Gwinlet," Luke said gently. "I thought you would be with Mama."

She shook her head.

"What is it then, little one? Why are you not in bed?"

She lifted one shoulder, turning her head toward it so that she looked like a bedraggled little bird. Luke went to her and knelt, taking her hands in his. "Talk to me, Gwin," he said. "Where is Erlys?"

Painfully, as if it hurt her to open her mouth, she said, "With—with him."

"You mean—with Axl?"

She nodded.

Luke sat back on his heels. "Where is that, little one?"

"The room at the back. The hunters are at the door."

The room near the waste drop was the one no one wanted, where no one stayed. It would be the one space available to keep Axl under guard until the Magister could decide what to do with him. But that Erlys would be with him. . . .

He stood up. He felt unbearably weary, too tired for a bath, too tired even to eat. He kept Gwin's hand in his, and led her toward the inner door. "Come, Gwinlet. You and I will go home. Sleep. I can't even think right now."

When he tucked his little sister into her cot, he almost didn't hear her whisper. "I stayed for her. For Mama."

Luke turned back to her, and knelt again beside her bed. "What's that?"

Gwin sat up, her blanket falling from her shoulders. Her voice broke as she said, "I wanted to go to Conservatory, Luke, but Mama . . ."

"Ah." Luke stroked her tousled head, struggling for words. "I see, Gwinlet. But she needs him, I guess, in some way we can't understand. You will go to become a Cantrix, and I will have a family of my own one day. . . ."

"And she will be alone with him," Gwin finished.

"Yes. That may be part of it."

"He is a very bad man."

"Yes. I think he is a very bad man. But Erlys made a promise to him, and I suppose she is standing by it."

"He will hurt her."

"That may be." Luke helped her to lie back on her pillow, and smoothed the blanket around her again. "But we can't protect her, Gwinlet. She has to protect herself."

# Twenty-Eight

"A RIDER WILL be dispatched to Lamdon the moment we're finished here," Magister Kenth said. "The party from Conservatory will loan us their itinerant. But I want to be very clear about what happened before I write the letter for the Committee."

They all looked back at him, Cantrix Mreen, with Lispeth at her side, Cantor Josu, who looked considerably stronger this morning, and Emle herself. Luke had been summoned from the stables and had brought Gwin, who sat as close to her brother as she could manage, looking as grim as a little child could look. Gwin had not spoken a word, not even responding to the greetings of the adults around her.

Luke leaned forward a little. "What do you need to know, Magister?"

"Let's begin at the beginning," Kenth said. His secretary sat beside him, quill poised over a sheet of paper. Luke glanced at Emle before he began.

The complete recounting of events took perhaps an hour.

Gwin would not speak, but Luke spoke for her, explaining how Axl had taken her, still sleeping, from her cubby, and that she had wakened only when he lifted her up with him on Brother. He had smothered her cries with his hand, Luke said, until they were out of earshot of the House. Luke went on, with occasional details from Emle and from Josu, to tell of their pursuit of Axl and Lev and their captive, down the cliff path, turning into the Southern Pass, hurrying to make up the distance between them.

When they came to the actual confrontation between Luke and Axl, Emle took over the narrative. It was as clear in her mind as if it had happened moments ago, and she told it objectively, describing every action, every detail. At the end, she finished with, "The telling has taken longer than the events, Magister. There was no time to plan, or to make choices. I did not mean to blind the *hrussmaster*, but I did certainly intend that he should not murder Luke. And so—" She spread her hands, and glanced at Mreen. Mreen had already assured her of her understanding. "My Gift chose that moment to heal itself, to realize its full strength. And I swear by the Spirit that had it not done so, Luke would not sit here with us today."

Kenth let out his breath in a great sigh, and nodded slowly. "Tarus is grateful to you, Singer," he said. "We would hate to have lost him. We have need of young, strong Housemen." His secretary, at his left, bent toward the Magister and murmured something. Kenth nodded again, and turned to Luke. "I believe your master contracted to send you to Arren to repeat your apprenticeship."

Luke said in a level tone, "So he did."

Kenth sighed again. "No matter what the Committee decides, Tarus has lost its *hrussmaster*. I'm told there is no way to know if his sight will return."

Emle bit her lip. Mreen, seeing, sent swiftly, *Emle. It is not your fault.*

Without meeting her gaze, Emle responded, *I know it is not. It is still upsetting.*

Kenth, unaware of their exchange, went on. "Luke, you have proved you do not need further apprenticeship. I hope you will choose to stay here, instead, and to take over the stables here at Tarus. To become our *hrussmaster*."

Luke sat a little straighter and met the Magister's gaze. His voice rang with confidence as he answered, "So I will, Magister. Thank you." He glanced down at Gwin, who leaned close to him, her cheek on his sleeve. He lifted his eyes again, and said, "What of my sister? Of Gwin? What will happen to her?"

Kenth cleared his throat, and looked unhappy. "The Committee—" he began.

Mreen signed something, and Lispeth lifted one hand. "Excuse me, Magister," she said softly. Kenth looked at her, brows raised. Emle saw that Luke glanced her way, as well. She suspected he had not noticed Lispeth until this moment.

Lispeth colored charmingly and put a long, slender hand to her pale hair. Emle belatedly remembered she had promised her an introduction. She looked down at the table, suppressing a painful stab of envy, and chiding herself for it. She could not, after all, have it both ways. She promised herself she would present Lispeth to Luke at the first opportunity.

Lispeth had more than fulfilled her part of their bargain.

Lispeth said, "Cantrix Mreen wishes Conservatory to decide about Gwin."

Kenth frowned deeply. "Cantrix Mreen, of course I want to . . . I mean, if you prefer . . . but Lamdon . . ."

Emle said, "Magistrix Sira was very clear about this."

Mreen nodded, and Lispeth sat back, satisfied that she had done her job. Emle saw how she glanced sidelong at Luke, and then, pointedly, in her own direction. Emle almost laughed aloud, and Lispeth's eyes danced.

By the time the meeting concluded, the hour for the *quirunha* had arrived. Josu rose to go with Mreen to the Cantoris, but she held up her hand. *You must rest, Cantor Josu,* she sent. *I have been working alone these past days, and I can do it on my own once again.* She turned to Emle, and dimpled. *Or Emle can help me.*

Emle bowed. *I am not fully trained,* she sent. *But I am more than willing.*

*You are trained in Cantor Theo's tradition,* Mreen sent. *A crooked path, but a sure one. You have served as an itinerant Singer already! And your support will be appreciated.*

And so it was that Emle mounted the dais beside Mreen, with Josu's *filhata* in her lap, to assist Mreen in the daily *quirunha*. Mreen led with a familiar melody in *Iridu*, and Emle sang, hesitantly at first, and then with increasing confidence as her tone resounded against the walls and ceiling of the Cantoris. When the ceremony was over, Emle began the closing prayer. Mreen stood beside her, her nimbus bright as morning.

*Smile on us,*
*O Spirit of Stars,*
*Send us the summer to warm the world,*
*Until the suns will shine always together.*

As they made their way out of the Cantoris, she sent, *I will miss you, Emle. But you will soon make a fine Cantrix. I am proud of you.*

Emle's heart felt full to bursting.

THE NEXT DAYS passed in a blur for Emle. Even though Josu recovered quickly, he and Mreen allowed her to sit on the dais with them for the *quirunha*, where she followed their leads with careful respect, but with the abundant energy of her newfound ability. She warmed the water of the *ubanyix* and the *ubanyor* until it grew so hot that Mreen, with her soundless laugh, begged her to stop before someone got cooked like a haunch of *caeru* meat. She packed and repacked her meager belongings, and worked with Gerta to see that her tunics were clean and mended. And she practiced, alone in her small apartment, until the air was so bright it hurt her eyes.

She was not alone with Luke again until the day before Tarus's rider was expected back from Lamdon. She had, as promised, introduced Luke and Lispeth one morning in the great room, but had not had the chance to speak to Luke since then. Josu commented to her that it had been six days since the rider's departure with the itinerant Singer, and that the Magister expected a decision at any moment. Emle knew that the moment of farewell was coming.

She turned left beneath the staircase as she left the Cantoris, smoothing her tunic with her hands, tucking an errant strand of hair into its binding. She noticed every detail of the House as she passed, the polished *obis*-carved panels, the hangings that softened the bare walls, the smoothness of the stone floors beneath her feet, the faint tang of salt that permeated the air even indoors.

She opened the door to the stables and stood for a moment, savoring the rich scent of *hruss*, of sea air, of fresh straw. She would remember this particular fragrance, she was sure, all her life. And when she did, it would conjure up Luke's dark face, his tall, lean figure, the gentleness of his big hands as he guided the *hruss* in his care, or caressed them. And she would always, she supposed, feel the same pang she felt now, thinking of Luke and what might have been. That it was her own choice gave her scant comfort. The Gift, in truth, left her no choice.

"Emle!" It was Luke, putting his head out from the tack room. "Need something?"

She shook her head, feeling a little shy. He cocked an eyebrow at her, and she laughed. "It seems I will be leaving soon. I just—I wanted to talk with you one more time."

He stepped out into the passageway, a hackamore in his hands. "One last time, you mean," he said. His voice sounded a trifle flat.

"I hope not, but I suppose—yes, it could be."

Together they walked down the passageway. The half-door stood open to the fresh air. They stood side by side, looking out to the paddock where Brother and his pair of mares enjoyed the thin, cold sunshine. The stallion lifted his head to whicker at them. Mreen's intensified *quiru* had faded days before, of course, and the air beyond the stables was too cold for humans to go out without furs. The water of the bay had already frozen solid near the shore. Emle said, "It grows colder every day."

"So it does."

Emle put her hands on the lower door. Even the iron-wood seemed colder under her fingers. But she did not want to talk about weather.

"Luke—how goes it with your family?"

He considered for a moment, rubbing the braided nose-piece of the hackamore with his thumb. "My mother refuses to discuss anything that happened. She lives in the belief that Axl will regain his sight and resume his position as *hrussmas-ter*, and that everything will be as it was."

"And Gwin?"

He sighed, and his jaw flexed. "Gwin will not go near the room where Axl is being kept. When Erlys comes out to fetch meals or clothes, Gwin will speak to her, but she refuses even to walk down the back corridor. And Erlys . . ." His voice trailed off, but Emle felt his grief.

"Perhaps she cannot help it," Emle said quietly.

Luke straightened and faced her, his face set in hard lines. "Not help choosing a cruel, dishonest man over her child? What kind of mother is that?"

Emle hesitated. "Luke—strange things happen, sometimes, when the Gift invades a family. It is such a great sacrifice . . . and it is hard for parents to say good-bye to their children."

"But soon Gwin will be off. . . . She has so little time left with her."

"Oh, Luke, I know. My own mother . . ." She remembered the day of her leaving Perl, her brothers staring at her, at the riders come to take her away, at the Magister as he made his proud speech about Perl's achievement in producing a Gifted child. She remembered her father's look of relief. And her mother—her mother had fussed over her clothes, her saddle-pack, her hair, her furs. Emle had always believed her mother had cared more about how her daughter looked than that she would not see her for five long years. But now, she was not so sure.

"Your mother . . . ?"

"Oh, Luke. I do not know enough to advise you on this. My mother, I think, distracted herself with other things. Perhaps it is this way with Erlys."

"No," he said harshly. "My mother is as much a child as Gwin is. She seeks the easy road. She wants to be cared for more than she wants to care for her daughter."

Emle, tentatively, laid her hand on Luke's sleeve. "In the end, Luke, it makes no difference. Gwin will go to Conservatory, when she is ready."

"She's ready now," he said. His voice cracked a little. He, perhaps more than Erlys, was grieving at his sister's departure.

She started to lift her hand from his arm, but he suddenly covered it with his. It was not proper. But Luke was in pain.

"Watch over her," he begged, stiffly. "Promise me."

"Of course. Of course I will watch over her. And I will write to you about her progress."

"Can't read," he muttered, his eyes on his boots.

"Someone will read my letter to you. Cantor Josu. Or the Magister. Or—" She took a deep breath. "Lispeth reads. Cantrix Mreen's Housewoman. It was one reason she was chosen for the job."

He swallowed and released her hand. "Thanks. I will ask Lispeth, then."

"You must dictate an answer, too," she said. "So I know what—how you are."

He swallowed again, and looked out the open half-door, his profile hard-edged against the afternoon light. She knew she must leave him alone. He would never forgive himself if he broke down in her presence.

There were no words for what lay between them. She knew it and hoped he did, too.

# Twenty-Nine

ON THE DAY of Emle's departure, Mreen descended the staircase to the foyer with a tiny leather pouch in her hands. Lispeth preceded her, carrying her furs. There was to be a formal farewell on the steps of the House, as if Emle was a full Cantrix instead of merely a young Singer returning to her studies. Mreen and Josu had discussed it, and Kenth had agreed.

Housemembers, streaming out to stand on the steps for the brief ceremony, bowed to Mreen as she moved among them, and she smiled and nodded to them. She knew their names now, knew what work they did, knew their children. She had treated a number of them for various ailments, and she knew what worried them, what they cared about. They had become her community. She sent a quick prayer of gratitude to the Spirit of Stars that this was so.

Lispeth held her furs for her, and she slipped into them, letting the hood fall back onto her shoulders. The morning meal was just being laid in the great room, but Emle's traveling party had already eaten. They would make the most of the chilly daylight on their first day of travel. As Mreen stepped out through the big doors to take her place beside the Magister and his mate, she saw that Emle was already mounted. And Gwin, little Gwin who was almost as silent as Mreen herself, sat behind Emle's cantle, clinging to her waist.

Mreen, with a gesture to the Magister, went down the steps to present Emle with the little leather pouch.

*A parting gift, my friend. With much appreciation for the support you have been to me.*

*Mreen,* Emle responded. Her eyes reddened, and she gave her head a little shake, as if to deny the emotion. *What is it?*

*Two tiny bits of metal,* Mreen told her, with a smile. *Do you remember them? They come from my home of Observatory. I have no need of them now.*

Emle held the pouch to her breast, and gave Mreen a tremulous smile. *Thank you. I will treasure them, though they send me no pictures as they do you.*

Mreen shrugged a little. *They are so old. The pictures are fading. But I will keep a picture of you always in my heart, Emle.*

Emle took a deep breath. *And I you, Mreen. Always.*

*Send me letters so I know how it goes with you.*

*I promise.*

*And the next time I see you, you will be Cantrix Emle.*

Emle brightened. *By the will of the Spirit!*

Mreen reached up to touch Emle's hand, to squeeze her fingers. She smiled at Gwin, whose cheek pressed against Emle's back, but whose eyes followed every movement around her. *Do not be afraid, little one,* she sent. *Singer Emle will take good care of you. And you will love Conservatory!*

Gwin lifted her head and sent, fuzzily, but with enough

clarity to be understood, *I will have my own* filla *soon.*

Mreen laughed and sent an image of Gwin playing a *filla.* The child gave a whisper of a smile, and Mreen nodded to her. It was all she could expect now, she supposed. *Farewell, both of you. Safe journey.*

She climbed the stairs again, and stood listening as Magister Kenth made his formal speech. Kenth spoke, in his ponderous way, of Tarus's gratitude to Emle and pride in Gwin. He made no mention, of course, of Axl, who had been banished to the house of Manrus, beneath the ice cliffs in the far north. Erlys, with torrents of tears and pleas for her children to understand, had gone with him. Mreen understood that Axl's sight had begun to return, in brief flashes of light, vague perceptions of shapes and movement. He was, she had heard, to be put to work in Manrus's stables when he was able. If he was able. The itinerant Lev had disappeared.

But Tarus's new *hrussmaster* rode proudly at the head of this traveling party, ready to lead them to Conservatory. When speeches were over, and final good-byes said, Luke turned his beautiful black-maned stallion toward the cliff path, to wind to the east, and then north into the Southern Pass. Mreen sighed, remembering her own journey here, the beauty of unfaded stars, the crispness of the snowpack . . . and Emle's beautiful voice rising into the night sky:

*Sing the light,*
*Sing the warmth,*
*Receive and become the Gift, O Singers,*
*The light and the warmth are in you.*

Emle heard her thought, and smiled through a rush of tears. *Farewell, Mreen.* Her *hruss* followed Brother's sure steps around the side of the House, through the stone arch, out of the stableyard toward the cliff path. *I will miss you.*

Mreen sent more good-byes, assurances that she would write. The rest of the Housemembers turned to go, but Mreen, pulling her hood forward for warmth, stood on the steps a long, long time, her head bent.

When she knew the traveling party was truly gone at last, she lifted her head. A wave of loneliness gripped her, but there was no time for weeping. She had Cantoris hours to face, and the daily *quirunha*. She sniffled, and went up the steps. To her surprise, she found Lispeth standing just outside the House doors, waiting for her.

"Are you all right, Cantrix?" she asked.

Mreen nodded. She signed, —*Sad. A little lonely.*—

Lispeth smiled at her. "Yes, me, too. I'll be watching for our new *hrussmaster's* return."

They started into the House together, Lispeth pushing open the door for Mreen, and then standing aside for her to pass through. "The morning meal is ready, Cantrix," she said.

Mreen signed, —*Not hungry*—, but Lispeth shook her head.

"You must eat something," she said firmly. "Shall I bring a tray to your apartment?"

Mreen hesitated, about to accept this offer, but then she paused, looking through the open door into the great room, where the Housemembers had gathered at the long tables.

Kenth and his mate were already seated, and Josu with them. Children laughed and cried, and their parents laughed with them, or soothed them. The kitchen girls hurried between the tables with baskets of bread and plates of the fish that was so much a part of Tarus's life.

She took a deep breath, feeling the knot of loneliness beneath her breastbone loosen just a little. —*No*—, she signed to Lispeth. —*I will have my meal here.*—

Lispeth grinned. "Good idea, Cantrix," she said cheerfully. "As my mama says, nothing like a bit of company to ease a heavy heart. You go and sit, and I'll bring you a cup of fresh tea first thing."

And Mreen, Cantrix Mreen v'Tarus, walked into the great room to have her meal with her House. As she passed, people smiled and bowed, and she smiled, too, nodding back at them. She took her seat beside her senior at the high table, and looked out over the bright tunics of the members of her House. She would miss Emle for a long time. But she was home.

# *Epilogue*

EMLE ROSE FROM her stool to bow when Maestra Magret joined her in the practice room.

*Emle,* Magret said, looking at her closely. *It is good to see you. You have grown in your absence.*

*Do I seem much changed?*

Magret nodded slowly. *So you do, my dear. Your face . . . something about the way you look.*

*I have learned a great deal, Maestra.*

Magret settled herself, with difficulty, onto a stool, and laid her carved stick aside. *I would like to hear all about it,* she sent. She folded her hands in her lap. *But now, Emle, I would like to hear you play, if you please.*

Emle nodded and resumed her seat. She took her *filla* from its pocket inside her tunic, and ran her fingers over its polished surface. *What would you like to hear, Maestra?*

Magret smiled. *You may choose, my dear,* she sent. She closed her eyes, and leaned back against the wall of the practice room. *I will listen.*

Emle was tempted to show off, to play something elaborate, something to demonstrate that she had kept up her facil-
ity with trills and turns. Instead, after a moment's thought,
she moistened her lips and began the old melody, the one
Magret herself had taught her, and as she played, the words
floated through her mind:

*Look back, O Nevya,*
*Look back to the Six Stars,*
*And cry aloud,*
*"Where? Where is the Ship?"*
*From the Six Stars it came,*
*From the reaches of the sky,*
*Look back, O Nevya,*
*And cry aloud,*
*"Where? Where is the Ship?"*

Emle remembered the night in the Marik Mountains, with
Mreen playing her *filla* and Emle's voice rising like a wisp of
smoke into the star-filled sky. So much had happened since
that night.

She came to the end of the tune and opened her eyes,
confident of what she would see.

Magret's faded blue eyes glowed with pleasure in the
intense warmth of Emle's *quiru*. Its light gleamed on her white
hair, glistened on the polished wood of the practice room,
the worn stone floor.

*Very nice, Emle.* Magret's sending was mild, as if this were
not, in truth, a momentous event. *Very nice indeed.* The Maestra

struggled to her feet, leaning heavily on her carved staff. *I see you have kept up your practice.*

Emle rose, too, and bowed again. *So I have. And—if I may presume—*

Magret, at the door, raised her eyebrows.

*If I may help with the pain that troubles you, you have only to ask, Maestra Magret. Perhaps in the evenings, before you sleep . . .*

Magret smiled again, and nodded. *Indeed,* she responded. *I would sleep better, I am sure. And the practice will stand you in good stead when you have your own Cantoris.*

*So it will!* Emle sent with energy. She laughed aloud, hardly able to contain the joy that sang through her. She opened the practice room door and stood back to allow her teacher to precede her.

As she followed Magret down the corridor, a little flock of new students passed them. In the way of the first level, they were still noisy, bursts of spoken words blending untidily with psi. They laughed, teasing one another, tumbling along the hallway like *caeru* pups dashing toward their den.

In the midst of them, Emle caught sight of Gwin. The child's face was alive in a way she had never seen it. Her eyes shone, and her cheeks and chin were beginning to round. She caught sight of Emle, and paused in her headlong rush to smile up at her.

*Singer Emle! Hello!*

*Hello, Gwin. How was your class?*

*It was wonderful!* Gwin declared. *But now we are going to receive our fillas, our very own fillas! Is that not wonderful, too?*

*Oh, yes, Gwin,* Emle sent. *That is wonderful, too.*

The little girl grinned, and dashed after her classmates. Emle moved down the corridor at a more sedate pace, thinking. She would write to Luke and to Mreen this very night, to have letters ready for the next rider to set out for Tarus. It would comfort them to know of Gwin's happiness. And of her own.

Emle pictured Lispeth, tall and slender and blonde, bent over her letter, reading it aloud for Luke, and she sighed. They would make a striking couple. She hoped Luke would be open to the possibility. And she prayed that, one day, she would see them both again.

*Louise Marley* is the author of a number of science fantasy novels, including three others set on the ice planet of Nevya: *Sing the Light, Sing the Warmth,* and *Receive the Gift.* Her novel *The Glass Harmonica* shared the 2001 Endeavour Award with Ursula K. Le Guin's *The Telling,* and her novel *The Terrorists of Irustan* was on the preliminary Nebula ballot and was shortlisted for both the James Tiptree, Jr., Award and the Endeavour Award.

Louise Marley has degrees in music and has sung professionally in many of its genres, including folk, opera, and concert repertoire. She lives in the Pacific Northwest with her husband and son.

Visit her Web site at www.louisemarley.com.